SMALL SCALE TOUR

Also by Caroline Ross and available
from Honno

The War Before Mine

SMALL
SCALE
TOUR

by
Caroline Ross

HONNO MODERN FICTION

First published in the English language by Honno Press in 2013
'Ailsa Craig', Heol y Cawl, Dinas Powys, South Glamorgan, Wales,
CF64 4AH

1 2 3 4 5 6 7 8 9 10

A catalogue record for this book is available from the British Library.
Published with the financial support of the Welsh Books Council.

ISBN 978-1-9-906784-95-9
Cover design: Rhys Huws
Text design: Elaine Sharples
Printed by Bell & Bain Ltd, Glasgow

For Teddy, with love

Acknowledgements

An earlier version of this novel formed part of my submission for an MPhil in Writing from the University of Glamorgan. I would like to thank all the tutors and students on that excellent course for the helpful feedback and encouragement in workshops. My thanks go especially to Philip, whose generosity with time went far beyond what I could have expected and whose wisdom and enthusiasm were an inspiration and a joy.

The author wishes to acknowledge the award of a Writers Bursary from Literature Wales for the purpose of completing this novel.

Epilogue

It was January. Thirty years is too long ago to remember the exact dates, though I can still recall the exact intensity of the cold. Cold as only northeast England on a direct trans-Siberian windway could be. Cold like it used to be cold; the earth rock hard for months; trains going north from London iced up on the inside before they hit Doncaster; a cloud of dragon breath fogging the view every time you opened your mouth.

Perhaps travelling there in the truck made it feel like a show. One final gig on the tour. A get in, a performance and a get out, which is what theatre people call packing up the set after the play. Cuff's get out, to be precise. His last, because there was no getting back in once you were nailed down under half a ton of frozen earth.

The truck groaned out of the city, past the Vickers tank factory and along bombed-out Scotswood Road, the newish Cushy Butterfield pub a big red sore amid amputated terraces and wasteland. Skinny kids trying to play football on the rough ground hugged themselves and moved in slow motion. Stafford drove, with Greg and me crammed in the cab beside him.

It was the second funeral we'd been to in four weeks, which perhaps explained why nobody felt like saying anything. I thought about that other, empty ceremony as the city slowly petered out, the truck starting to climb through brown villages interspersed with scrubby woodland.

1

Greg and Stafford chain-smoked with the windows half down. Finally, I complained, 'Fuckin' Arctic in here,' after which they silently finished their tabs and wound the windows up. Outside, the landscape turned into Northumbrian tundra, the tarmac disappearing under the wheels of the truck paled to ashen, nothing but a spatter of crows in the sky. Up here, the wind blew so hard it stunted and contorted the trees into bent, spiked things that looked like Martha Graham dancers in something alienating. No, actually, that's as I want to see them now, conscious of employing a sophisticated image that will mark me as knowing something about art. Back then, none of us – with the exception perhaps of Greg – knew or cared who Martha Graham was.

'You going to make a speech or anything?' I asked, just to break the silence.

Greg shook his head. 'Sam's reading.' He paused before adding, 'Alice and Maureen are doing something.'

Stafford rolled an eye towards him. 'They never are!'

'A duologue,' said Greg, glumly.

There was silence again for a bit while we all pictured Alice and Maureen doing their duologue.

Greg looked really depressed and I realised he was going to miss Cuff more than anyone. It's one thing to speak the lines, quite another to nurse an idea to life together. Cuff and Greg, the writer and the director. I remember watching them in Cuff's garden, working on the play – *that* play – and I see Cuff frowning, stroking the soil from a bunch of carrots, nodding his frizz of grey hair as Greg declaims, pacing the veg patch, restless and dangerous-looking, banging his forehead with the heel of his hand to summon up ideas, 'C'mon. C'mon…'

How Greg ever found his way to directing a theatre company in Newcastle upon Tyne I'll never know, because he'd been brought up in South America, his mother some Peruvian aristocrat, his father American. He was about thirty when Cuff died, but seemed younger. Black hair, short black beard, he looked like someone who'd swung in across the Atlantic on the end of a rope, Errol Flynn style, and, true to the type, he'd actually served as a soldier in Vietnam. One time, walking with him down the Bigg Market, a car backfired. He dived for cover into the gutter, entertaining a passing group of lasses no end.

Meeting Greg was a bit like waking up and finding a hoopoe in your garden. It looked so vivid and exotic a bird you thought it couldn't possibly belong, but, strangely, it did. His productions were good. That outsider's eye for the truth of the thing. Think of Altman doing *Gosford Park*, or Ang Lee doing *Ice Storm*. So it was with Greg directing plays about working-class northerners, which was Kicking Theatre's brief, back then.

I suppose Cuff had worked with a lot of directors over his fifty-odd years and come to value a good one, so despite the big age gap he and Greg were close, which in a creative partnership is oddly both more and less than being best friends. I see now why Greg was so shattered that morning in the truck. They'd fed off each other. Cuff dying put Greg in danger of starvation.

Greg's feet, in green striped pumps, were up on the dash, above them, thick red socks pulled up over blue jeans, brown leather jacket, something bright and ethnic wound around his neck. Even looked like a hoopoe. Stafford and I both wore hand-me-down dark suits. Not that I went in much for colour at any time, in terms of species being what twitchers call a little brown job. I think I liked the idea then of looking like a nobody offstage who magically became a somebody on. In my opinion those are the best actors. Not that my opinion counts for anything.

The village was little more than a huddle of cottages, now surrounded on all sides by haphazardly parked vehicles, including the company minibus, *Kicking Theatre Company* emblazoned in red letters on its side A few people still hurried down the narrow lane to the church, but most of the mourners were obviously already inside. Stafford slammed the truck into reverse, bucked it up onto the verge and we climbed out. The bell stopped tolling just as we got to the wooden gate. Faces turned as we entered the church and I couldn't help myself – I looked for Jane, hoping perhaps she'd come on her own, had saved me a place… Then I saw her back, and beside it, her husband, Gerry's, back. We squeezed into a pew and sat down.

Alice and Maureen, poised to perform, had placed themselves as near to Cuff's family as was decent. I could sense, almost hear it humming in the air, the pent-up power they were about to release on the congregation. No wonder the vicar looked unnerved as he stepped up to the pulpit, though he managed the first bit all right, wisely leaving all the plum parts to the actors, first calling on Sam to say a few words. My old mate Sam, teetering on the brink of fame as he was then, his big part at the funeral first proof of the privileges celebrity brings. I'd certainly acted in as many of Cuff's plays as he had so it rankled a bit – but only a bit. I noticed something funny, though. Rather than addressing Cuff's wife and children, Sam seemed to be projecting his words to a place about five rows back.

Then Alice and Maureen did their duologue. They were big women, and usually played mams or wives, the sort that wore housecoats, tied their hair up in scarves knotted at the front and wielded their brooms like mattocks. The strong women at the heart of our northeast culture, enduring, protecting, occasionally doing a bit of philosophising. Cuff had done them proud over the years.

Their competitiveness came out, of course. 'This is something he wrote for me.'

'And this is something Cuff wrote for me…'

A couple of times it was definitely something he hadn't written for either of them, but that's actors for you. Give us a moment in the limelight and there's only one person gets promoted. I'd like to think I was different; able to give credit where credit was due, not always hug it all to myself, but I've had so few moments under the spot, I don't really know.

Actually, they didn't do badly, Alice and Maureen, and the bit where Cuff used Bede's comparing human life to a sparrow fluttering briefly in the roof space of the feasting hall before flying out, got to me. I looked at the simple coffin and thought about Cuff and the poet in him and it wasn't a performance any more, but something real.

More fool me. I should have put one and one together by that time, because they, too, were aiming their performance to the middle of the fifth row, the same place as Sam.

The vicar began burbling through his bit and we all started to feel the cold. There were heaters on, but only the type that warm up the parting in your hair, so it was a relief when he got to the end of the prayers. I imagined it was just going to be outside into the graveyard and heave ho into the hole for poor old Cuff, but blow me if Maureen didn't get up again, walk gravely to the front and start singing 'Speed Bonnie Boat'. There wasn't a dry eye in the house, then, and Maureen cried best of all, big shiny tears rolling down her face. Not a tremor in the voice, mind. Bravura performance. From the tense set of Alice's shoulders I could tell this was a little extra Maureen had not seen fit to share with her. I thought then how much Cuff would have enjoyed his own funeral.

Outside, I felt a hand on my shoulder and turned to see a face I didn't at first recognise as Jenny's. Cuff's wife. Cuff's widow. She looked younger than ever, her face shocked, like a child's just after a vicious seeing-to with a damp cloth. She whispered a request that I tip the first shovelful of earth into the grave.

This was easier said than done, because the pile was frozen solid and I had to hack into it to get a clod free. I stood there gasping and looking down the hole, which seemed unnecessarily deep, as if they'd been digging for oil or something, before finally dropping it in. It landed with a juddering crash on top of the coffin and for a horrible moment amid a collective sharp intake of breath, I thought it was going straight through the lid. Then out of the sea of black a voice came quite clearly, 'That'll sharp wake the bugger up.' It was as though Cuff's spirit was speaking at his own funeral, still coming up with a good line.

On the frozen trail back to Cuff's house, Jenny told me who he was, Mr Fifth Row Back, the slight young man in the black polo-neck and slim leather jacket, and I tried to think of something I could to say to impress him. Maureen and Alice were in there straightaway, hovering, constant reminders of their superior performances in church. Sam engaged him with confidence, letting him know his credentials. To do the bloke justice, he seemed much more interested in talking to Jenny about Cuff. Poor old Cuff. He chose the wrong time to die. His play for the Royal Shakespeare Company was just about to go into rehearsal.

In the end I decided to try and get drunk with Stafford, who was spicing up orange squash with whisky from his back pocket. 'What about the Fat Cows then?' he said. 'Best bloody performance they've given in a while.'

Maureen homed in just at that moment to scold him. 'You might have changed your shoes.'

'What's wrong with Doc Martens? Black aren't they?'

'Haven't even polished them,' Maureen tutted, moving off.

Stafford tipped another slug of whisky into our paper cups and looked after Maureen's departing arse with hatred. 'Bitch.'

There's always been a bit of the polecat about Stafford, who I still see occasionally. Put him down a hole and he'd certainly come up with a rabbit. He's lightweight but very strong, and dark skinned, so dark he's got away with playing Romanies, though in reality he's a wily borderer, last in a long, long line of poaching Picts. Stafford's in his element garlanded with dead animals, or laying bets at some rural racetrack, or boozing with red-faced farmers in some all-night lock-in.

He started a couple of years after me as the company driver, gradually taking bit parts, then larger roles. Never did any training. With a company as small as ours, becoming an actor didn't mean he stopped driving the truck. He carried on at the

7

huge wheel, especially on the homeward journey, because he was the only one, everyone agreed, whose driving improved after eight pints. As a matter of fact his ability to drive at all, let alone drive well stottin' drunk, was a bit of a miracle but I'll come to that.

He's done well as an actor, better than me, made a bit of a speciality of low-budget independent films. The face was always good, meaning characterful not handsome, and it's aged well, by which I don't mean he's stayed young looking – more cured well, like Parma ham. That face has kept him in roles all through his acting life. So on the day of Cuff's funeral, had he but known it, his future looked pretty bright. But he was obviously very miserable, and obviously not just about Cuff. I didn't ask him where Nic, his gorgeous girlfriend, was. Rumour had it she'd left him.

He rubbed a sleeve across his face. 'Hope this is the last bloody funeral I go to for a while.' That shut up the both of us. We stood there drinking and looking down at our scuffed toes. 'To Cuff,' Stafford said at last, raising his cup to mine. But we were both thinking about somebody else.

I'd given up on impressing the RSC director and on snatching a moment with Jane, who'd disappeared, so I wandered out into the garden. Cuff's sprouts looked just about fossilised with cold. He grew loads of vegetables to save money and I remembered him saying gardening, especially hoeing, helped him think out his plots. Beyond the sprouts, the little wooden hut where Cuff wrote his plays seemed to beckon me over.

I pushed open the door and found Greg sitting by the Olivetti, Jane resting her bum on the rickety desk. She smiled at me and I saw her eyes were full of tears. 'This is the place to say goodbye,' she said.

There was still a piece of paper on the roller and a few lines of dialogue, the typeface blurred a little by the damp. Greg said: 'It'll never happen again. I'll never work with another writer as good.' He looked into his lap and made circles with his thumbs.

'You're right,' I said. 'And no one will ever write us such good parts.'

I'm not sure, now, I really believed that. We were young, after all, and our theatre lives, full of wonderful roles, stretched ahead of us.

We silently said our goodbyes, while our warm breath melted the ice on the inside of the window into little streams. I thought of Cuff looking out over his sprouts, tapping out words, hundreds of thousands of words, keeping the wolf from the door with his plays, making the parts fit the actors in the company. Cuff had written plenty of things with Jane in mind, or me. We just didn't talk about it as much as Maureen and Alice. Looking back, I suppose that might explain why our careers petered out. Sad, because of all the women in the company, I reckon Jane was the best actor, because she could *be* anyone on stage: a madwoman, a beauty, a sophisticate, a tart, an old granny, and pull it off better than any of the others. It comes from inside, that kind of acting. Offstage, she was dead shy, pale skinned, with a mass of dark red hair. A nice-looking woman rather than a stunner; but for me, then, the most desirable woman on earth.

She wore a new fitted jacket; well, not new, probably 1940s, off a market stall, but new to her. I nearly told her how great she looked, but managed to stop myself. Shortly afterwards, she said 'I'd better go,' and left. Story of our relationship.

Greg rolled a joint and the two of us stayed there till the cold got into our bones and we had to move or freeze solid. I don't know about heart attack. I reckon Cuff died of frostbite. Walking back through the garden, I saw the truck lurch off the verge. Stafford's head looked back towards us from the driver's window. Greg set off at a run but I thought, bugger it, I'll catch a bus or something, I didn't want *noise*. Jenny was saying goodbye to people and I felt a twinge of guilt for hardly having spoken to her. 'Stafford was looking for you,' she said. I rested a hand on her shoulder and she started to cry. 'I wasn't a good wife to Cuff, I wasn't, you *know* I wasn't.' I gave her a hug and felt her shoulders trembling.

'You were fine,' I said. 'He understood. He loved you.'

She blew her nose on a big old hankie. One of Cuff's, I thought. 'There's just a few people staying for a cup of tea,' she said. 'You'll come in, won't you?'

I followed her into the house.

INTERIOR, CUFF'S HOUSE. SLIM YOUNG MAN IN BLACK STANDS ALONE. JENNY ENTERS FOLLOWED BY HAM.

JENNY	You two know each other?
MAN IN BLACK	Yes. *(he holds out a hand)* Good to see you again, Ham.
HAM	Have we met before, then? Sorry, I don't recall…
MAN IN BLACK	In the pub. The last night of the play. Remember?

10

That awful night. I must've blocked him out. Anyway, we got talking and later shared a taxi back to Newcastle. Shortly afterwards, he offered me work at the RSC, but that's another story and, strange to tell, not such an interesting one.

It's all such a long time ago, but it's only recently I realised Cuff's dying was *the end* – in more ways than one – of the central drama of my life, a bit of illumination I owe to my current role as a minimum-wage shop assistant. Stacking shelves gives me time for reflection, in fact seems to force me to go over the stuff I've been dodging for the last three decades.

Soon after Cuff died, the company broke up. Sam already had his telly and, as it turned out, his West End run as well; Maureen and Alice followed him to try their luck in London; Greg lost heart and went back to America. So I suppose that explains why Cuff's funeral felt like the final performance on the tour, before the set gets broken up, the writhing, argumentative whole that is the company divides, and thin, indistinct figures flit away to the shadowy real world.

Act I: The Play

I. 1

In the two weeks I've been in the shop I've discovered my employer, Mr N Khan (proprietor), sells allsorts – whatever he can get hold of at a bargain price.

'Academic diaries?' I said when he plonked a big pile of books down by the till. 'Shouldn't have thought there'd be much call for them round here.'

His eyebrows came together in a line thick as a cat's tail. 'It is true, Mr Nicolson, the customer may not know he requires this diary. It is up to us to convince him it is a desirable purchase.'

I couldn't picture the sort of aimless kids, old biddies and giro wallahs we get in the shop being persuaded, however good our sales patter, but I thought I might get one for myself, thinking I needed some deadlines with the writing projects. I flipped through the diary. The dates went from August to August and since we were already in September I thought Mr Khan would be lucky to sell one, let alone the fifty or so he'd bought in. 'How much are they?' I said. 'I'll take one off your hands.'

'Two pounds.'

'Do I get any discount?'

'As I informed you at interview, none at all until after the first month.'

'Don't remember that.' But now I came to think, I did remember *something* about it, buried among the more memorable oddities of the afternoon I got the job.

When I'd pushed open the shop door and seen the advertisement *'Dependable assistant to the proprietor required. Enquire within,'* I'd got four pounds and 17 pence in my pocket, had just worked out I'd been out of acting work for more than a year and all I had in the fridge was a Tesco Value loaf and half a tub of margarine. I'd come for a bottle of cider but instead found myself telling this grizzly bear in a sort of cage behind the till, 'I'm interested in the job.'

He raised a big brown paw and I thought for a moment he was going to scoop me up like a salmon, but instead he unlatched the door to the cage and came round to meet me. There was only one other person in the shop; an old wife with an empty basket. 'Madam!' he shouted, so loudly she dropped a pack of pan scourers. 'I need to conduct an interview. Will you be happy to remain here if I lock up the shop for a short time?'

She looked too frightened to protest and he led me through a plastic curtain to the cave-like back area of the shop, where a bare light bulb illuminated slatted shelves filled with bottles, cans and cardboard boxes, and, pinned to the far wall, what looked like a map. As a set it interested me, and the bear, who'd introduced himself as Mr N P Khan, made a good character study. He sat himself down on a giant can of vegetable oil with all the confidence of some big-wig executive holding court. 'Take a seat.'

But there didn't seem to be anything to sit *on* and for a moment I was back in this interview training film I'd made years ago, in one of those role-plays where the applicant is deliberately wrong-footed. *Do sit down. Where?* Still, you didn't expect that kind of sophisticated trick when the job you're going for is minimum wage shop assistant. I lowered my arse to approximate seat level and folded my arms.

'Where'd you get this chair?' I said. 'It's dead comfortable.'

Mr Khan slapped his knees delightedly and grinned. 'Forgive me.' He got up and pulled a wooden box from under a shelf. 'Please. Be seated.' I sat. 'What are seven times eight?'

'Err... 56.'

'Correct! Place the following in order of importance: loyalty, industriousness, truthfulness, punctuality.'

'Em. Well. Truthfulness first, I reckon. Then mebbes industriousness.'

Mr Khan nodded encouragingly, and looking at him sitting there, perched on his vegetable-oil throne, I thought if he'd been an actor he'd have blown every bugger else off stage. 'What does God mean to you?' he demanded, and then, 'Would you call yourself a Pietersen or a Flintoff man?' and then, 'What are thirteen times thirteen?'

Da had drilled me on times tables and calculations as a lad so I just about managed the sums, and quite enjoyed the bizarre questions. Finally, Mr Khan reached a hairy mitt towards mine. 'Welcome to the establishment,' he said. 'You may wonder about the questions. I must tell you my last assistant failed badly in point of arithmetic...and also, regrettably, in point of ethics.'

At that moment the old wife appeared in the doorway,

plastic strips draped over her saggy cardigan. 'Can I go home now, please?' she said.

Mr Khan left me for a minute and I took the chance to get a look at the map. Had to get close in to make it out. I suppose I was expecting Pakistan, but the shape looked completely unfamiliar. Then I saw 'Kandahar' and I knew.

'Afghanistan,' said a deep voice behind me. 'My home.'

Mr Khan's a touch *superior* but I'll just have to hack that because it's the sort of undemanding-on-the-brain-job I need now, letting me concentrate on my writing when I get home. I thought I'd be able to do a bit of scribbling at work too, but just about all I manage is looking up the odd word in the dictionary Mr Khan keeps by the till, because he likes to keep me busy. Particularly on the tomato front. He's had a load delivered. Flood damaged or something. This gadgie arrived one afternoon last week, upended a tipper truck in the backyard and sent two thousand cans all over. Since then I've been collecting them, stripping off the remains of the labels, shining up their outsides and piling them into big baskets under a sign saying 'Best Italian tomatoes: 35p'.

Having been stuck on tomato detail for two days, I was pleased when Mr Khan asked me to go on the till for an hour so that, as he put it, he could 'assess my performance with the public'.

Well, he did ask for a performance. So when a fat blonde woman brought a pint of milk, together with her giant pair, to the counter and said, 'Hello pet, you new?' I went into action.

'Aye gorgeous. Me first week.'

16

'What's your name?'

I leaned in, mouthing, 'Bond. James Bond.'

'Eeeh. Having me on.'

'Need a diary?' I said.

She smiled. 'Bit early for Christmas, isn't it?'

'These are different. Go from now till next September. In case you didn't get one like, when you should of.' I held a diary open, shuffled the pages like a hypnotist. 'Take a look at all the information there is here. Sunrise. Sunset. Birthdays, useful addresses.'

She blinked. 'Never use a diary, me. Just as long as I know when Thursday is…'

'Gan on. Bet you have a busy social schedule, admit it. Must have all the lads after you.'

'How old are you, anyhow?' She straightened up, not liking the idea of being chatted up by an old git. People often ask me that. I've got one of those neutral-type faces that hasn't changed much, and I've kept my sandy-coloured hair. A face you can draw a character on, I tell myself. But I've realised, thanks to my nasty sister-in-law, Frances, that when people think I'm a lot younger than I am they're not just talking about how I look – it's how I sound. 'Why don't you listen to yourself? Who do ye think ye are, Peter Pan?' It's her favourite refrain. I don't think actors grow up like other people. Maybe playing make-believe and having to be hopeful in the face of so much rejection requires protracted immaturity of the kind I was showing now, flashing my full set of pearly whites at Blondie.

She looked at me with her head on one side, considering, 'Ye must be about 35.'

17

'I'm a little bit older than my teeth,' I said. A lot older actually, my dazzling smile having been constructed by a London orthodontist in the early 1990s after my agent told me I was up for a Hollywood film.

She relaxed onto the counter, one finger toying with a loose strand of yellowish hair. 'How much are they, like?'

'Two pound to you, petal.'

'Gan on then. Do you know what? I fancy a bit of chocolate as well. Give us some of them Ferrerroshy things.'

She opened a pink furry purse, counted out the coins and sighed. 'You're dead persuasive, you. Should be doing adverts.'

'I've done a few of those.'

'What? Are you an actor like?'

'Resting one.'

'Do you know that Jimmy Nail?'

'Met him, aye.'

'He's dead sexy, him. So, what have I seen you in?' I mentioned a few things, none of which she remembered, conversation faltered a bit – her aware of having spent too much, me aware of how washed up I was – and she turned to go. 'Nice meeting you,' she said. 'I'm Sue.'

'Ham.'

That cheered her up. 'Never met a Ham before…'

Mr Khan emerged from his reconnaissance position behind the shampoos to open the door for her. 'Ye want to keep this lad on the till,' she said, laughing. 'He's dead canny.' Slapping past the window in her flip-flops, she blew me a kiss.

Mr Khan turned towards me. 'I didn't know you trod the boards, Mr Nicolson.'

'What did you reckon, then?'

18

'About what?'

'My performance. On the till.'

'Hamlet! Of course. That explains your unusual first name.'

'So what did you think?'

'Forgive me Mr Nicolson, but you do not sound like an actor. How did you become such a thing?'

'I sold her a diary, didn't I?'

He shook his head. 'Success with that foolish person means little. A sterner test is required. At a later date. Now. You have work to do. We can talk later.'

Or not, I thought, edging out of the cage to let him in and trudging backstage to the tomatoes. Set him right on one thing, though: 'My name, Mr Khan. It's religious. Nothing to do with Hamlet.'

'Religious? Please explain—'

But I was out of the door among the cans and (after taking out some resentment through a bit of savage label removal) back among my memories.

It must have been the second week in September, thirty odd years ago, when excitement about the new play took me down to the quayside and The Building. We always called the Kicking office The Building, which makes it sound very important, though at that time it was just a big, leaking warehouse where the technicians built the sets, together with a small room for the administrator and a very chilly rehearsal space on the top floor. The rest of it was derelict, waiting for a big grant from the Arts Council to convert it into a theatre.

Now I come to think of it, that day was the first time I saw Matt – hanging around uncertainly at the end of the alleyway that led to The Building. No one started down the alley unless they wanted something to do with Kicking Theatre, though even in the moment I had to register his appearance, I had my doubts Matt was in the right place. There was something stranded about him, something hunched-up and helpless, like an oil-slicked guillemot awaiting rescue.

If you'd glimpsed him at the scene of a crime you'd be hard pressed to recall what he was wearing, though I do remember his hat. It was a sludge-green, knitted type of thing, not usually worn in late summer, pulled over his ears with dull brown hanks of hair emerging underneath. Otherwise, the general impression was shapelessness with a suspicion of grime. Altogether an unlikely person to have business with a theatre company and I thought he might be up to something – something low-grade and pitiful, like chucking a brick through a pane of glass, or making off with a piece of scrap metal. And I'm pretty sure I adjusted the dialect setting to strong, without him even saying a word. 'What are ye lookin' for, bonnie lad?'

He silently handed me a piece of crumpled paper on which was written: *Kicking Theatre. 2pm. Ask for the Administrator, John Hardleman*, in a bold, authoritative hand.

'I'm ganning there meself. I'll take ye.'

So he trailed through the gate after me and up the stairs into Hardley's office, where Hardley himself sat at his desk. 'Ham,' he said, apparently not entirely pissed off to see me. 'Thought you'd be away like the rest of them.'

'I missed the place,' I said. It was true. I hated the two-month break from theatre over the summer.

Hardley was older than the rest of us. Late thirties then

seemed really old, and he was the sort of person that it was hard to imagine young. His hair had been grey as long as I'd known him and he was a gaunt, angular person, seeming to fold up when he sat down, so that you'd have thought he never ate a square meal, though actually he was famous for getting through huge plates of scran.

'Come and look at these.' Two sketches lay on the desk. In one, a couple of crudely drawn women – Victorian by the look of their long bloomers – were doing a knees-up above the words *Kicking Theatre Presents: 'The Blaydon Races'.* The second showed the front sections of two horses racing neck and neck. One had a balloon coming out of its mouth with the same message.

'Got to be the lasses,' I said.

'I think so, too.' Hardley scrunched up the horse drawing and with perfect aim threw it across the room into a wicker basket. That was when he noticed Matt.

'This lad here's got an appointment with you. Name of Matthew. That's right isn't it?' Matt nodded and handed over his piece of paper.

Hardley had a particularly hard and disapproving stare – perfected for us actors – and I could see Matt was ready to run. 'So you're interested in the work experience place?'

'Aye.'

'Do you know anything about touring theatre?'

'Nuh.'

'You know the placement is for twelve weeks?'

'Aye.'

Well. I'm sure we can make use of your talents.' He paused. Matt shrugged. There was another long pause, during which Hardley decided to move the problem along.

'Ham – could you take Matthew along to meet Greg? He's the director, Matthew. If it's all right with him I'll sign you up.'

Since Greg was the man I really wanted to see, I was happy to oblige. 'Where is he, like?'

'Where do you think?'

Greg was in his usual position at the back of the pub, right arm rising and falling. I tapped him on the shoulder. 'Hang on a minute.' He pulled down the lever again and we watched the fruits line up. Lemon, lemon, plum. 'Shit. Good to see you, Ham.' Greg lifted his glass of lager from the top of the fruit machine and drained it in one. 'Wanna beer?' He looked even more exotic than usual because a recent visit to his family somewhere hot had made turned his brown skin darker still. The whites of his eyes and his small sharp teeth gleamed. I introduced him to Matt. 'You wanna beer?'

Matt shook his head and looked at his shoes.

'Hardley said to ask you if it's all right if he does the work experience YOP thingy,' I said.

Greg tipped a packet of peanuts down his throat, wiped his mouth on his sleeve and looked at Matt. 'Can you write plays?'

'Nuh.' After a pause, he added, 'But I can fiddle them machines. Need a screwdriver, like.'

'Can you? You sound like our kind of guy. Whaddya say your name was?'

'Matt.'

'Tell you what, Matt, you go back to the office and tell Hardley I said okay and he'll sign you up. Get the dates from him and I'll see you soon.' Matt scurried towards the door. 'Don't forget to bring your screwdriver!'

22

Greg bought another pack of peanuts and led the way over to a table. He threw himself down in a chair and let out a huge, groany sigh. I took my cue. 'Did you mean that about the play?'

'Fuck, Ham,' he said. 'We're in the shit.'

'How much have you got?'

'Fuck all. About twenty pages. Twenty pages of shit, that is. Why didn't anyone tell me the bastard's an alcoholic?'

'What, the writer? Where is he, like?'

'Up at the house. I've told him he's got to get the first half finished today.' He drummed his fingers on the table top and closed his eyes in apparent agony. 'It's all my fault, too, should never have commissioned a fucking London writer.' He stood up and stuffed his rolling tobacco in a back pocket. 'You coming?' The door swung shut behind us and we stood blinking for a moment in the evening sun.

Greg unchained a bicycle from a lamppost and rolled a trouser leg above a tanned, muscular calf. He didn't get on, but wheeled it beside me as we walked slowly up the hill towards Newcastle town centre. 'I need to see how he's doing,' he said.

'The writer?'

'Writer, my ass. The fucker couldn't write his way out of a wet paper bag.'

'You never know. Perhaps he's finished the first half by now.'

Greg sighed as he lifted his leg over the crossbar. 'You'll get the bus, then? See you back at the house.'

Sunset should have been at 19.35 according to my diary, but it was 10 minutes after when I watched it go down from the backyard and it finally became too dark to continue gathering tomatoes. We closed at nine and I walked home to my flat thinking at least I'd be able to make the rent this month.

I'd planned to settle down to writing the soap opera straight away, but thought I'd set myself a few deadlines before I started. Then I got distracted filling in the front, *personal details*, section of my new diary. *Name* and *Address* went fine, but I soon ran into trouble with *Telephone* (cut off last Wednesday) *Mobile* (refused contract) and *email* (no computer).

Vladimir in *Waiting for Godot* would say things were getting alarming by the time I came to *Pension details* (n/a) *Blood group* and *Allergies* (haven't got a clue). *Birthday*. I wrote down October 17th, felt better and turned over the page to *The Year at a Glance*. I started inking in self-imposed deadlines. *September 30th finish screenplay; November 20th send off first two episodes of soap opera…*

That kept me happy for a while, though for some reason Vladimir kept on whispering behind me, 'This is getting really insignificant,' so that I finally did get something written – though not what I'd intended.

LIGHTS UP ON 'THE HOUSE', NO. 12 JARVIS GROVE, A MILE AND A BIT OUTSIDE TOWN, WHERE HARDLEY, GREG AND STAFFORD LIVE, ALONG WITH STAFFORD'S GIRLFRIEND, NIC, AND VARIOUS TEMPORARY RESIDENTS CONNECTED WITH PRODUCTIONS. AN UNTIDY LIVING ROOM. SAGGING SOFAS, EMBOSSED WALLPAPER PAINTED MOSSY GREEN, DIRTY BEIGE SHAG-PILE CARPET. WINDOW TO LEFT SIDE OPENS ONTO BACKYARD WHERE WASHING HANGS AND GREG'S RED BIKE IS VISIBLE, PROPPED AGAINST THE WALL. RIGHT OF CENTRE IS SMALL GALLEY-TYPE

KITCHEN. SINK PILED WITH DISHES AND BACK DOOR AT REAR.
TO THE FAR RIGHT OF THE LIVING ROOM IS AN OPEN PLAN
STAIRCASE, CARPETED THE SAME. BACK DOOR OPENS. HAM
ENTERS THROUGH THE KITCHEN AND COMES INTO THE LIVING
ROOM. SHOUTING AND THUMPING FROM ABOVE.

VOICE OF WRITER	Let me out, you bastard!
VOICE OF GREG	You're under contract. I need a play.
VOICE OF WRITER	Fuck your play! You can't keep me locked up!
VOICE OF GREG	Stay there. I'll bring you up some coffee.

FOOTSTEPS HEARD APPROACHING STAIRS.

WRITER	*(voice rising)* Where are you taking that?

GREG'S FEET AND LEGS APPEAR AT TOP OF STAIRS – ONE TROUSER
LEG STILL ROLLED UP.

GREG	Out of your reach. You can't write a play intoxicated.
WRITER	Listen you fucking foreign twat give me that bottle.

GREG'S LEGS DISAPPEAR UP THE STAIRS AGAIN. GASPS AND
GRUNTS. A THIN, SPIDERY MAN – THE WRITER [DUE TO THE
FACT THAT THIS IS HIS ONLY APPEARANCE IN THE PLAY, THIS

25

CHARACTER CAN BE PLAYED BY AN ASSISTANT STAGE MANAGER
IF NECESSARY] COMES STUMBLING HALF WAY DOWN THE
STAIRCASE BEFORE TAKING A GIANT LEAP SIDEWAYS INTO THE
LIVING ROOM. HE FALLS OVER, STARTS TO PICK HIMSELF AND IS
ON HIS KNEES WHEN HE CATCHES SIGHT OF HAM

WRITER   He's mad! He locked me up!

GREG STARTS TO WALK HEAVILY DOWN THE STAIRS CARRYING A
WHISKY BOTTLE THAT IS ABOUT ONE-QUARTER FULL. THE
WRITER SCRAMBLES UP IN APPARENT TERROR.

WRITER   Don't come near me! I resign! I
                      resign!

HE LOOKS WILDLY FOR AN ESCAPE ROUTE AND THEN RUNS
THROUGH THE KITCHEN AND OUT OF THE BACK DOOR,
BRINGING CROCKERY CRASHING ONTO THE FLOOR AS HE GOES.
THERE IS A LONG PAUSE. GREG SITS DOWN IN ONE OF THE
SAGGING ARMCHAIRS, UNSCREWS THE TOP OF THE BOTTLE AND
TAKES A LONG SWIG. HE COVERS HIS EYES WITH ONE HAND AND
HIS VOICE ADDRESSES THE WHOLE WORLD.

GREG   I don't have a play and we go into
                      rehearsals in *ten days' time.*

THERE IS ANOTHER LONG PAUSE.

HAM   Have you thought about 'phoning
                      Cuff?

I. 2

'The day tea came off ration, you came along,' Mam said. She'd thought she was past having bairns, her youngest, our Harold, being 11 by then, and had been looking forward to putting her feet up and having as many cups of tea as she liked. She lived for tea.

Mam went to Scottish Presbyterian chapel and must have enjoyed the story of the Great Flood, because she named my two elder brothers and me after Noah's children: Shem, Japhet and then me, Ham. They started using their second names as soon as they realised just how abnormal their first ones were, but my parents hadn't bothered to give me a choice. So while Shem became Joe and Japhet changed to Harold, there was no escape from Ham, and seeing her love of Noah all but flooded out of the family by wilful sons, Mam was determined to have more control over me.

'Excuse me, Mrs Nicolson, but Ham tells me he'd like to be called Huntley from now on,' my primary teacher told her.

'Ham he is and Ham he will remain,' my mother retorted and marched me out of the playground. 'Huntley! What do you think you are, a biscuit?'

Well it seemed better than Sandwich, which was inevitably my nickname at school. I kept on trying with Huntley, so by the time I got to secondary school a few of my friends and some of my enemies addressed me as 'Hunt' – the enemies adding their own unforeseen-by-me little rhyme – but by the time it came to choosing a stage name it had lost its appeal completely. There are loads of actors on the Equity register called Nicolson, so though I tried quite a few names, they all got knocked back as repeats. I was twenty-three and Mam had just died so I ended up sticking with Ham as a way of respecting her memory. It's got one good thing going for it anyway; always breaks the ice at auditions.

I grew up in a three-bedroom terrace in Pity Me, County Durham. Doesn't sound real, does it? But the place is real and the pit was real, and my father was down it daily until he retired one sunny day in 1965.

I remember he came in the door and gave Mam his bait tin saying she may as well use it for her rock cakes, as he'd be at home for his dinner from now on. I was thirteen and the day felt important to me, but he just rested his big stained hand on my head for a minute and said, 'Well that's it, lad. Do you fancy coming down the allotment for a bit?'

I'm glad he didn't work till the seventies and all the pit closures, and I'm glad he had a bit of his life on the surface of the earth, rather than crawling underneath, though that was the place he seemed to be at home and even in a way wanted to get back to. For over a hundred years my forebears on the paternal side, right down to my father and eldest brother Joe, were all down the pit, living their lives underground, digging up something dead. Even after Da retired he looked down all the time, as though unable to stop himself burrowing. He collected fossils; at weekends he used to take me to the coast looking for specimens, saying he needed my young eyes to find them for him.

Now, I wish I'd been more enthusiastic, but except for some lovely golden ammonites we once found on a holiday down south, looking for fossils bored me rigid. I was for looking up

– at the birds balancing on the wind in the grey sky, or clinging to the cliff at Marsden Rock. I didn't know what they were called then, but I knew them one from another. There were oyster catchers, guillemots, black-backed gulls, and on the trudge home, lapwings, rising in huge flocks from the ploughed fields, where now you'll be lucky to see one or two.

Da knew *those* all right, because he couldn't avoid them, there were that many around. Peewits, was the name he used, telling me to listen to their mewing, whistling cry that some people said sounded like 'pity meee!' and explained how the place where we lived got its name. Not that he believed in that particular derivation.

'Doesn't sound anything like Pity Me does it, son? You only have to take a look around you to see where the name comes from. Imagine trying to get a crop off that. It was the farmers who wanted pity, like. We went down under the ground because there was nowt to be had on top.'

Even leisure activities meant digging. It was root veg – spuds and parsnips – Da took most pride in growing, and I don't need to tell you about miners' leeks. At night, some of the men used to take their dogs and go badger baiting.

Pity Me was a hole above a hole, and it took some climbing out of, as though the great, scoured world below sucked at your soles, rooted you where you were. Pit villages are often set in beautiful country, surrounded by hills and copses and hedgerows and all the wildlife under the watery sun, but they were never country places. The sun couldn't quite reach between the tight rows of houses because everything was under the shadow of the pit. The coal coloured the place, darkened the brick and kept on trying to black out the windows, only just kept at bay by strong wives armed with vinegar and newspaper.

When I was a – let's-face-it-verging-on-the-cissy – kid, the idea of the pit terrified me. I imagined it like Hell. A place of fire inhabited by black-faced monsters with teeth showing savage white. I suppose that was a memory of seeing Da and my uncles just finished work.

I finally went down a coal mine in the 1980s when I was in a play about the Hartley Grange disaster. It wasn't the pit where Da worked; this one was Easington, only a few miles away, but a place I'd never set foot in before. That's another thing about pit villages – they were tribal. Lads from Pity Me got beaten up if they wandered into the territory of another mining tribe from Houghton, or Hetton-le-Hole or Easington; reckoned we were after their women, you see.

It was beautiful and romantic, the pit at Easington. High-ceilinged, like a great vaulted cathedral under the ground, and the air so unchanging that you could still smell the pit ponies in the stables they'd left 10 years before. A silent place, where huge machinery lurked, dusted silver in the dim light, and then a clanging roaring place, where men jumped on and off the fast-moving rubber belts, preferring the perilous ride to the mile walk to the coal face. Every so often the pressure in the tunnels had to be broken by wind locks; great dusty doors banging shut behind me as the heat grew and grew and the ceilings lowered and lowered until I was on my knees in the place where my father had spent most of his life, watching a huge mechanical claw tearing at the rock – where he'd used a pick – and the belt bearing away the shining coal.

But that was much later. The pit gave me nightmares as a

child and as far as it was possible to worry Mam, I do think she felt a bit anxious about what she called 'Our Ham's funny dreams.' Not that she did anything about it. She just poured herself another cuppa and waited for things to explain themselves, which they did when I told her I wanted to be an actor. It was her grandad's genes coming out. 'Eeeh it's bad blood, that's worritis,' she'd tell Da and he'd look over to me with a smile and say, 'He's just got an over-active imagination, that's all.'

But Mam wasn't convinced. Her grandfather, Sidney 'Cheeky Fella' Reay, did music hall and then did a flit, leaving his wife with six bairns and no money, so as far as she was concerned 'actor' was synonymous with 'adulterer'. She was probably right, as a matter of fact. But I'm glad I found out about my granddad because it gave me the idea that *once*, somebody had escaped and done something really different.

When I got five good 'O' levels and Miss Short, my English teacher, sent a letter home recommending I go on to the Grammar school to do 'A' levels, my parents were having none of it. Da said I needed to come down to earth, behind which I think was the idea I needed to stop reading all those books and be more of a *man*, though he certainly didn't want me in the pit. Instead, he fixed me up a 'nice, outdoor, healthy job for life' with a mate of his in the seafaring line. The mate turned out to be a captain on a collier, one of the ships that still took coals from Newcastle down to London. I couldn't blame Da for his inability to see a future for me without coal being in some way involved.

So in 1968, by which time Eric Burdon had made Newcastle *the* place to be, there I was, plying the cold North

Sea in an old ship loaded down with best bitumen coal – me, another lad called Jacko, and Da's friend, Captain Pike.

It was a dirty, boring job, but coal being the sort of stuff that lies quietly after loading, we at least got time to read on the voyage south. I read Tolkien and Jacko read *Mayfair Magazine for Men*. Jacko was seventeen, a year older than me. He wasn't exactly a man of few words, but there wasn't much variety in the words he used. 'Canny' covered everything good, as in 'Canny tits, hor, do you not think, Ham?' 'Shite' was bad, and 'ye fucker!' expressed extremes of canny, shite and/or astonishment. To use his words, Jacko was a canny enough lad, though his taste in music (which ran to the Tremeloes and Herman's Hermits) was shite, and ye fucker! was how I felt after being stuck on a boat with him for five days.

Probably because of knowing Da, Captain Pike went easy on me and took most of his bad temper out on Jacko. He said Jacko was dense whereas I had a few brains, enough to warrant him now and again opening up the giant sea chest he kept in the cabin, digging out a little glass-topped table and a chess set, and challenging me to a game.

Mam said I'd see a bit of the world in the job, but I think what she had in mind was a glimpse of Hull on the way south, rather than Captain Pike's unscheduled activities at North Shields with Betty the Prostitute. Every Monday, Betty would be sitting on a capstan down by the quay, beefy red legs crossed at the ankle, waiting for us to come down the Tyne. We'd tie up and she and old Pike would go below for a bit, then she'd reappear, straightening her skirt, and Pike'd order me to accompany Betty and a sack of coal home to her place before we'd resume our journey south.

When Betty came aboard we lads were usually given orders of some kind to keep us out of the way, like going down the quay to pick up a couple of crabs for the captain's tea, and there was no chance of peeking in the cabin windows because the curtains were always tightly drawn. But Jacko realised it would be possible to bore a spy hole through the back of the coal hold. It took a couple of weeks of surreptitious activity with a gimlet to get a half-crown-sized opening which Jacko then plugged with a lump of coal until the next Monday came round. Then, after getting our marching orders from the captain, we crept back, lay down on top of the coal and took it in turns to peep through.

Pike opened up his chest and took out the little glass-topped table. Then he lay down on the floor while Betty stepped out of her bloomers, planted the table over his face, hoisted up her skirts and squatted over him. It looked like a kind of grown up version of 'I'll show you mine' until Betty started straining, which was when Jacko pulled me off and took my place.

'Ye fucker! Ye dirty fucker!' he whispered.

Remember, I was into elf maidens at the time and they obviously didn't go to the bog at all never mind shit on elf warrior's faces, and as I walked Betty back to her house with her bag of free coal, part of me was in shock. But I was also fascinated by the weirdness of it, and sort of thrilled by listening to Betty rabbit on about how the country was going to the dogs and it was all Harold Wilson's fault – after seeing her doing *that*. Cuff had a line for the mad way people behave in one of his plays: 'People. Think owt. Do owt.'

'Perve' was the word the incident added to Jacko's vocabulary. From that point on, his feelings for the captain changed from dislike to a murderous disgust that took only a few days to come to blows. It was their fight on the quayside that finally got me off the collier. Jacko had his say before leaving Cap'n Pike's employment with a split lip, and somehow or other news of this reached Mam. Though we never talked about it, she was suddenly persuaded that the Tech might not be the option most threatening to my morals, after all. So a few weeks later, I was signed up by a very dubious Mr Adrian Sylvester, MA (Cantab), to study music and drama at Newcastle College. The Animals may have broken up, The Club A-Go-Go may have closed, but Newcastle, lovely Newcastle, still seemed the centre of the world to me.

It was at the Tech I met Sam. Since he came from a village a few miles away from Pity Me and we were the only two working-class lads on the course, it's no surprise we became good friends. After leaving college, we went on to join Kicking Theatre together. *Alive & Kicking Theatre Co,* that is, to give it its full name – the company where you'd have to say Sam and me 'honed our craft' for quite a few years up to just after the time Cuff died. He went off to TV and the West End and I joined the RSC for a couple of seasons. Amazingly enough, the company survived our loss.

As it happened, the colliers from Newcastle to London only ran for another six months. So much for Da's job for life… I should have taken more note of that, because once I got where I wanted to be – on stage – I never thought I'd have to get off. But that's life: people die; love doesn't work out; you lose the job you thought you'd have for ever. You tell yourself it's a learning curve, and of course it is, but believing that is also what prevents us from jumping off the nearest bridge.

I. 3

Greg spotted Cuff's frizz of greying hair bobbing in the garden as we pulled up outside the house. He leapt out of the van, vaulted the fence and sprinted towards him, firing words as he ran. I shut the passenger door he'd left hanging open and took the slow way round via the gate and path. From a distance you could read the scene like a mime. Greg danced round the still figure of Cuff, who stood leaning on his fork, muddied but attentive. He had a way of listening with his head on one side, like an oldish male blackbird. 'So-oo Ham,' he said, in his soft Scottish stretched-out voice, 'It would seem I'm to write a play.'

I grinned stupidly at him. Cuff had the effect of making you feel happy and foolish at the same time. 'Jenny will be pleased to see you,' he said, stroking his chin, and transferring smudges of dirt onto his stubbly jowls. 'Perhaps we should all adjourn to my shed for a while?'

'Do you mind if I sit in?' I asked Greg.

He shrugged. 'Up to the writer.'

Cuff pulled open the flimsy wooden door. 'Away in, Ham.'

The shed wasn't much more than a large hen house containing a chair, a desk and a typewriter. As he wrote, Cuff could look out over his vegetables through a long horizontal slit into which a pane of glass had been haphazardly inserted. A couple of ancient canvas chairs were folded up in case of visitors and Greg and I erected these and sat down. The planked floor sagged.

I wish now I'd paid more attention to their discussion, but

as most of it was about history and politics, I went off into a bit of a dream while they talked. Periodically, Cuff put on his large tortoiseshell-rimmed specs and thumped something into his old Olivetti. I only woke up when they started to talk about casting and mentioned Sam. I told them, 'He's got this audition for a telly series in London.'

'I know,' said Greg firmly, 'but even if he gets it, it won't start till after the run.'

Cuff looked at me. 'But suppose we don't have Sam, I'm thinking, as long as we've got Ham…' the unspoken message being what he'd really like to do would be to write a one-man show for me… Of course it was flattery, and of course I lapped it up.

'…and Rod…' I said, magnanimous.

'Hmmm, yes.' Greg and Cuff exchanged glances.

'And Stafford,' I added, helpfully.

That seemed to cheer them up. 'Stafford, yes… good. What about the girls?'

'Alice and Maureen are perfect,' Greg said. 'You know, broad peasant faces…'

Just as well they're not around to hear that, I thought.

'Aye, aye,' Cuff took up the idea enthusiastically, 'Russian Women of the Revolution throwing off their chains…'

'And their voices… I see choirs, Cuff, marching men…'

'There's Jane, too,' I said, beginning to get worried for her.

'O yes. Jane's essential,' said Cuff.

'And Lynette.'

'A child?' Cuff looked at Greg.

'I've been promising her an adult part, if you can do it.'

'Well perhaps… So how many have I got in total?'

'I can guarantee you eight. Four men and four women. We've got the funds for that.'

'No chance of twenty-eight, then.'

'RSC's spoiled you,' Greg laughed. He wanted Cuff to write about Stalin. The 'tyrannical end of the Communist dream' was how he put it.

What about the Wallsend pensioners expecting a nice knees-up about the Blaydon Races? I thought.

Cuff nodded along, stroking his chin as Greg built up steam, then said quietly. 'A lot of people won't like us attacking the Soviet Union.'

You can say that again, I thought.

'I don't give two shits what they think.' Being American and an ex-soldier, and not inclined to apologise for either, Greg had had a few run-ins with actor members of the Workers Revolutionary Party over the years, mainly in the pub after shows. Within the company, we didn't go in much for politics. Most of us came from working-class backgrounds and the WRP seemed like a bunch of privileged private school head bangers. I suppose we saw ourselves as 'left wing' meaning not much at all except voting Labour if you could be bothered, a kind of blind support for trade unions and ritual slagging-off of American behaviour in Latin America. Russia wasn't imperialist according to my thinking then, and if I'd had the confidence, I'd have jumped in and told them the play to write was about Chile and Allende. But since I knew next to nothing about Allende except he was a hero, I just listened.

Cuff said. 'How long did you say I've got?'

I could see Greg working out the best words to use. 'Sixteen days,' he said at last.

Cuff laughed. 'We can forget the Stalin play, then. We do get a bit carried away, don't we?'

Greg sighed. 'Shit. Okay. But we've got to do this next, okay? Maybe in spring?'

'Well perhaps, yes. Doesn't sort out your problem for *now*, though,' Cuff said.

'Have you got anything we might use?'

'It's supposed to be a comedy about the Blaydon Races?'

Greg nodded.

'I may have something. An adaptation of a Feydeau farce I started for another company years ago. I've been thinking… I feel quite attracted to the idea of looking at it again. You know the kind of thing, unfaithful wives, lecherous old men…' He stood up and pulled from a shelf a pile of dog-eared cardboard files, extracted one and handed it to Greg. 'Have a look.'

Greg flipped it open began to read.

I think I must have a filmic kind of memory because it's usually the pictures I remember. I can still see the last of the day's thin September sun striking the dusty window and haloing their two uncombed heads. Through the glass, Cuff's wigwam of runner beans fluttered a little in the breeze, and an unpruned rose bush rambled over and around itself in a riot of blowsy pink blooms. The concentrating going on in that shed was intense, but it's restful being in the presence of others thinking without being under any obligation to do any oneself, and pretty soon I dozed off.

It must have been an hour later when Greg woke me up with 'Yep! There's something here. But it's an opportunity, Cuff, to do something *more*. Okay, it's farce. On the surface. But there's a build…or we can *make* a build, all this human mess coming to a climax the day of the Blaydon Races, June 1913, yes! The last time it was held before all the men disappeared to World War I.'

Cuff folded his arms and twinkled at him. 'You can't let go of your marching and your choirs, then?'

'Come on! We've always wanted to do something like this, a comedy that turns into a tragedy that leaves the audience in shock. Now's our chance! It's an opportunity.' Greg rolled a wad of Old Holborn into a narrow cigarette of liquorice paper and filled the shed with its sweet-smelling smoke. 'You'll need to make them working class, of course...and change the names, not the drawing room, but the backyard, a summer's day...'

It was Cuff's five-year-old daughter, Sally, who brought the meeting to an end. A tinkling sound approached across the garden and the handle of the shed moved downwards without opening. Cuff gave the door a shove and Sally's face peered in. She had little cymbals slotted over finger and thumb of both hands.

'Hellooo Sally.' Cuff held out his hand and she took the huge step up into the shed.

'Mam says can you do dinner,' she whispered. She pointed to a neatly plastered knee. 'Johnny pushed me over.'

Cuff lifted her onto his worn corduroy lap. 'Did he? Did he do that to you?' He brought her small hand to his mouth and kissed it. 'Shall we go out and find some greens to have with our chops?'

Cuff and I picked beans while Greg walked in a circle barking questions. I soon lost the plot, but Cuff, all the time groping expertly for beans, seemed to be keeping up, slipping from Feydeau's farce to something, as he put it 'more Greek tragedy'.

'A chorus! Yes! That's it!' Cuff stopped picking, stared at Greg and nodded slowly. 'But still comic,' Greg insisted. 'A big-scale intimate family drama.'

Even I found that funny, and we were all laughing as we went inside. 'You're talking Eisenstein, man. You'd need hundreds to do it justice.'

'You let me worry about the numbers. Just give me a script.'

Cuff stooped to clear a path for us through a load of children's bricks on the kitchen floor. His wife came into the room. 'Ah,' he said, straightening. 'There you are. We have visitors.'

I hadn't got to know Jenny well, then, but had seen enough of her to gather she didn't find it much fun stuck out in the wilds with two young kids. She was Cuff's second wife; he had another family from a previous marriage. From all accounts this second brood, and the financial and domestic cauldron into which it pitched Cuff, was the consequence of a middle-aged man's weakness for a schoolgirl; Jenny was only seventeen when they met.

Two kids later she'd put on a bit of weight, but still had the round face and little soft mouth of a girl, brown eyes sparkling at the sight of us, or to be more accurate, at the sight of Greg.

'You'll stay to dinner?' she said, a little breathlessly. Her long dark hair looked freshly washed. 'Cuff's doing chops.'

'Lovely,' I said.

Greg started up again, standing at Cuff's shoulder as he scraped carrots at the table. 'You know we can do it – done it before, haven't we? And we've got the *voices…*'

Jenny watched them for a while before realising the situation was hopeless and turning to me, 'Come on Ham. It's nice out. Let's leave them to their boring play.' I followed her down the garden path.

On the few times I'd seen Jenny – first nights mostly – there'd be a distinct I'm-not-going-to-miss-all-me-chances-of-having-fun-air about her. Cuff never seemed to mind her flirting; he certainly never said anything, and smiled on whatever she was up to as though it was no better than he deserved. Perhaps it was the sense of guilt that made him so useful about the house. He grew vegetables, cooked meals, washed-up – as well as writing endlessly in his shed to keep the family afloat.

Jenny picked a bloom from the rioting rose bush and tucked it behind one ear. 'How do I look?'

'Champion.'

She just wanted someone other than Cuff to notice her. I remember feeling awkward at the time, even a bit resentful. All that clumsy flirting, more like a fourteen-year-old than a woman of twenty-four, but it must be hard to have your seducing days over before they even get started. One shy smile and you're six months' gone.

We arrived in an untidy play area and Jenny climbed onto a kids' climbing frame and peered at me through the bars. Around us, the fields sloped away into other fields, patches of woodland, the odd cottage. 'Have you got a cigarette?'

I lit two and passed one over. She snorted out a long plume of smoke and looked at me. There was something appealing about the way her expressions told you exactly what she was thinking, even when, like now, it told me my company was only marginally better than no company at all.

'Have you heard of the Bhagwan Shree Rajneesh?' she said.

'Can't say I have.'

'He's like a guru. I met some people the other day who follow him. They're having a weekend, soon. You can take your kids. Or I might leave them with Cuff.'

'Sounds good,' I said. I wasn't much into gurus, but tried to sound interested because she obviously needed a bit of cheering up.

'Shit. Forgot to bring in the washing.' Jenny started taking greyish sheets off the line and piling them into my arms. Across the field we watched as a bus on its way to Newcastle groaningly approached the village stop, awaited by a small cluster of teenage girls setting off for a Saturday night out. Jenny's peg-filled hand paused in its work. The bus stopped, and, faintly, the high, excited voices of the girls drifted across the hedges to us. 'They'll have to stay the night,' Jenny said, with a short laugh. 'Last one back here is seven o'clock.' As the bus moved off the girls appeared on the top deck, weaving their way to the back seat.

Jenny added the last sheet and the pegs to my pile. 'That's what I miss most, you know. Getting ready to go out. Girls putting on their make-up together.' She turned and started walking back to the house. 'You live at number 12 too, don't you?'

'Some of the time.'

'It must be great, living there. Always something going on.'

'Yeah. It is good.'

'All the other mothers here are much older than me,' she said. 'I don't fit in. And there's nowhere to go – even with the kids. There's not even a park.'

I could have told her there was plenty of room for swings and sandpits in the garden, but that wasn't the point, of course. I liked her and felt sorry for her, which is, I suppose, why I got ambushed later, when we were finishing our meal, and Greg finally told Cuff exactly how long he'd got before opening night.

'I can't write a play in ten days!'

'You can. I know you can.'

Jenny gave Cuff a murderous look and told Greg. 'He can't. He promised to take us away. You *promised*, Cuff.' The two children stopped eating ice cream and watched their parents' faces.

'Yes,' said Cuff. 'That's right. I haven't forgotten. I promised to take Jenny and the children away for a few days.'

'I'll take them,' said Greg, and then, as Jenny threw him a scorching glance, 'or Ham will. Won't you, Ham?' Both children's eyes slid from Greg to me. 'Yes that's the best idea. I'll stay and work with you.' He looked at Jenny, 'And Ham will take you wherever you want to go.'

I was about to say *Hold on a minute, will you; just hold on one fucking minute here* when I caught sight of Jenny staring into her lap like a spaniel who's just been offered a juicy bone and had it snatched away. I had a horrible feeling she might burst into tears.

'Well, I don't know, maybe…'

'You can take the minibus,' said Greg, dead generous, like it was my birthday and he was giving me a wonderful present.

I still hadn't definitely said yes when the kids went off to watch *Dr Who* and Cuff took his accustomed place at the sink. Since Greg denounced drying dishes as an unhygienic British

43

perversion, that left me holding the tea towel. Jenny, brightening up at the prospect of having a few minutes alone with Greg, invited him into the next room for a smoke.

Cuff favoured big yellow gloves and a sponge thing on a stick. He made dreamy circles with this on the grill pan. 'She gets bored, poor thing.' The *r* rolled wonderfully on his tongue. He smiled. 'Life's guilty pleasures, Ham.' We watched the scummy water slide over the tray. 'This play,' he said, looking at me sideways through his steamed-up glasses, 'I think there'll be a good part in it for you, young Ham.'

'Will there?' I gripped the sopping tea towel.

'O yes. The main role, probably. At least, that's my thinking, at this stage. A miner, perhaps.' Cuff squirted a little more washing-up liquid into the greasy water and stirred it to a grey foam.

'My dad was a miner.'

He put a yellow finger up to pull his specs down a little and peer at me over the top. 'I know.'

I saw myself, the Tom Courtenay role in *Dr Zhivago*, a great orator, leading the miners into action. I saw a big musical number. Me and Julie Christie… Then I remembered it wasn't going to be a Russian play any more. What *was* it going to be, again? Cuff still looked at me. The wise blackbird again, so interested in me, so hungry for my thoughts. 'So I'm thinking you'll be able to bring a lot to this role.' My heart swelled. There was a pause while Cuff moved on to the pile of plates. 'I'd take it very kindly, Ham, if you would accompany Jenny and the children to see this Guru person…'

I don't think it occurred to me then I'd been seduced. Somehow, Cuff didn't get suspected of anything underhand,

44

though of course he must have been at times; his survival as a writer proved it.

'I'd be glad to,' I said. It may even have been, 'I'd be honoured,' so filled was I with a sense of personal sacrifice in the cause of *art* (or rather as I see it now in the cause of *me*) and so elevated an atmosphere now prevailed above the chipped sink.

Jenny came back, quite skittish, a bit flushed. Greg followed slowly. She touched Cuff's shoulder. 'Nearly finished? Shall I make some tea?'

'That would be lovely.' He tipped the bowl and the scummy water drained slowly away, food fragments eddying in circles to settle in the plug hole. Cuff rooted for them. 'Sooo Ham, though it's been a bit of a surprise, I'm looking forward to writing this play. I think it could come very much from the heart.'

Writing's an odd business. Over the course of few hours one idea had changed completely into another, and dramatic effects dreamed up for one play would enhance a totally different production. Now, I just wish I'd got someone to work with, to bounce ideas off, like they had.

Greg and I left soon afterwards. I drove us back through the Northumbrian countryside on a beautiful evening, the light soft but intensely defining, every contour of the land clearly etched against the sky. Greg didn't say much, but I felt his excitement matched my own. After *The Blaydon Races* would be the Stalin play, and after that… It looked like their partnership would go on, getting better and better, with loads of great parts for me, especially since soon Sam would be out of the way.

We reached the city's western outskirts, which at that time, years before it all was demolished to make way for 'Europe's Premier Retail Park', consisted of row upon row of cramped terraces. The sun going down over the Team Valley blazed suddenly, fierce and red, and momentarily the world of Newcastle's poorest, a world Cuff had spent years bringing to life on stage, took fire.

I. 4

'Good-morning-Goodman-Fisher-Douglas-this-is-Angie-how-may-I-help-you?'

I'd rehearsed in my head the call but the words still stuck to the back of my throat 'It's Ham Nicolson.'

The little sigh followed by a pause gained Angie immediate status points because it forced me into grovelling mode. 'It's all right; I don't want to speak to him… I was just wonderin'… I mean following up…that audition I did.'

I remember Greg telling us when we started rehearsing a new play that the way into our characters was to find the 'I want' behind every line spoken. Sometimes, there's a great big 'I want' behind all the lines a character speaks. Mr Khan is constantly saying things under which pulsates *I want your respect*, because so many of the toe rags that come in the shop seem to be intent on delivering *I want you to get back in your dusky immigrant kennel.* They don't need words to deliver that message.

Once you become aware of them, you hear these struggles for status going on around you all the time. Sometimes the battles get bloody. And none bloodier than my encounters with Angie of the sing-song voice.

'Now, Mr Nicolson.' Note the phrase. Its weight. Its pretence of patience. An address to kids or the bothersome old. 'Which audition exactly?' The tapping of fingernails on computer keyboard. 'We've got that many clients and that many auditions.'

'Pork Scratchings.'

'Oh yes... The local radio thing. I think they recorded it the next day. Yes. Here's your file. "Unsuccessful" it says.'

'You might have let me know.'

'Mr Nicolson. Believe me I tried. I've noted here *cannot be contacted by phone*.'

'Oh aye. Sorry. Been having a bit of trouble with phones lately. Sorry.'

'And still no email address?' Note the placing of that 'still'. And the vocal achievement of keeping the chime in the voice but somehow slipping in *scathing*. It's one to think about – professionally I mean.

'You can get me at this number,' I blurted, rashly giving her the shop landline. 'I'll let you know my new mobile next week...' I rallied the troops in a bid for surprise offensive/rearguard action '...once I've got some satisfactory answers out of my provider.' A different kind of pause. Yes! A patch of higher ground gained. 'So, Angie, got anything else for me?'

An intake of breath. 'Hold on.' And away she went, leaving me with Liza and a different kind of fear taking hold; that Mr Khan would be back any minute and I'd lose the job on the grounds of failing the *trustworthiness* test.

But Angie didn't take long. 'Nothing *what so ever*, I'm afraid.' Killer line, usually, especially slowed down like that, but my spark of resistance glimmered on.

'Fine. Well that will give me a bit of time to finish the series I'm working on.'

'Series?'

'Yep. In a rush to make a meeting, I'm afraid. Cheers Angie. Talk soon.' I put the phone down.

For a moment I felt elated. Just for a moment.

I've been with a few agents down the years. For a brief period with the RSC I had one with sofas and coffee machines in reception and a big pile of *The Face* magazines to pass the time until one of a couple of gorgeous women ushered me into the presence. But my career's been on the slide for a decade and I know all the scenes /duologues that take actor and agent towards the parting of the ways.

'They loved you, Ham, but they've just gone in a different direction...' followed a thin month or so later by, 'The problem is they have a choice...' or the verging-on-the-cruel, 'The director thought you were great but in the end the producer wanted to go with a name...'

And then you get called in for a chat. 'I don't know if the photo's working any more...' or 'Have you changed what you do in auditions?'

I've heard agents talking about other actors, so I know what comes next, 'Problem is he's past his sell-by date,' or, 'We just can't move him.' And finally:

'He's dead in the water.'

Sitting there at the till I realised the warning signs were all flashing with Goodman Fisher Douglas – the seedy agency I've been with for the last eighteen months. I only ever got to talk to Angie these days, and no doubt Angie would soon be instructed to tell me the partners really didn't think the relationship was working any more and I'd be better off elsewhere... Which I suppose will at least give me the satisfaction of telling Angie that there are no other agencies to try, Goodman Fisher Douglas being the absolute shite-ist, bottom-feederish, etc. around. In fact I decided to phone up and resign right then – just for the brief surge of pleasure it would give me to tell her what a crap job she'd got.

But at that moment Mr Khan came back. 'Great news,' I said breezily, 'sold the last of the tomatoes.' *Trust me.*

'Good, good,' he said, going in the back to put on his white coat. Thing is, now I've been there a few weeks, he does seem to trust me. Doesn't make a fuss when he catches me reading or looking up words in the dictionary at the till, because as I've found out, Mr Khan approves of knowledge. He told me he thought when he came to England everybody would be quoting Shakespeare, but instead discovered, as he put it, 'There is much ignorance.'

'We used to be keen on education here,' I told him, 'but we've gone off it.'

Made me think of my father going down the WEA and coming home with wonderful stories about the Greeks. Mr Khan knows a lot about them, too, and recently, after closing, we've been kind of swapping stuff about Shakespeare for stuff about the Greeks, so he must have accepted the idea of me being an actor, however far I am from his Laurence Olivier idea of thesps. Once I've got rid of the last of the cider drunks and lowered the metal shutters, we go upstairs to Mr Khan's little room, he gets out a couple of glasses and opens a box of out-of-date cheesey snacks. 'So Mr Nicolson,' he says, pouring the cooking brandy, 'Richard the Third; are you for, or against?'

In the only production of Dick the Shit – or Richard the Turd, a joke lost on Mr Khan – I've ever been in, I played Second Murderer, Gentleman and (veiled) Handmaiden to the Queen, but it isn't just sour grapes when I say it was a crap show, mainly down to the monstrous ego of the leading man. I know Richard's dominant, but the actor who played him might has well have performed all by himself. We did all call him Dickshit behind his back and I was just grateful I only had one scene with him, because he'd stoop to any trick – changing the moves, suddenly coming downstage, literally shoving people out of the light, hopping about all over the shop – to keep the focus entirely on him for the whole three hours. Yes, it was that bloody long, too, because he loved pauses, anything up to 12 seconds (we counted) *'Now is the winter of our* (six-second pause, head swivel right, head swivel left, suck teeth) *dis con tent.'*

It's enjoyable, talking about 'the bard' as Mr Khan calls him, and he loves to hear about the Shakespearean roles I've played. It sounds glamorous, and I'm dead proud of having worked for the RSC, but I always find myself somehow steering the conversation around to the old days. The fact is, for me, nothing ever beat the thrill of Kicking Theatre on form, so I started to tell him about *Myself. You. All of us.*

Greg did *Myself. You. All of us.* just before we went on stage to perform *The Life and Times of Mary Angell* for the first time. In the usual run of things, Greg wasn't one for drama exercises, warm-ups often being a swift pint down the local pub, but things were looking very grim. We'd had a disastrous dress run and with only two hours to go till curtain up, he'd just told us there were yet more rewrites to go in. Cuff scribbled away at the back of the hall. I caught his eye a few minutes later. He looked like a rat in a trap.

As well he might. The play was based on a real family, and it was opening in their home town. Fifty or so descendants of

Mary Angell, plus a couple of hundred of the Angells' friends and acquaintances, would be watching. The fact it was sold out meant another two hundred would be in, just expecting a good night out. *That's* the kind of audience that makes you nervous.

Kicking came under the label of a small-scale touring company, but that didn't mean small productions or small audiences. *Mary Angell* had a cast of nine, played several five-hundred-seaters, and the set was huge. The get in had taken three hours so we were all knackered and some bits didn't fit. The teccies hammered away still, making last-minute alterations to the boxing ring that formed the main playing space, turning what our Buddhist designer had envisaged in the round into the three-quarter thrust stage most of the venues demanded. There'd been a huge row between her and Greg and she'd disappeared, presumably off to set light to a few joss sticks.

Greg was doing his tiger-in-a-zoo pacing, stroking his short black beard, a red shirt making him look even more satanic than usual. Then he took it out on the chairs, shoving them violently aside to clear spaces about the hall. He put his fingers to his mouth and whistled. 'Can you all come here, please? Yep, you as well, Cuff.'

He put us in positions so the whole space, from the stage to the swing doors at the back, was covered. Told us we had to say 'myself, you, all of us' in turn. We were not impressed.

'Fuck's the point of this…?' Sam said, arms folded over his long Catholic priest's costume, and for a moment I thought he might lead a rebellion by stalking off to the pub, but Stafford, who had his first lead role, chipped in, 'Nothing to lose is there?' He was stripped to the waist and gleaming with sweat from his last bout with the punchbag.

'Great vocal exercise,' Greg said.

I touched my chest and said 'Myself', then looked at Stafford and said 'You', then took in the tired and gloomy lot of we, 'All of us.'

'You've got to reach every corner of the space,' Greg said.

When you think you're going to die a death, how much does it matter if people can hear you? I thought, but I raised my voice. 'Myself.'

'Don't fuck around,' Greg shouted. 'Think about the word you're saying. You can't fake this exercise.'

After knowing Stafford for 10 years I knew who he was, all right. Though he certainly looked different. He looked fantastic, in fact. The five weeks' hard training had made him every inch the lightweight boxing champion of South Shields 1936 he was going to be on stage later. 'You,' I said. *Angry. Dangerous. Dedicated.*

Difficult to explain to Mr Khan. The nearest thing is taking you back to being a kid again, when a group of other kids turn up at your door and say 'You coming out to play?' and you search their faces and see they really have something big on, and before you know it you're running with them, stone deaf to your mam's questions following you up the back lane, off on some mysterious adventure together.

'All of us.' I could feel the words swelling in my diaphragm and building and connecting with the other voices, and all the people who would soon be our audience.

At this point, I tried to show Mr Khan how it worked. He felt a bit awkward, I could tell, but he came out from behind

53

the till and boomed out a 'Myself' that had such a strong sense of his own identity it nearly sent me out through the plastic doors into the storeroom. His 'You' sucked me back. We vocally embraced ourselves, each other, the condiments, the cakes and biscuits and the chest freezers.

Back in that 1980 first night, when Greg called us together to rehearse in the rewrites, not one of us complained. Half an hour after that, the place began to fill up.

Mary Angell started on time. We got a laugh where we'd expected one in the first scene; then, just afterwards we got a huge laugh where we hadn't expected it at all. It's when things like that happen you know the show is a wild horse, and your job is to ride it, keeping your body flexible so that if it shoots off in an unexpected direction you can stay on, feeling the energy underneath you, keeping your reactions sharp. You start pausing where you've never paused before – not Dick-the-shit *look at me* pauses, but a pause where the piece needs to take a breath, or roll over and have its tummy tickled – and you might have to jump out of the way if that happens.

The love scene at the half took things to a new height when Jane's blouse popped. Hanging out the washing as Mary she stretched and two buttons undid themselves, those tiny buttons on 1930s frocks that are really hard to do up, and she being a respectable girl, can hardly talk to her Johnny with her underwear showing. So there she was, all the rehearsed pegging-out moves up the creek, holding her blouse together, breathless in the company of Stafford as her Johnny, the man she loves but thinks she's lost.

It's when you get ambushed like that that things get special. She's trying to peg out clothes with one hand, keeping her blouse closed with the other, when Stafford ducks under the line, magically does up her buttons without looking ('cos he's a respectful lad); takes her in his arms, and kisses her. *End of the first half.*

We knew we were flying, the only problem being lifting it even higher at the end.

Jane, under a spot, standing in the middle of the boxing ring that'd become – by flying in bunting and playing 'happy crowd' sound effects mixed with a bit of brass band – the quayside, at the launch of *The Mauritania*.

Mary's handsome Johnny is dead by now, there's no work to be had, hardly a roof over her head, but in her memory she watches the ship slide down the slipway, *'The great beautiful size of it… All that wood and iron, hammered and sawn into that lovely shape. Slippin' away in a few minutes an' just for a few minutes fillin' your eyes wi' dreams…'*

We watch her watch the ship, in her shapeless cotton dress and squashy hat: *'Look it's the most beautiful thing in the world and us made it. Us rough and raggy Tyneside folk, us made it.'* And me, you, and all of us wonder at how lovely she's become.

She stops speaking. Silence. Total silence. Then that first dull slap of left palm on right. Then many palms slapping. Then cheers. Then roars.

The Angells were ecstatic and the ordinary punters loved it as well. The funders and the local press said very complimentary things and the *Guardian*'s stringer scuttled out in a hurry – to file his copy that night, we hoped. In the event, Monday's paper called *Mary Angell* 'regional theatre at its best,' and I reckon it got that right.

Even the three-and-a-half-hour get out couldn't dampen

our sense of triumph. After we'd stuffed the set into the truck we all went down to the fish quay. Cuff treated us all to crab, still warm from the big boilers on the dock, washed down with a barrelful of beer. Three a.m. and the place was buzzing; fishermen and actors – seemed like a good mix.

We'd pulled it off, Stafford and Jane maybe most of all, because they had the main parts, but *we'd all done our bit to make it work.* I can see that cast now, drinking, eating and laughing under the orangey lights of the quayside, the backdrop a silvery sea, Cuff and Greg to one side, gassing. I knew who they all were and we loved each other and that's how we'd carry on, carry on, a few spats notwithstanding, working together as one on that tour. *Myself. You.*

I think I got it across to Mr Khan, too, because I swear by our third 'all of us' the fish fingers were sitting up in their boxes, ready for the show.

I. 5

A week or so after our visit to Cuff, Hardley called an emergency meeting. We weren't keen on meetings, but he made it sound really important – said the future of Kicking depended on it.

I remember that Matt was sweeping the yard outside The Building when I arrived. He nodded at me and I asked him how he was getting on. ''S okay,' he said. 'Nowt much to do, like.'

'Wait till we start rehearsin'.' He looked at me, unconvinced. 'Coming to the meetin', are yous?'

'Didn't know I was invited.'

'Oh aye. Everyone gans to meetings.' I wanted to give him the impression he belonged. He set the brush against the wall and followed me in.

No doubt I ignored him after that because it felt like a bit of a party inside – everyone having just come back from their summer holidays. After we'd told each other what we'd been up to for the last couple of months, people started to ask about the new production and Hardley said bookings for *The Blaydon Races* were going well because everyone loves a laugh… I gathered, a bit uneasily, that I still had to keep my mouth shut about the change of writer. After a few minutes of gossip, Hardley tried to call order. He'd have liked a bit of help from Greg, but Greg seemed only half there. I supposed the other half was off in somewhere epic with Cuff's play.

Finally, Hardley got us sitting in a circle on various chairs and boxes. He counted up. Thirteen. 'Eeh that's bad luck,' said

Lynette, with a sharp intake of breath. At only eighteen, Lynette was the youngest in the company and her specialism – gasping, wide-eyed amazement, 'eeh you never did!' or 'never in the world!' – was combined with an absolute belief in ghosts, omens, tarot cards and superstitions in general. 'One of us will have to leave!'

Rod, an actor who greatly resented wasting any of his time on company business, looked at her. 'I'll go.'

Last time I saw Lynette she'd moved on to more sophisticated fears regarding inorganic food, air quality and carcinogens, though still expressed with that breathy horror that took you straight back to the playground. Back then, with her mass of blonde curls and big blue eyes, she was brilliant at playing kids.

Hardley cleared his throat. 'Sit down, Rod. We *all* have to be at this meeting or it will be bad luck for everyone.' He waited for silence. 'I need someone to take the minutes.'

Rod, writhing in anger at spending Saturday morning in The Building rather than at the pub, spat out, 'You're the administrator aren't you?'

'Yes. But I can't run the meeting *and* do the minutes.'

'Who said you could run the meeting? I thought we were all equal here.'

Hardley folded his arms. 'All right then. *You* run the meeting.'

'Don't know what the fuck it's about do I?'

Stafford cut in. 'Shut up then, ye workie ticket, or we'll be here all day.'

I offered to do the minutes.

'Thank you Ham.' Then, remembering I wasn't much good

at it, Hardley added, 'Just get –the gist down and I'll tidy them up later. Names first. Oh, and one apology. Sam phoned.'

'Where is he, like?' I swear it was in unison from Maureen and Alice, tensed for action on my left flank.

'London, I think he said.'

Lynette gave an excited squeak. 'It'll be that series!'

'They're auditioning the men first,' said Maureen. *I'm in touch with the producers* was the message. I wasn't convinced.

'If we could get on…' Hardley glared at Greg, whose eyes were directed downward to the task of rolling a thin wad of tobacco in a liquorice paper. Jane twisted her wedding ring nervously, and I remembered how she hated conflict. She was looking good after the summer break. Tanned. 'Just from the garden,' she'd said, like an apology.

Minutes

J Hardleman (administrator) called the meeting to order and informed those present that Northern Arts had requested the company adopt a recognised UK company structure as soon as possible, and certainly before the next round of funding decisions. Northern Arts felt they could not continue to provide financial support to Alive and Kicking without an acceptable structure having been agreed and put in place.

'What's wrong with it?' Rod said. 'Works all right. Let's leave it as it is.'

Greg woke up. 'The problem is it isn't anything right now. It's not a collective, though we all get equal pay, it's not a management structure, though you could say Hardley and I act as managers…'

'Oh aye,' Maureen interrupted, 'and I suppose you want it to be a management thingy so yous two can get paid more than the rest of we.'

Mrs Maureen Buckley questioned the desirability of adopting a traditional management structure with the likelihood of administrative and artistic functions attracting higher salaries than those given to the performers.

'That's right, Maureen, up the workers!'

Mr W Stafford supported this view.

'What's a collective then?' Rod was more interested now, sniffing a dispute in the offing.

Greg closed his eyes and went back to Playland. Hardley tried to explain. 'In a collective everyone has a say in every single decision the company makes,' he went on, looking hard at Rod.

Alice made a big circular gesture with her hands, 'You know,' she said enthusiastically, 'like in the Soviet Union.'

Only two abstained from the collective murmur of approval that followed her words. My mind filled with pictures of happy Cossacks raising their glasses in vodka toasts...of strong, smiling women, bearing baskets filled with golden loaves for all to share. Imagining those women, I could see why Cuff and Greg had got excited about Alice and Maureen playing Russian...Then I had a thought.

'Isn't Scally Roo a collective?'

The mood of the meeting changed. *Escalier Rouge*, universally called Scally Roo on account of pronunciation difficulties, was a smaller company than Kicking, specialising in what they called 'revolutionary theatre'. Alice and I had both worked with them at different times. Seemed like an honour at the time to work alongside intellectuals. Now I think we just fulfilled their need for a token pleb or two in the cast, helping bridge the yawning gulf between what their audiences wanted to see and what they wanted to show them.

Alice followed my drift. 'They have a meeting every day. Gans on forever sometimes.'

Rod gaped. 'Every day?'

'I remember one about bog paper,' I said. 'Andrex or Bronco in the toilet.'

'What did they go for?'

'Bronco in the end. Solidarity with the workers, like.'

Stafford snorted. 'We share your sore arses comrades!'

'Aye,' said Maureen, 'that's what they call theirselves you know. That comrade shite.'

'Hey, Ham,' said Stafford, 'that show you did, where you had to take your kit off...'

I didn't need reminding. In their self-devised *Arcadia in Ashington*, the Scally Roos showed pre-industrial paradise by having us all nude in the first half except for garlands of paper flowers round our necks and then, after the interval, during which time capitalism had arrived, we all blacked up and put on miners' helmets. Nobody 'got' the production, the miners of Ashington least of all, but the fact there were two nubile young lasses in the cast meant the audience figures for *Arcadia* were apparently still the best in Scally Roo history. Stafford was just about killing himself laughing at the memory. 'That guy. I divvent know how he dared...' He raised a curled index finger. 'No bigger than that, it was. Mi-nute. Do ye not remember?' The whole meeting dissolved into a discussion of one of the leading Scally Roo's very small dick.

'What kind of paper you got in your bog?' Stafford asked Rod. 'I won't just take your word for it, mind. I'll be needing a look at your arse.'

Hardley shouted 'All right, all right. Quieten down. If you don't like the idea of a collective, what about a partnership, then? That's another alternative.'

> *J Hardleman (administrator) explained that each individual could become a partner in the company. Mrs M Buckley expressed her concern that a partnership structure would not adequately recognise the members of the company who had contributed most over the years. She suggested a sliding scale, with those most recently joining the company regarded as junior partners, which could be reflected in the pay given.*

Stafford, who always drove the truck, looked up from cleaning his nails with a matchstick. 'You can carry the next play's set on your back to the venues if you gan for that option.' There was no love lost between Stafford and Maureen.

> *J Hardleman went on to explain that in a normal partnership, partners shared profits equally and had equal liability for any losses.*

'What fucking profits?' said Rod.

'Well precisely,' said Hardley. 'We don't make profits. But you shouldn't forget we could make losses.'

'What? With a tight-fisted bugger like you?' Rod said. It was true. Hardley's control on the purse strings was such that we usually had a slight surplus at the end of the financial year and, for all his eccentricities, Greg also took a pride in bringing shows in on budget. It was what, among other things, differentiated us from the Scally Roos and plenty of other community theatre companies around.

Though making a loss might appear unlikely given the present controls, J Hardleman wanted everyone to keep clearly in mind the possibility of future debts in making the decision as to whether to opt for a partnership structure. In the event of a loss, there would be a call on the partners' assets, so for instance it might come about that a partner's house would have to be sold.

'Well that counts me out, then,' said Maureen, who'd been simmering by my side for a while. 'I'm not putting my bairns' future on the line.'

Maureen had three kids, all of them in my view well past being called *bairns*. One of them worked in a bank. But I didn't say anything. For most of us, the idea of having any assets under threat was pretty remote. We either rented rooms or still lived at home. The only person apart from Maureen who owned a house was Jane. Hardley looked at her. 'What do you think?'

Jane flushed. 'I like the idea of a partnership,' she said. 'And I trust you not to get us into debt.' She hesitated then seemed to take courage. 'That's what makes me feel good about it – the idea of us trusting each other to do our jobs, whether we're actors, or set builders, or lighting designers or like you, the administrator, or the director, like Greg.'

Greg gave Jane a soft look. I think if you could have photographed the males in the room at the moment, they would all have their heads on one side, internally smiling at Jane.

I see now how alike we were, Jane and me. A pair of romantics, in love with the company. Of course we were ambitious, wanted opportunities, like Sam and his London auditions or like Maureen would get with her soap, but it didn't sour the present for us. The privilege of being in the company was what we felt. I'm not sure we'd really have wanted anything more than staying there for ever, if only it had been possible.

'Well! More fool you to be so trusting,' said Maureen, nodding significantly towards Hardley and Greg.

'I think we ought to ask an astrologer,' said Lynette. 'There's a good one on Thursdays in the Bigg Market.'

Rod stood up. 'Don't be fucking stupid, Lyn. If we don't get a shift on we won't get last orders.'

'I want a partnership,' said Stafford. 'Let's have a vote on it.'

'Hang about.' Alice raised her hand. 'Hardley – are you saying everything'll go on as it has – you doing the money and Greg the directing?'

'And we won't have meetings all the time?' added Rod.

J Hardleman assured those present that nothing in the day-to-day running of the company need change, if all were happy with procedures as they were. Only the structural basis would be different, and that was in order to safeguard the funding from Northern Arts. H. Nicolson proposed a vote in favour of a partnership, seconded by A Taylor. The result of the vote taken was eight in favour two against and one abstention.

People immediately got up and moved for the door. Then someone said 'What about Sam?' and it was agreed he be offered the choice to become a partner or not. As it turned out, he decided not, I suppose Kicking having become rather small fry by then, and the prospect of owning assets looming large.

The need for the pub having become pressing in a number of minds, the meeting broke up in a hurry after that. Maureen stalked off home to her *bairns*, but it seemed everyone else was up for a drink, including Jane. She didn't usually come and for a minute I basked in the idea of an hour or so in her company. That was until Greg, in a hissing whisper, reminded me that we were due at Cuff's. Him to work with the writer – and me, idiot fool me – to accompany Jenny and the kids on a three day visit to the Guru place.

That depressing prospect to one side, I should tell you the outcome of the meeting was successful, since Northern Arts showed their satisfaction with our improved 'corporate underpinning' and our continued 'artistic excellence' by handing out an increase in the next funding period and agreeing a capital grant to develop a small theatre space in the building. They'd liberated the funds by making a few cuts, and one of the victims was Scally Roo.

LIGHTS UP ON CUFF'S KITCHEN. CUFF, LOOKING TIRED, IS SWEEPING THE FLOOR. HE PAUSES FOR A MOMENT, LISTENING

TO THE SOUND OF RAPID FOOTSTEPS AND CHILDREN'S VOICES IN THE ROOM AND THEN STOOPS TO PICK UP A RABBIT SOFT TOY, BLOWING THE DUST FROM IT BEFORE SITTING IT CAREFULLY AGAINST THE SUGAR BOWL ON THE TABLE. THERE IS A KNOCK ON THE DOOR. BEFORE CUFF CAN MAKE A MOVE GREG BOUNDS INTO THE ROOM, FOLLOWED BY HAM.

GREG   How's it going?

CUFF PICKS UP A SHEAF OF PAPERS FROM THE TABLE AND GIVES IT TO GREG

CUFF   There. Today's offering. *(Greg flings himself down in a chair, takes some bent glasses out of a pocket and starts reading)* And hello there, Ham. The man of the hour. I'm very grateful to you and I know Jenny is too. *(Cuff exits briefly and can be heard calling up the staircase)* Jenny? They're here. *(he comes back)* I think they're nearly ready.

THE SOUND OF RUNNING FOOTSTEPS ON THE STAIRS. THE CHILDREN, SALLY (5) AND JOHN (9) COME INTO THE ROOM. THEY ARE BOTH WEARING CLOTHES COLOURED A STREAKY ORANGE. PAUSE.

CUFF   Well you both look…very cheerful.

JENNY ENTERS, CARRYING A LARGE HOLDALL. SHE IS WEARING AN ORANGE SMOCK OVER COTTON TROUSERS AND HAS OBVIOUSLY MADE AN EFFORT WITH HER HAIR AND MAKE-UP — BUT SHE LOOKS FLUSTERED.

JENNY	It doesn't suit me at all, does it? *(Ham looks at her. Greg glances up briefly from his reading)*
CUFF	You look very nice.
JENNY	Ham?
HAM	You look canny, aye.

JENNY LOOKS AT GREG WHO TAKES OFF HIS GLASSES AND CONSIDERS HER.

GREG	Too much orange. It bleaches your face. Maybe keep the trousers and change the shirt. Something blue? Then you could have a bit of orange in earrings – or in your hair – if you want. You need to get some focus on your eyes. You've got good eyes.
JENNY	*(angrily, to Cuff)* I told you! *(she flounces out of the room and all listen to her pound up the stairs. There is a pause as she can be heard banging about in her bedroom. Cuff looks at Greg, now reading intently again)*
JOHN	I wish you were coming, Dad.

67

CUFF	Your mummy needs a break from me. And I need to work. *(he ruffles his son's hair while addressing Sally)* And you, Miss, have you not forgotten someone? *(he reaches for the rabbit and gives it to Sally)*
SALLY	Robert! *(she hugs the rabbit to her face and leans against her father's legs, thumb in her mouth. Greg is still intent on his reading, apparently oblivious to all else)*
CUFF	*(mischievously to Ham)* I notice you are not wearing the sacred hue?
HAM	You're cracking jokes aren't you?

JENNY RETURNS, NOW WEARING A BLUE BLOUSE. SHE AIMS HER CHALLENGE PARTICULARLY AT GREG.

JENNY	Better? *(he nods)* So. *(raises her voice slightly)* We all set?

HAM PICKS UP THE HOLDALL AND GREG PUTS ASIDE THE SCRIPT AND STANDS UP.

HAM	Come on you two. Let's go on holiday.

THE CHILDREN AND CUFF FOLLOW HAM OUT OF THE DOOR. JENNY AND GREG STAND AWKWARDLY.

JENNY	Bye then.

GREG   Have a good time. *(Greg sits down and takes up the script)*

JENNY   OK. See ya.

SHE GOES OUT. VAN DOORS SLAM, VOICES SHOUT GOODBYES, SOUND OF VAN DRIVING OFF. CUFF RETURNS AND SHUTS THE DOOR, LEANING ON IT FOR A MOMENT. WITHOUT LOOKING UP FROM THE SCRIPT, GREG PATS THE VACANT SEAT BESIDE HIM.

GREG   It's getting there, but we've got a lot of work to do.

I. 6

Soon after I paid my bill and got my mobile working, Sam rang me up out of the blue. Hadn't seen him for nearly a year and after his behaviour *then*. I should have cut him off as soon as I'd realised who it was. That I didn't was partly because I wanted to have my say. 'I saw your book.'

'Oh. Yeah.'

'Selling well, is it?'

'Couldn't say. Leave that to my agent. Anyway, how are you me old mate?'

I was on the brink of remarking, 'As an old mate, like, why wasn't I worthy of a mention in your book?' but it just seemed a pathetic thing to say and it always feels good, sort of *warming*, to hear his voice. So I gave him what I suppose he expected, the usual spiel about waiting to hear on a really good part, funding being almost in place for a film… then added, 'matter of fact, I'm doing some writing meself.'

'Are you? What kind of thing?'

'Soap opera, for one. Security guards in a shopping centre.'

'Canny idea, like. Didn't they do one of those already?'

'Don't think so.' But a hole opened up in the conversation through which my hopes started to drain. I filled it, finally. 'What about you, then?'

'Not a lot, to be honest.' He seemed a bit down, and I suppose I'm unimportant enough to be confided in, so I ended up in the ridiculous situation of consoling him because he hadn't had a TV series in a couple of years. 'Not like the old days, is it?' he said. 'Load of crap writing. Some of the things

I get sent – you should see them.' There was a pause. 'I was thinking ye knaa, that last play we did at Kicking, that was one of Cuff's, wasn't it? That *Blaydon Races*.'

'His last.' The hole got a bit bigger. Then I couldn't resist: 'Tell you what else is funny. You don't mention it in your book.'

'Not commercial is it? Not what they want. They just want to know about meeting famous people, going to Hollywood, parties, wild nights, that kind of stuff.'

'You never told me you met Ava Gardner.'

'Aye well. Ye didn't ask.'

'Did you though?'

'Down there in black and white, isn't it? Look what's up with you, anyway? I phone up for a chat about old times and all I get is a fucking interrogation. Autobiography's just another project. Get it out, get it on the shelves for Christmas, we've all got to do one.'

'Who's all?'

'Ye knaa. Everyone who's so say *made it*. Your agent sorts it out. Tell you the truth – I didn't write much of it.'

That bit of honesty did the trick. Fact was, I really wanted to talk about Cuff, that play, the Feast. 'You know, Sam, *'The Blaydon Races'* was when everything changed. Like we all confronted our destinies. I mean life and death… Things happened then I've never forgotten, I've lived with ever after. Remember the feast?'

'Good party.'

'And Matt?'

'See what you mean.'

'Cuff, too.'

71

'He was a great writer, mind. Parts I play these days, you can say the next line before you read it. What was the first one we did of his?'

Well that started off a long conversation about Cuff and the state of British playwriting, with Sam asking all the right questions as far as I was concerned, and it was a good half hour before he said he had to go because Denis Waterman was coming round for a game of snooker. Even though he said that, I put the phone down with very friendly feelings towards him, that-Sam-he's-canny-really sort of thing. I think I even said, 'Hope things look up for you,' before ringing off.

But who do I see when I turn on the telly a month or so later? Sam. Doing a bit of public remembering. About Cuff. Turned out it was 25 years since he died. Sam reminiscing. And what do I hear among his own recollections of working with the great man? *My* words talked back to me, Sam spouting my memories, and passing them off as his. Bastard.

There were one or two familiar faces on the programme – people who'd known Cuff and then gone on to do well themselves – and a lot of other successfuls, who as far as I knew had never worked with him at all. The irony was that none of the people who really knew Cuff were on the programme. There was no Greg, no Stafford, no Jane. No me. They didn't even have Cuff's wife, Jenny, on – and I would've liked to see her again, though come to think of it she'd probably told the producers to fuck off.

Anyway, since Cuff didn't know most of these 'great friends' from Adam, they'd all had to take the 'adopt a memory' approach. One young lass, now on *Emmerdale*, who must have been about seven when Cuff died, said his words had been in

72

the air she breathed; it was as though they'd always been part of her. Sadie, her name was.

The whole Remember-Cuff-Twenty-Five-Years-On must be a nice little earner for Sam, so I can stop worrying about him, because the announcer said afterwards they're doing five of Cuff's best plays on Sunday nights in October to commemorate the anniversary. Starring Sam. That's when I stopped feeling angry and started feeling the old clutch (weak, but still there) of ambition. Must be a part or two in it for me, I thought. I phoned up the BBC the next day and it turns out they're shooting now – in Manchester – and it's all been cast.

That hurt. I asked to be put through to the producer and when she finally came on the line I said, 'Don't you want actors that know the plays?' She gave me a bit of flannel about being well aware of the fine work I'd done in the past but what they were really after was *freshness*.

'Why are you using Sam, then?'

'Well obviously because he's an established television presence. I'm sorry I don't have time to talk further. Do keep in touch.'

I told Mr Khan about it. Didn't expect him to have much to say, but he leaned over, topped up my glass and said, 'Ah! Fickle fortune! But you know all about that from your Shakespeare, of course.'

It seems Mr Khan's slipped down a bit, too. He started to tell me about his great granddad, a man of noble family possessed of a harem of gorgeous women and also a great warrior, who, mounted on an Arab steed of surpassing beauty, led his men into battle at the Khyber Pass. Mr Khan's shoulders went back, his neck extended, I swear his nostrils flared at the thought of his ancestor, and I almost expected him to pull out some huge shining scimitar from behind the till and strike off my head. As it was, I could see the horse prancing, the air swirling with sand and grit – and Mr Khan's glittering eyes as he raises his blade and the line of horses plunges forward.

In his youth, he said, his family had still owned a lot of land in Afghanistan, so he's seen his fortunes change a lot, too, his domain reduced to a little shop where he has to be nice even to the 'Oy Pakkie' morons around here.

Mr Khan takes a very kindly interest in my non-existent career. He seemed pleased to hear I'm writing, but not impressed by television sitcoms. 'The movies, old boy, that's the way to make a big death.'

A big killing, I think he meant.

I explained I'd tried screenplays a few times and never got anywhere, so the obvious message coming through was 'give up', but I keep trying. I've written a 'Very *Get Carter*' thriller, and a soap opera about a funeral parlour (finished a week before BBC 1 screened the first episode of a soap opera about a funeral parlour).

But somehow, however much I get knocked back, September always brings a whiff of hope with its sharper air and the idea I can still succeed provided I put in sufficient *endeavour*. I suppose this sense of renewal goes back to schooldays, *I will try harder this year*, and theatre seasons begin in September, too. This is the time of year I feel things are about to start up again and if I can only squeeze through the turnstile, get past the lad collecting the money and jump on, just as the Big Wheel starts to lift into the air, you never know…

'Now Mr Nicolson, what do you know of Archimedes?' Mr Khan opened out a pack of crushed Hula Hoops, took a handful, and looked at me with gleaming deep-grey eyes. We were in the little upstairs room.

'Nowt, as it happens,' I said, looking around. 'Where's that?' I pointed to a picture, showing a great, crumbling citadel, round towers set in its sandy walls.

He came to stand close beside me in front of the picture, his bellows of lungs releasing the word like a sigh, 'Herat.'

'Where you come from?'

'Yes. My home.'

I stared at the picture. Beneath the walls of the castle people drove goats along the dusty street. 'It's beautiful,' I said. 'Looks really ancient.'

'Oh yes. Very old. Herat is the town of Alexander.'

'Alexander the Great?'

'Yes, yes, who else? Alexander built Herat. Come. Sit.' He lowered himself on to a pile of carpety cushions and placed the brandy, glasses and Hula Hoops on a squat table between us.

'Very comfortable.'

He smiled as he poured. 'My little piece of Afghanistan.'

'Why did you leave?'

'You really know nothing of Archimedes? That is indeed a great chasm in your education.' I took the hint and didn't pursue the question, instead learning about catapults, and machines that lifted enemy boats out of the water, and the mathematical pie thing that is, after 2500 years, still the rule, until he said, 'Nice to wag chins, isn't it? Your turn now, Mr Nicolson.' He threw back his glass of *grape spirit* with all the panache of Omar Sharif between rounds of backgammon. 'What about Hamlet? Did you ever play the part?'

I told him I played Rosencrantz once. The director's concept was me and Guildenstern were a couple of Geordie lads who teamed up with their old chum the prince to form a hard-drinking out-on-the-toon-type trio. Mr Khan lapped it all up and then told me the problem with Hamlet was he lacked valour.

'He is brave, in the end.'

'Ah yes, in the end, perhaps, but to no purpose!' Mr Khan got up, dusted the crumbs off his trousers and looked at his watch. 'My word, Ham, it is very late.'

The only downside to our cultural exchange is getting home about midnight. Still, Mr Khan told me as he locked up what a privilege it was to have in his employment so cultivated an individual. First time anyone ever called me that. 'It's only because I'm an actor that I know it,' I said. Selling myself short, which is a bit of habit of mine, because the one thing about 'resting' for the last five years (and if not fully at rest taking it very easy for another five before that) is I have read a lot of books, mostly about theatre and theatre history.

I found out that as an actor I'm more of a sock than a buskin, for instance. A sock is an actor in a comedy, whereas a buskin plays tragic roles. Comes from the sort of boots they wore, apparently. So Robert Armin – the clown who played the funny parts in Shakespeare – was a sock, and Edward Alleyn a buskin. Which led me to imagining Armin, on getting a first look at the Scottish Play and seeing unrelieved violence and slaughter, saying to the great man, 'Why don't you put a sock in it?' and hence the drunken porter scene…

Armin, Alleyn, Kempe, those are the names we remember, but there were hundreds of others who didn't become famous, stopped getting the parts, fell out of favour, tied their whatever it is to the wrong comet and ended up – well not quite working in Mr Khan's – because I suppose they ended up starving in the street, if syphilis or plague didn't get them first.

We were talking the other day about the great Wheel of Fortune idea. I imagine it like the Big Wheel at the Hoppings, the huge fair that comes to the Town Moor every year. Always the ride with the longest queue and that sense, reinforced by the skinny little devils that work it, of danger. I ask myself now if it was possible, back in those Kicking Theatre days, to tell which of us was going to get on and stay on, getting another turn and another, who'd get just one short go, and who'd arrive a day late and find the fair had packed up and gone, leaving them standing in the middle of a churned-up field with all the lights out.

In Shakespeare, the characters rise to the top and then, because of the sins they have committed in their ascent, satisfyingly fall off, but in my experience it doesn't happen like that – some people seem to stay up there in the top spot while the rest of us are still waiting for a go.

Perhaps we were all, except that thieving bastard Sam, victims of the Curse of Cuff. You see he died on the point of being rich and successful: in the little car, safety bar down, feeling that powerful upwards lift into the sky – only to fall out and land splat, dead on the muddy ground.

LIGHTS UP ON GREG AT PAYPHONE IN A PUB CORRIDOR, ROCK
MUSIC IN BACKGROUND. HE HAS A PENCIL BETWEEN HIS TEETH,
A SHEAF OF PAPERS CLUTCHED IN ONE HAND.

GREG   Cuff? *(beep beep beep beep)* Shit! *(he
spills papers in his struggle to find a coin,
pushes it in slot)* Hello? *(retrieves papers
from the floor)* Got the script? Okay.
Start page 37 halfway down, Rose's
line: 'I can't go on.' Got it? *(shuffles)*
Shit shit shit okay to 40 bottom of
page 'exit Morris'… cut. Yes. Cut the
lot. It's not working. Look.
Everything's in place and this is where
we need to spring the ambush –
comedy's got to become tragedy in
three pages. Okay? *(music gets louder as
elderly woman comes out of the bar. Greg
shouts)* What? I'm in Redcar – with the
Redcar Arts Association. Believe it or
not we'll be playing Redcar. Listen I'll
be up tomorrow – about ten, TEN, all
right? Oh one last thing *(shuffling)* shit
shit shit Page 30, last line of the scene
'Bugger off' how about changing that
to 'hadaway and shite'?

HE PUTS THE PHONE DOWN. THE WOMAN STEPS OUT OF THE
GLOOM WHERE SHE'S BEEN WAITING TO MAKE A CALL.

WOMAN   I don't know what they speak like where ye come from, bonnie lad, but in my opinion ye need to wash your mouth oot.

I. 7

LARGE, DARKLY FURNISHED BEDROOM IN ASHRAM MANSION.
JOHN AND HAM ARE BUILDING A SMALL LEGO CAR. SALLY IS
DRAWING.

HAM   There can't be only three wheels. Have
                       you checked in the bag?

JOHN SEARCHES IN THE HOLDALL. ENTER JENNY.

JENNY   You should have come, Ham! We all
                       blindfolded each other and then did
                       this breathing. Really fast. For ten
                       minutes! Then he said do whatever
                       you want to and I just felt—
JOHN   Mu-um you didn't pack all the Lego
                       bits—
JENNY   I just felt like shouting – anything that
                       came into my head—
JOHN   This bit's bloody Playmobil.
JENNY   It was amazing, kind of – electric –
                       never felt anything like it before—
JOHN   Can I come, tomorrow?
JENNY   It's really for grown-ups—
JOHN   Please.
JENNY   Shush a minute, I'm talking to Ham.
                       So anyway then he, Graham – you
                       know the one with the really stary

	eyes? – told us to jump up and down like this *(she jumps)* and when you land go Hoooo aaaa! Hooo aaaaah! All your air goes out of your lungs – you feel dizzy and tingly—
JOHN	Sounds like it's for babies.
JENNY	Melissa says it's emptying out all the thoughts you don't really need. All the rubbish just goes. Then we had to be silent and still for fifteen minutes and it felt like I was a bit drunk, you know, the tingly-all-over kind of drunk… Then we went really wild for the last bit, dancing about. Kept bumping into each other and laughing. It was great! Then we took off the blindfolds and – then I thought I'd better come back and see you lot.

HAM PICKS UP A PAPER FROM THE BEDSIDE TABLE AND READS FROM IT.

HAM	'Don't look for God in the sky; look within your own body.' *(pauses)* 'Love is prayer.'
JENNY	That's just what Graham said to me.
HAM	Well you know what he's after, don't you?
JOHN	Is it like Sunday school? I don't want to go, then. I've decided I'm an atheist.

81

'I don't suppose,' I called over to Mr Khan during the lunchtime lull, 'there's much theatre in Afghanistan?' Stacking shelves, I wanted something to get me out of the Feast scene. The scene I can't get out of my head – and can't seem to get down in writing either – because the night everyone involved in *The Blaydon Races* got together for a pre-rehearsal meal, things went seriously weird. And when people start behaving in a very unexpected way it becomes difficult to make it believable. I'd tried daydreaming the scene while restocking the tea and coffee section, done it again as I moved on to tinned fish, imagined the words on paper as I started on soups, and it still looked a pile of shite.

Mr Khan had been at the till all morning, frowning into his tax return. He flashed over one of his 'you just made my day' looks, and I immediately regretted opening my mouth. 'Surely you know where theatre began?'

'The Greeks?' I said, not completely destabilised. Yet.

Mr Khan put down his pen and slowly spread his fingers out on the counter in the manner of a Presbyterian preacher about to start a very long sermon. 'From the festivals of the god Dionysus, to be more precise. Bawdy, drunken revels in the forests, celebrating the god of wine in song.'

'Oh yes.'

'Yes indeed, Mr Nicolson. And one day, in the midst of these lascivious cavortings, a young man stepped forward – a young man like you once were.' He cleared his throat, 'A young man named…Thespis. And this young man, this Thespis, a name that should not be unfamiliar to a fellow *thespian* – ah, I have your attention now, I see! This Thespis started to act out a story about his god, Dionysus…' He leaned forward, fixing me with his gaze, 'This was the very first play.'

'Yes,' I said, and moved out of sight into the far aisle.

'And Mr Nicolson?'

'Yes?'

'Of course you know who was a follower of Dionysus and loved theatre?'

I shoved a few more cans of condensed mushroom on a shelf, muttering to myself that I was *not*, on any account, going to be persuaded into staying late for a wag fucking chin and might even ask him right out what it was that he didn't like about going home on time. But there was no escape. His voice sailed loud and clear over the bags of flour. 'Alexander!'

'Ah.' Alexander had frequently come up in our chats before. *Alexander Goes to Afghanistan*. I reckon there ought be a Ladybird book about it, and Mr Khan would be the one to write it. He told me his mam was red-haired and blue eyed, and that was on account of the fact she had the blood of one of Alexander's soldiers still 'coursing through her veins'.

Once Alexander was loose in the shop there was going to be no stopping Mr Khan. I wanted to stay behind the stacks, but unfortunately my trolley was empty. I walked towards him, giving him the longed-for cue, 'So you're saying…'

He was resting his weight on his fingers now, leaning forward, like some eager beetle. 'Precisely! Theatre began in Afghanistan!'

A poet and he don't know it. 'Well I never,' I said.

'Literally *thousands* of years before your Shakespeare we had plays in Al Khanoum. Archaeologists have found the remains of a theatre—'

83

'So why,' I interrupted, 'isn't there any theatre there now?'

He sat down and fluttered my irrelevant question away with his fingers. 'So much for the West and their culture. You were still painting your bodies blue and fighting like savages while *we* were at the theatre.'

Crap, I thought, but when I looked Dionysus up in Da's *Book of Knowledge* later, I found the bugger was right. Seemed appropriate that theatre came out of religion, but then, it's been *my* religion for years. Started off with everyone getting pissed and ecstatic in the forest. Actually, it started with *women* getting pissed and going wild in the woods, worshipping Dionysus, who could be anything – a pretty boy, a bull – then men cottoned on, probably, now I come to think of it, to regain some control. In an uncontrolled way, that is, the rituals being all about losing inhibitions and going savage as hell. Dionysus was all over the place, not just Greece and Afghanistan. My childhood would have been a lot more fun if Mam had worshipped him. Could have got up to no end of fun in the copse.

I found myself back at the bookshelf, blowing the dust off a volume of Greek plays I'd picked up in charity shop years ago and reading *The Bacchae,* starring my new friend, Dionysus. It gave me the idea of writing the Feast scene like a play. For a while I scribbled away, dead excited at finding a solution. But the number of entrances and exits was still so difficult that I gave up and went to bed, lying awake for a while as I tried to puzzle my way through.

In theatre we call working out who comes in where, *blocking.* In writing, I call it *blocked.* No use wishing now I'd paid more attention to Cuff when I had the chance, or could get hold of Greg – who did a Sean Flynn into the urban US jungle decades ago.

Next day, in the middle of sweeping the shop floor at the same time as blocking the Feast, using little piles of dust to represent characters, I became aware of Mr Khan watching me, arms folded. Uh oh, I thought, but he said, 'Theatre's not just jolly fun, is it?'

'I read up a bit on Dionysus, last night.'

'Ah.' He nodded approvingly, then said after a pause, 'Like your exercise.'

'Exercise?'

He stabbed himself in the chest with his huge thumb, 'Myself!' pointed at me, 'You!' spread his arms wide, 'All of us!' What is this if not the summoning of a god?'

'I don't see it like that—'

'A ritual – is it not, that takes away the silly self and replaces it with the big "*one*"?' He peered at me. 'You knew this, surely, O son of Thespis?'

'Well—'

'Of course you do! Theatre is a ritual. A very powerful ritual. It can unite, as in your 'All of us!' But it can also be dangerous, very dangerous.'

'I don't see that *at all.*' But even as I said the words, something started knocking in my head.

'No? No? Your Shakespeare knew this but you, Mr Nicolson, do not?' He paused and puffed out his cheeks, always a preliminary to the *N Khan Lecture* I was about to receive. 'In theatre we worship the god Dionysus. His spirit enters us and – perhaps – sends us out in the world all jolly good and at peace with our fellow human beings – or perhaps

– at war with our fellow human beings? Is it not like your church, your communion? You eat the flesh and drink the blood and from your small silly self you become one with god.'

I don't think Mam's bit of dry bread and sip of Ribena in chapel made her feel at one with God; the only thing that seemed capable of that was a good funeral. But then, that was a ritual, too. With a death at the centre. The knocking in my head got louder, but I still didn't want to listen. 'What do you know about it?' I demanded. 'You're a Muslim.'

Mr Khan shook his head in disappointment at my level of argument. 'Religions are all the same. All the same. And, anyway, I am Afghan first, *then* Muslim.' He held up two fingers about a centimetre apart. 'Islam only goes a little deep in Afghans. We are not so very Muslim. Now Mr Nicolson, Special Offers. Get on with that, please.'

Fuming, I set about filling the bargain baskets with the bottles of Indian shampoo called *Silkee* Mr Khan had got hold of from somewhere. So what if theatre came out of religion? It wasn't a religion *now*.

I thought about Shakespeare plays, plays involving large casts, mad happenings, love, lust, jealousy and betrayal… Yes! *A Midsummer Night's Dream*. Respectable girls go running off into the forest led by some spirit of lust or rebellion and are followed by lustful, jealous youths… It all felt a bit Dionysian, now I came to think of it – and should all have ended in tears except Will made everything all right by the use of *magic*. But I couldn't get away with fairies now, could I? Or, like in the Greek plays, gods? And what about plays with feasts? But that took me to the Scottish Play and pitched me right off course into a bout of envy and rage.

1. 8

The last time I saw – *Macbeth* – there, written the bastard, was when Sam was in it, last spring. Playing the Porter. Nice opportunity for a clown, and a very quick evening's work since you're only on stage for about five minutes. It being the National Theatre, you don't have to play anyone else so are free to go off to the pub for a few drinks until coming on to take more than your fair share of applause at the curtain call.

I had it in mind to get to the theatre early, and look out for an old face or two. You never know who might know someone, or tell you about something going on; that's how it works, especially in London, where I lived for five years. Not that you'd know that if you'd seen me on the night in question *twice* getting on the wrong tube and finally arriving as the last of the punters disappeared into the theatre. The woman at the ticket office gave me a doubtful look when I panted out my name and asked for the comp Sam said he'd leave for me. 'I'm sorry,' she began, even though I could see the envelope, plain as fuck, with *H Nicolson* on it in Sam's writing. By the time I'd convinced her, the play had started and the girl at the stalls' door told me and one other heretic latecomer we'd have to wait until the first scene change.

By that time I was steaming hot from running, my heart hammering in my chest and the idea of schmoozing Sam or meeting any other actors I knew filled me with a crawling sense of horror. *I'm past all this*, I thought, and felt like turning round and going straight back home. But…but… The skinny hope that had lured me to London kept me waiting the wrong side of the baize-covered doors, until the girl put her fingers to her lips and granted us admittance to the holy shrine. I found my seat just as the witches came on for the second time.

It was what Greg would've called a *not exactly goddam subtle* production featuring naked sexy witches, tons of dry ice and gallons of best blood. At Kicking we usually had to make do with blackcurrant squash mixed with cochineal; the good stuff costs a fortune. I sat there resenting it all: the money, the reverence, the fact that it's so much easier to get away with crap work when the audience are all wearing 'cultured person' badges and things look posh. But the language, 'A drum a drum! Macbeth doth come!', well – you can't say it better than that – and I relaxed, even started to enjoy myself. Until Sam came on.

Sam and I based our drunks on this old gadgie we got to know in the pub. Arthur, his name was; he lived in the Sally Army hostel and got entertainingly palatic every night. We made Arthur a bit of a pet, for the very selfish reason that for an actor he was a gift. He stuttered, he did wide-eyed bewilderment and gawping surprise funnier than anyone we'd ever seen. I was the acknowledged Arthur specialist, though Sam did a good line in the tipping forwards walk and the slow collapse sideways, accompanied by a high, whining fart.

Geordie drunk was a part I'd seen Sam play hundreds of times. And he'd seen me play it, too, over and over again. I went cold watching him. He was doing my stutter, my pauses. Not very well, but he got lots of laughs. With *my* stuff.

Resentment filled me right up to the tonsils. I don't remember anything about the rest of the production, except that it went on too long, because I was burning to have my say with Sam.

I found him afterwards in the sort of dressing room Maureen would've killed for, drinking champagne with Macduff. Sam introduced us, poured me a glass and started to take his greasepaint off in front of the mirror.

'Enjoy it?' said Macduff. He was one of those hearty types.

'Canny, aye.'

'Ah. A fellow Newcastle-ite, I take it?'

'Pity Me,' I said, and while he was working that one out, turned to Sam. 'Eeh, it was almost like watching meself up there.'

He stopped his cottonwool pad in mid circle. 'Come again?' The face reflected in the glass glowed cartoon innocent, like he didn't know what I was talking about, was completely guiltless of the cheap trick of ripping me off. And for a minute in the brightly lit pause I wondered if he *could* have forgotten. There is a silvery cloud that descends over the successful through which they only dimly see their pre-success pasts. Like *through a glass darkly*. So it's possible he'd forgotten. But I doubt it. Sam never forgets about work.

I downed the champagne. Banquo and Lady Macbeth came in. They were all off to a restaurant. I said I had to be going. Sam said nothing to stop me. Thieving bastard. And not even any good. Would never have pulled it off in Wallsend.

Came up with a killer parting line, though, 'You know what? Put Ham and Sam together and what do you get? Sham! That about sums up your friendship, marra.' Unfortunately I came up with it in the corridor, the minute *after* I'd left Sam happily drinking the last of the champagne and about to go out for a slap-up meal. Mean fuck, too, I thought. Probably didn't want to pay for me to eat, especially as he'd already given us the pleasure of seeing him for free. Not that I'd wanted to go with them. Couldn't have faced being the one Have Not with all the Have Lots. I don't mean money. Work. Acting. If I'd had some small thing – *anything* – it would have been enough. A tin-pot Theatre-in-Education drugs play tour of East Anglia. But I'd not worked for four years and we both knew it.

It was a beautiful night on the South Bank. October, but quite warm, the sky so clear that even with all the light pollution you could still make out stars. I climbed the steps up to the footbridge across the Thames and stood for a moment looking down at the water rushing seawards; above me a train trundled towards Waterloo. People leaving the Festival Hall gathered in little clumps, then separated, walking quickly in all directions. The great body of London vibrated to the movement of people as cars crossed bridges, buses streamed down the Embankment and people swept around me, keeping the great body of the city alive with the pulse of human ambition. Standing in the middle of the bridge I was a clot in the bloodstream that busy people had to skirt around. Everyone had somewhere to go. Somewhere to be. Except me, a *myocardial infarct* blocking the life force, like the one on Da's death certificate.

But I wasn't the only blockage on the bridge. At the far end, I found a young lad sitting on a blanket, begging. 'Homeless old sea dog' the placard read, 'give generously.'

'What's happened to the old sea dog, then?' I asked.

'In the pub.'

What did it matter if Sam had ripped off my Arthur? I didn't need it. Even poor old Arthur himself didn't need it, since he'd been ashes these 20 years. I dropped 50p in the kid's plate and set off for Victoria and the night coach back up north.

So what did I do when Sam called a few months later? Let him rip me off again. Pathetic isn't in it? But now, when Sam comes on telly, I make myself switch off. I don't need to keep the envy muscle in any better trim. Though actually, it's not all the TV he gets that makes me suffer: it's theatre, that waiting in the wings shitting yourself before you go on and then the radiance as you hit the stage – like stepping into the bright light of death – and for a moment you're blinking and then you can see where you are, and you start talking, and it feels like…home.

HAM IN DOUBLE BED READING A BOOK WITH THE LIGHT ON. JENNY ENTERS. HAM GLANCES AT HER AND THEN RETURNS TO HIS READING. JENNY HOVERS AWKWARDLY.

JENNY	Is Sally okay?
HAM	She's asleep. *(Jenny perches on the very edge of the bed.)* Wore her out with games of hide and seek.
JENNY	*(after a long pause)* I lost John – is he?
HAM	Said he'd been wandering around on his own. *(pause)* He's in bed too.
JENNY	Oh. That's a relief. Thanks.
HAM	I suppose he got in the way? *(when Jenny does not respond Ham puts down his book and folds his arms)* When I say hide and seek, it was more like dodge the shaggers.

91

JENNY	*(quietly, as she picks at her fingernails)* Just trying to make me feel bad.
HAM	You can do what you like far as I'm concerned. You want some orange twat to fuck you stupid that's fine by me—
JENNY	*(flaring)* You jealous or something?
HAM	Jealous? What? Of that tosser?

SILENCE.

JENNY	It's all right for you… You don't know—
HAM	Oh aye it's been great, running around among the rutters, playing mother all day with a permanent hard-on—
JENNY	You don't know what's it's like to be me! I'm all the time at home thinking *(her voice catches)* I'm young… Where's the fun for me? Where's *my* wild time? You don't know what it's like to be stuck in the middle of nowhere with someone twice your age who's only got time to write fucking plays– who everyone thinks is some kind of *saint* and they all look at me – like *you're* looking at me now, like I should be locked up for cruelty to Cuff—

SHE BREAKS OFF. THERE IS A LONG PAUSE.

92

HAM	Look. I'm tired. And I don't have any right to judge you, okay? How about getting some sleep?
JENNY	I'm not tired.
HAM	You *should* be…
JENNY	Very funny.
HAM	You're not saying old Guru Graham wasn't quite—
JENNY	It was great. He was great. Triple fucking great. Okay?
HAM	Well good. I'm pleased you had a good shag. Everyone needs a good shag now and again. Now can I go to sleep?

PAUSE.

| JENNY | Can I stay here? |
| HAM | Long as you don't mind sleeping in the chair. Take the blanket. And a pillow. |

JENNY GOES OVER TO THE CHAIR AND SITS. SHE COVERS HERSELF WITH THE BLANKET. HAM TURNS OFF THE LIGHT.

| HAM | Night. |

AFTER A PAUSE JENNY SPEAKS QUIETLY INTO THE DARKNESS.

| JENNY | It wasn't good. |
| HAM | Oh? |

JENNY   They *are* a lot of wankers. That
         Graham. You know what? I had to be
         naked but he kept his stupid
         underpants on until he got under the
         sheet. It was like…like some kind of
         nasty spider crawling all over me,
         pinching and squeezing – pinching so
         it hurt. I think he thought that was
         dead arousing instead of fucking
         painful. Then he starts giving me
         orders – say this, say it again, say that
         – god I can't repeat it, it's too
         embarrassing *(laughs)* – and every time
         I tried to touch *him*, to try and make
         him get on with it, he wouldn't let me.
         It went on and on and on: pinch
         squeeze, pinch squeeze, knead knead
         knead – like he was making bread.
         Honestly my tits are so sore. *(she snorts
         with laughter)* I wanted to say, 'Look
         Pet, you just bugger off and I'll see to
         myself.' *(Ham laughs)* Wish I had said
         that now. After a bit I just imagined
         myself sitting in the corner watching.
         If it'd been on the telly I could've
         switched it off. *(long pause)* I thought –
         I'll just get it out of the way, the sex,
         and I'll be all right, I'll go home and
         behave myself. But it wasn't any good.

HAM	It matters who with, you know. You've got to like them. *(pause)* Sorry. About what I said.
JENNY	You don't hate me, do you?
HAM	Course not. I like you.
JENNY	In a friend way, yeah? *(pause)* Do you think I'm pretty?
HAM	Yes, you're pretty. But—
JENNY	Do you think I'm attractive?
HAM	Yes, you're attractive.
JENNY	And sexy?
HAM	Yes, sexy, you are sexy. But—
JENNY	Thank you. Thank you for saying that. Thanks.
HAM	The thing is there's somebody else—
JENNY	I just want a hug, Ham, a bloody hug. Don't want to *do* anything. Cuff wouldn't even *mind* if I did, but I don't anyway. I don't even fancy you—
HAM	Someone I want but can't have.
JENNY	So shall I, then? Come into bed with you. I've got all my clothes on. So do you. Just for a hug. I'd really like a fucking hug.

THE DOOR OPENS.

JOHN	Mum?

HAM TURNS THE LIGHT ON. JOHN, WEARING PYJAMAS, COMES

INTO THE ROOM.

JOHN   You remember when you spilt tomato
                soup on the cat's tail?
JENNY   I think so. Yes, yes I remember.
JOHN   There's someone yowling like that in
                the room next door. I can't get to sleep.

HAM SIGHS, PUSHES BACK THE BEDCLOTHES.

HAM   I'll sleep in the chair.

JENNY AND JOHN GET INTO BED, HAM SETTLES IN THE CHAIR

JENNY   I was thinking – for our last day,
                maybe we should go somewhere more
                fun? Like the seaside?
HAM   Now you're talking. Whitley Bay here
                we come. Turn off the light, Johnny
                boy.

I. 9

The Feast was a company tradition, taking place the last weekend before rehearsals started. I was between flats at that time, officially staying with my older brother Joe and his nasty wife, Frances, in Hetton-le-Hole (a place quite aptly named in my opinion) but often kipping on the sofa at no. 12. There, in addition to escaping Frances's savage tongue – 'I was saying to Joe, wasn't I, Joe, to my way of thinking you don't look much like an actor' – I felt much more in the swing of things.

As well as Greg and Hardley, Stafford lived at no. 12 with his girlfriend, Nic. It was pretty obvious to see what Stafford saw in Nic, because she was a beauty. What Nic saw in Stafford seemed harder to fathom, even once you knew about his secret wealth. It had happened a few years before I knew him and I don't think he's ever told anyone the exact details, but one windy winter afternoon, in some Cumbrian-back-of-beyond pub not too far from a racecourse, Stafford gained a fortune.

I imagine the event. The public bar is thick with cigarette smoke and steam rising from the oiled coats and corduroy trousers of recently rained-on countryfolk. Stafford's smile's grown wider as the afternoon's gone on; he's among friends and friends of friends. He's just discovered a distant relation on his mother's side who's going to show him a little stretch of the river Eden where he can catch salmon. If he didn't know the barman by name yesterday he does now, and as he lowers his slight frame a touch unsteadily from the bar stool, he orders another pint for himself and for his cousin, and confirms, 'Bog's out the back, isn't it Alan?'

'Mind you don't get washed away,' Alan replies and there's a genial guffaw from around the bar because they've all been drinking since noon and it's now nearly dark. Out of the door goes Stafford, a roll-up cigarette clamped to his lower lip. Cold rain hits him in the face as he crosses the pitted car park towards the shed of a toilet. No light. Fuck. He sits there in darkness until his thin knees and the torn off pieces of newsprint threaded on a string at his side are suddenly illuminated by a flash of lightning. *One thousand, two thousand,* the thunder rolls. He looks up – and hits the jackpot. Another flash of lightning shatters the skylight and propels a shard of glass deep into his right eye.

The sight was lost, but the case against the brewery was won. Exactly how much Scottish and Newcastle had handed over none of us knew, but it was enough to make Stafford, in comparison with everyone else in the company, fabulously rich, in possession of a secret deposit account. He didn't go round in taxis, nor own a car, but he and Nic went on exotic holidays, indulged in regular cannabis, occasional cocaine.

As for Nic… In one of my many moments of reflection in the shop I've thought about Nic, who came across as a kind of groovy chick, happy to chat to anyone while in the bath, for instance, with a tanned, slim legginess that must have made Stafford feel like a Rolling Stone. Nic was a demo-attending, badge-wearing feminist who'd ironically ended up more trapped than the wife of the most male chauvinist pig husband.

Instead of clearing up after one man, she cleared up after three, plus occasionals like me. I don't suppose Anita Pallenburg or Marianne Faithfull did a lot of scrubbing bogs, whereas Nic did plenty of that, plus washing up, tramping off to the laundrette, mopping the floor and trying to make something of the garden. She'd recently introduced the idea of composting, hanging a plastic bag next to the cooker for peelings. It wasn't much used and hung there emptily, a sort of sad symbol of her efforts against the odds.

Back then I think we in the company were all too busy with the drama of our own lives to wonder much about what she felt. Her looks were resented in a non-virulent way (the non-virulence explained by her non-thesp status) by the likes of Alice and Maureen; most of us just thought of her as decorative and friendly, quite accepting the image of liberated woman she showed the world. It would've been easy to scrape the surface and find that identity was more of an accident of birth than anything real.

As a middle-class girl who hit sixteen in the last gasp of the 1960s, she was virtually obliged to be a socialist feminist and to take up an approved occupation in the form of social work, suppressing her talents for the decorative arts, keeping an orderly house and gardening. In fact she endured just about the complete opposite to what she was most suited, having to put up with domestic chaos both at home and at work.

I reckon in her real self she might have been happier as the ideal 1950s housewife, more like my Auntie Joan in liking to create prettiness about the place, a posy on the table, a parsley garnish, than she was Germaine Greer. Better suited to the 1850s, even, because she was amazingly accomplished. She played the piano and sketched beautifully.

So it wasn't easy to understand Stafford's allure to Nic. The appeal of rough trade, perhaps. Rough trade intriguingly labelled 'actor' and 'homeowner' and 'purchaser of two tickets to Barbados'. And she enjoyed feasts.

Everybody involved in the play was invited to the feast, and since I'd spent the previous night on the sofa I was on hand to help get things ready. That was just as well because Greg had shot off to see Cuff early in the morning and there was no sign of Hardley. Stafford announced his intention of taking the truck off to Gateshead, where he had connections at the abattoir. His mate had promised to hand over a couple of bags of meat in exchange for a fiver. So as usual all the cleaning up looked like falling to Nic. 'Thank God you're here, Ham,' she said, handing me a broom.

Anyway, she being both gorgeous and likeable, the prospect of scrubbing and hoovering in close proximity was a lot nicer than it would have been otherwise. I swept the kitchen while she attacked the cobwebs and sprinkled Shake 'n' Vac over the carpet – which was even smellier than usual on account of Stafford's dad's two dogs staying for the weekend. Then I ran the ancient hoover over the shagpile. Greg came back, and, announcing he'd be down in two minutes to help, disappeared into his room. Beethoven at full volume came out but it was a while before he did, eager to get on with making a chilli sauce for some delicacy he had planned. Nic flinched, the kitchen having only just been set to rights, and sent him off to get wine and beer.

We lugged a table from upstairs, shoving it up against the existing one to make a great big feasting surface. Then Nic suggested peeling spuds outside in the last of the afternoon sun. Even peeling potatoes became art in Nic's hands, the skin curling off in dusky coils. We sat among her pots of flowers on the little terrace she'd created, a bucket between us, and fell into a peacefulness approaching meditation, the creamy spuds dropping into water with little splashes.

Nic started telling me about her family, about how her mum had died when she was only fourteen. 'I remember doing this with her. Afterwards, we'd get the paints and make designs.' She picked a leaf from one of her pots, studied it for a moment and cut deftly into the potato producing to my eyes a perfect replica. 'I love doing stuff like that.'

The peace suddenly filled with panting dogs. Two retrievers, one golden, one black, burst ecstatically onto the terrace. Stafford followed. 'They went fucking mental at the abattoir,' he said proudly as they leapt at him. 'Andy gave me this bloody gigantic great bone.' He gave the dogs an end each of what looked like the whole leg of a cow and they bore it off down the garden.

Nic swept the peelings into a colander and stood up. 'That was nice while it lasted. Let's go and see what he's bought.' As I followed her in with the bucket of spuds she smiled and murmured, 'You're a lot more peaceful to be around than the rest of them.'

Along with bottles of wine and cans of beer, two bulging red-smudged plastic bags had arrived on the table. 'Take a look at that lot,' said Stafford.

Nic inserted her slim fingers into the bag with the delicacy of a surgeon inspecting a wound and removed two legs of lamb and several pounds of chopped steak. 'Oh God what are these?' she said, peering into the bloody depths.

Greg leaned over her shoulder and announced, 'Beef hearts, that's what they are.' He dug out the three huge organs and held them in his cupped hands like an offering to the gods. 'I'm going to make anticuchos.'

'Antiwhatlike?' I said.

'Cuchos. I used to eat them in Peru when I was a kid. Hearts in chilli sauce on a stick. You eat them like popsicles.'

'Oh aye. Sounds delicious.' In just about every way possible, Greg was different.

CUFF'S SHED TWO DAYS EARLIER. CUFF AT TYPEWRITER, GREG — AS FAR AS IS POSSIBLE IN THE CRAMPED SPACE — PACING.

CUFF	I don't think I can do it. There's just not enough time.
GREG	Look, if we can get the shape of the first half working tonight, the second will write itself… And if it's not perfect I can sort it out on the floor. One more push…that's all that's needed.
CUFF	There's a limit. The RSC want a re-write too – and that's real money. I've been writing non-stop for months. I'm exhausted.

PAUSE

GREG	It's like this. The tour's booked and we'll be liable for the venues' losses if we don't show up. Northern Arts' grant has been spent and they'll want their money back if we've nothing to

show. The bank'll see that we're in shit
and refuse to pay creditors. Creditors'll
go to court and we'll be bankrupt. No
more Kicking. No commissions for
you or anyone else. It's that simple.

I can't procrastinate any longer. I've arrived at the Feast. But
how to get my cast from *there* – before the feast – to *there* –
afterwards? I know characters are supposed to go on *journeys*,
have a *trajectory*, but who could have predicted the kind of
shot-out-of-a-cannon type journeys that took place that night?

There's still a bit of time. Curtain goes up at eight, so at
seven, all the cast – and there's the director, the technicians,
the administrator as well as the actors – are in their various
dressing rooms, quite relaxed. They've done this particular
show, this Feast show, a few times now, there's nothing to get
stressed about. Greg's in his room, running through a
particularly difficult scene change to the accompaniment
Beethoven's Ninth at full volume.

Cuff? In his shed, of course, two-fingered tapping out the
lines, while inside the house Jenny is on the phone to her last-
hope babysitter. Maybe it's the crack in Jenny's voice that does
the trick; the babysitter says she'll be there in an hour. Two
minutes later Cuff looks over the top of his big glasses at his
young wife. Smiles. 'If that's what you want.'

Stafford, lying on his bed under a pile of dog, rests his one
eye on lovely Nic. *Mine*, he thinks, as she stands before the
mirror pinning up her long dark hair. 'Coming to talk to me
in the bath?' she says through a couple of hairgrips.

'Might do.'

Across the city, Sam shuffles into the shoulders of the new and expensive leather jacket he bought in London, glances into the mirror to adjust his thinning hair, slaps his cheeks with aftershave and whispers to himself, quite rightly as it happens, *This. Is. It. I'm. Going. To. Be. Famous.*

Matt, on the second leg of his journey from North Shields, sees a bus heading in the opposite direction and considers for a moment jumping off to grab a ride back. But even an evening with a load of weirdos seems better than returning home, and he sits down again, watching the shadows lengthen over the endless roofs as the bus takes him deeper and deeper towards the enchanted, dangerous world of theatre.

And me? I've helped shift the scenery, pushed the battered sofa and armchair to either side of the gas fire, and, with trestles and a couple of old doors, set up a huge table covered in two white bed sheets, upon which now rest a pile of cutlery, some unlit candles, various bottles and cans. Having done my bit, I crack open a lager and walk into the garden to fulfil Nic's last instruction: picking a few flowers from the garden.

There's only one thing in my head. Only one name: *Jane*.

And here she comes, through the steam and smoke of the kitchen, like a lovely dryad stepping from a woodland mist. Our eyes meet across the fragrant shag pile. She smiles, opens her mouth to speak—

Night, a smell, an expectation, the start of the process from which the magic grows...

I. 10

A BLACK BOX SET. LIVING ROOM DOMINATED BY A HUGE TABLE SET HAPHAZARDLY FOR A MEAL. OPEN SWING DOOR UPSTAGE RIGHT SUGGESTS CLUTTERED KITCHEN AREA. DOWNSTAGE EXTREME RIGHT STAIRWAY ASCENDS. CHORUS EMERGES FROM THE DARKNESS.

Lights up.

CHORUS   Fast darkens now the sky; and peering
                             through
                             The tiny holes you mortals call the
                             stars
                             The God peers down from his bright
                             heaven.
                             Tonight, the wind is in the trees and
                             whispers
                             'Drink, do what you please, free your
                             desires and find release…'

Whispering as goes off into wings

                             Dionysus is his name,
                             Frenzied raptures are his game…
                             Listen mortals! God is near
                             Dionysus now *is here*!

ENTER **DIONYSUS**, GOD OF WINE AND THEATRE, HIS BLACK CURLS ENTWINED WITH TENDRILS OF IVY, A THYRSUS STAFF IN HIS HAND. IN THE KITCHEN HE PAUSES, LOOKING BRIEFLY INTO THE SINK. HE COMES IN TO THE LIVING ROOM.

DIONYSUS	Who wrote *that?* One of the problems I have with theatre – just one of them mind, is language. Rapture, entrails! How words obscure the truth. Sex and blood. Sex and blood! *(he looks around in some dismay)* Not what I expected. *(he sniffs)* Still…smell of meat, smell of dog, hearts in the sink. Well, where are they all? *(he drums with his fingers and chants)* The calf is slain, the meat is cooking The wine is on the table, looking… *(he picks up a bottle)* Strange. You may ask me what I'm doing here… *(a door opens upstairs. Dionysus puts finger to lips)* Sshhh! I'm bringing out the beast.

LIGHT FOOTSTEPS. NIC DESCENDS WEARING A LARGE BATH TOWEL SECURED UNDER ONE ARM. DIONYSUS WATCES AS NIC OPENS A DRAWER, TAKES OUT A BOX OF MATCHES, AND PROCEEDS TO LIGHT CANDLES. STRETCHING TO REACH THE FARTHEST, THE TOWEL APPARENTLY UNFASTENS AND FALLS LIGHTLY AT HER FEET, LEAVING HER GORGEOUSLY NAKED. DIONYSUS LAUGHS AND NIC SEES HIM FOR THE FIRST TIME.

NIC	Oh my God! Where did you spring from? *(Dionysus reaches out a hand and gently squeezes a nipple between finger and thumb, as though testing a blackberry)*

106

DIONYSUS	Some say Thrace. Some say India. *(Nic, visibly entranced, accepts the towel Dionysus now produces from behind his back and wraps herself in it quite languorously, staring into his face all the time)*
NIC	Is that where you got that beautiful tan, India? You must be an actor. Nobody told me there was anyone new in the play. I'm Nic.
DIONYSUS	You're in the play too?
NIC	God no! I'm just a groupie.
DIONYSUS	A groupie?
NIC	You're teasing me... Like a camp follower, you know. My boyfriend – Stafford? Maybe you haven't met – he's the actor. I don't actually do anything in the plays... I'm just a social worker.
DIONYSUS	A maenad, not a groupie, beautiful one. And you couldn't be more wrong. You're essential. *(without taking his eyes off her, Dionysus picks up the bottle of wine, and inserts its neck into his mouth. He sucks out the cork, and in the same movement, spits it clean through the glass of the window, leaving a neat hole. Outside a faint exclamation of 'Ow!' is heard. Dionysus pours two glasses of wine, handing one to Nic)*

107

NIC	*(whispering)* God! How did you do that? *(she drains the glass of wine, gazing into Dionysus' eyes – he holds out his hand to her)*
DIONYSUS	How about a walk in the forest?
NIC	*(drowsily, the towel beginning to slip again)* You mean Jesmond Dene? Hadn't I better get dressed first? *(she reaches up a hand to touch his hair)* I don't know how you've done it, but I love how you've got your hair. It's beautiful. *(she is about to take his hand when)*

JANE AND HAM ENTER FROM THE GARDEN.

| HAM | *(to Nic)* We found a few flowers, and Jane said this creeper stuff would look nice on the table. There's enough wood for a bonfire later. |
| NIC | Lovely. Must go and change. You never told me there's a Greek god in the cast. Look after him won't you? I'll be back in a sec. *(she glides up the stairs)* |

HAM AND JANE LOOK AT EACH OTHER. DIONYSUS LOUNGES IN CHAIR DOWNSTAGE LEFT, ONE LEG HOOKED OVER THE ARM, AND WATCHES.

| JANE | Did you understand any of that? |

HAM	Greg did say there might be a part for Fergus. But she can't be talking about Fergus, surely? No one's ever compared him to a Greek god. *(they both laugh)*
JANE	Shall I get a vase?
HAM	More a case of a jar, I think. On the draining board.

JANE GOES INTO THE KITCHEN.

JANE	Whatever are these disgusting things in the sink?
HAM	Hearts. Greg is going to make some kind of Peruvian lollipops. *(Jane returns with the vase and reaches for the assortment of flowers, weeds and ivy that Ham has in his hand. He hands them over and there is an awkward pause)*
HAM	Nice bouquet for you. *(Jane busies herself arranging the flowers in the jar and coiling the ivy tendrils around the bottles and candles on the table, all the time avoiding looking at Ham)*
HAM	So Gerry's okay?
JANE	Fine! Fine! Really good, actually. Doing Chekhov in Manchester. Coming back the odd Sunday, you know. It's going well, he says.
HAM	Great. Great. Good for him. *(a silence)*
DIONYSUS	How sweet. Love. *(he turns his thyrsus*

109

	staff anti-clockwise. Jane takes a buttercup from the vase and holds it under Ham's chin)
JANE	Remember that thing about 'you love butter'?
HAM	Never understood it, did you? *(he takes the buttercup and pulls off a petal)* She loves me. *(pulls off another)* She loves me not. *(they laugh)*
JANE	Counting your prune stones, remember? Tinker, tailor, soldier, sailor, rich man, poor man, beggarman, thief. I was always going to marry a beggarman.
HAM	That didn't work, then. *(he sits on the stairs and pats the carpet next to him)* Come and sit with me.
JANE	Why?
HAM	Want to tell you a secret. Have to whisper.
JANE	*(Jane sits down next to him)* Budge up, then. *(Ham whispers in her ear)* What? Cuff"s written it?
HAM	Sshhh. Secret. *(he whispers again)*
JANE	No. I won't get that part. Alice will.
HAM	Bet you do. Adulterous young wife. In love with me. How do you like that?
JANE	Oh Ham, it would be great. I love Cuff's writing…
HAM	And I've got to be in love with you.

110

	Haven't done a romantic role like that for years. Bet I'll be crap. *(takes her hand, looks into her eyes)* I love you. *(pause)* See! I told you I'd be crap.
JANE	That wasn't bad—
HAM	I love you. I think about you all the time. Just now in the garden I wanted to say how beautiful you are… *(a long silence. Jane looks at her hand in his)*
JANE	I… What would she do? It would be a shock, hearing that, even though she loves him back… It would be really sort of – difficult – wouldn't it?
HAM	She'd get up, I think.
JANE	Yes. *(detaches herself. Stands, hands twisting in her skirt of her dress)* Maybe avoid eye contact? *(she addresses the door)* I thought about you all summer. I don't know why. Just when I'd be pulling up weeds or making spaghetti Bolognese, you'd come into my mind. I'd see you, Your face—

ENTER (HESITANTLY) MATT. AWKWARD SILENCE.

MATT	I… Is there a party on here?
DIONYSUS	Come in boy!
MATT	*(to Dionysus)* Who are you?
HAM	Ham. You remember me, don't you? This is Jane.

MATT	I didn't know if it was the right house…
HAM	What happened to your head?
MATT	*(fingering livid bruise on forehead)* Oh. I was just you know in the backyard, wondering you know if I'd come to the right place, and this…cork thing came flying out and hit me.
JANE	*(inspecting the bruise)* Maybe I can find something for it.
MATT	It's nowt.

ROD ENTERS FROM THE KITCHEN CARRYING A CRATE OF LAGERS.

ROD	All right? *(he sits down on top of Dionysus and tucks his crate under his knees)* Ye fucker! Springs in this thing! *(Dionysus glares as Rod selects a can and opens it with a little hiss)* Dig right into you.
NIC	*(running downstairs in a purple halter-necked dress)* Where is he then?
JANE	Who?
NIC	The Greek god.
ROD	I'm right here, petal.

NIC RUNS INTO THE KITCHEN. SHE SEES THE HEARTS IN THE SINK.

NIC	Shit! *(she picks up a broom and thrusts*

the handle at the ceiling three times making loud thumps) Greg! Come down here and sort out your bloody hearts! *(she runs back into the living room)* Is he in the garden? No? Why are you all looking at me? Something *bizarre* you know, Jane, looking at those hearts I thought I could just eat one raw, like mmmm you know?! *(she runs into the garden)* Helloooo?

AN ARM REACHES AROUND ROD, AND DIONYSUS'S HUGE HAND EXTRACTS TWO CANS FROM ROD'S STASH. DIONYSUS STANDS UP, PASSING THROUGH THE BODY OF ROD IN THE PROCESS, AND FOLLOWS NIC INTO THE GARDEN. SEVERAL THINGS NOW HAPPEN AT ONCE. STAFFORD ENTERS WITH MORE BOTTLES OF WINE, FOLLOWED BY ALICE AND MAUREEN IN PARTY BEST; GREG THUNDERS DOWN THE STAIRS SHOUTING AT HAM TO PUT SOME MUSIC ON. THERE IS AN EXCHANGE OF 'HI'S' AND A CRASH OF SOUND AS LITTLE FEAT BELTS OUT. FREEZE. LIGHTS GO DOWN ON THE SCENE LEAVING ROD SPOT-LIT IN HIS CHAIR WEARING THE AGHAST EXPRESSION OF SOMEONE WHO'S RECENTLY BEEN DISEMBOWELLED. HE FEELS AROUND HIS BODY, MAKING SURE EVERYTHING IS THERE.

ROD   Fuck me. What was that?

BLACKOUT.

Scene 2

LIGHTS UP TO CANDLELIT FEAST. ACTORS FROZEN IN MIDST OF GOOD CHEER. DIONYSUS LIES ON THE TABLE AMONG THE DEBRIS OF THE MEAL, DRINKING LAGER, HIS HEAD PROPPED ON ONE ELBOW. THE FEMALE CHORUS NOW SITS IN SHADOW ON THE STAIRS.

CHORUS	Everything all right?
DIONYSUS	I like it here. This Stella stuff's not bad.
	Quite strong enough to drive girls mad.
CHORUS	*(archly)* And is there lots of human passion.
	On which, in entertaining fashion,
	We may create some *art*?
DIONYSUS	It's building up to something interesting, yes. We have *envy* (*touches Maureen*), we have *pride*... (*touches Sam*) as well as just about the most gorgeous mortal I've seen since—
CHORUS	Since the last gorgeous one.
DIONYSUS	Leave us now. Things are hotting up.

A HUBBUB OF NOISE AS EVERYONE COMES BACK TO LIFE, APPARENTLY IN THE MIDST OF A COMPETITION, EVERYONE DOING 'TURNS'.

LYNETTE	You've got to do something, Greg.
GREG	I direct, I don't act.
STAFFORD	You do tonight.

114

GREG	What about Hardley?
JANE	*(shakes Hardley by the shoulder)* He's out cold.
	(the hammering on the door becomes louder and louder)
MATT	Do I have to do a turn?
ROD	Someone at the door.

SMOKE (DRY ICE) BEGINS TO ENTER THE ROOM THROUGH THE DOORWAY TO THE KITCHEN.

STAFFORD	Something's burning.
DIONYSUS	*(jumps from the table delightedly)* Fire! Lovely!
STAFFORD	Your hearts, Greg!
MATT	*(terrified)* I cannet dance or sing or anything…
NIC	Don't look at me, Greg. I'm staying right here.

GREG EXITS TO KITCHEN. SOUND OF BACK DOOR OPENING AND CLOSING AND THEN VOICES AS THROUGH THE MIST OF SMOKE THAT POURS INTO THE LIVING ROOM, CUFF AND JENNY ENTER. THERE ARE SHOUTS OF SURPRISE AND GREETING.

STAFFORD	Come and have a drink.

JENNY ACCEPTS A GLASS OF WINE, WHICH SHE DRINKS EAGERLY, HER EYES LOOKING BACK INTO THE KITCHEN AND HER BREATHS SHORT. DIONYSUS BEGINS TO MOVE HIS HANDS OVER HER BODY.

115

DIONYSUS	Lust! At last! *(he moves in close behind Jenny)* You can't help it. You only want a bit of fun. Some company your own age. It's no wonder you're excited. *(he blows softly on her neck)*
JENNY	Managed to…get a babysitter…at the last minute.
DIONYSUS	He is handsome, there's no denying it. And strong. Rumour has it he's killed. Killed men, I mean. In his time.
JENNY	Have we…missed all the fun?
GREG	*(shouts)* Best is yet to come. My anticuchos.
LYNETTE	Aren't they burnt to a frazzle?
GREG	They just need the chilli dressing and they'll be fine.
STAFFORD	*(shouts)* Don't think that lets you off, Greg.
JENNY	Lets him off what?
STAFFORD	He's got to perform something. You know, do a turn.
JENNY	I'll give him a hand. *(she goes into the kitchen and closes the door)*
MATT	I haven't got to do owt have I?
CUFF	We haven't met, have we? I'm Cuff.
MATT	My name's Matt. I haven't got to do owt, have I?
NIC	Did *you* see him, Matt – the big guy with the curly hair?
MATT	Only I cannet do it. Hate actin'.

116

NIC	Why don't you eat something?
MATT	Have you not got any chips?
NIC	I don't know why no one will tell me where he's gone! *(she drains another glass of wine) You* saw him, didn't you? Big guy. Beautiful curly hair…

GREG SPRINGS FROM THE KITCHEN TO CENTRE STAGE. HE CARRIES A DISH IN ONE HAND AND BRANDISHES A CHILLI-SAUCE-COVERED BEEF HEART IMPALED ON A KNIFE IN THE OTHER. QUITE A LOT OF THE CHILLI SAUCE IS ALSO SMEARED ON HIS MUSCULAR BARE TORSO. LYNETTE SCREAMS. JENNY WATCHES PANTINGLY.

GREG	Tis a heart! A heart! my lords, in which is mine entombed. *(he brandishes the heart at the feasters)* Tis Annabella's heart… I vow tis hers: this dagger's point ploughed up her fruitful womb and left to me the fame of a most glorious executioner! *(he takes a bite of the heart)*
LYNETTE	Eurghh! That's disgusting that is!
GREG	Who's for anticuchos?
MAUREEN	Is that it, like?
GREG	It's all you're getting. Great play. Love to do it.
ALICE	You're not getting away with that crap. That's not a performance!
ALL	*(shouting and banging on the table)* More! More!

117

LYNETTE	Was it a play then? What play?
GREG	'Tis Drag she's a Slag', of course. One of the greatest plays ever written.
LYNETTE	There's never a play called that, is there? That's disgusting!
NIC	It's called *Tis Pity She's a Whore*, really. I did it for my English degree. It's about incest, brother and sister incest, and in the end the brother cuts out his sister's heart.
LYNETTE	Eurghh.
NIC	*(dreamily)* It's very good actually. They really love each other.
DIONYSUS	It does sound good. Just my kind of play.
CUFF	*(sadly regarding Jenny, who's still looking hungrily at Greg)* And it's true. We're always cutting out each other's hearts.

HEART LOLLIPOPS HANDED OUT.

GREG	Matt?
MATT	Eh, I couldn't.
LYNETTE	Eurrghh, just looking at them makes me feel sick.
ROD	Come and sit on my lap, petal, I'll make you feel better.
STAFFORD	Fucking hell they're tough!
GREG	Mmm. Must have different kinds of cows in Peru.

118

DIONYSUS SITS IN VACATED CHAIR NEXT TO MATT AND BITES
INTO A HEART.

DIONYSUS	This animal was sacrificed badly. I feel his fear.
MATT	I divvent knaa how ye can…
MAUREEN	When are ye going to tell us about your audition, Sam? Keeping us old friends in suspense…
SAM	*(toying with his glass then looking up to meet her eye)* They're talking to my agent. Just a question of which part. I'm going down again Wednesday.
GREG	*(outraged)* You're in rehearsal!
STAFFORD	Howay man, you're not going to stand in his way. Both big parts are they?
SAM	Aye. Leading roles as they say.
LYNETTE	*(already quite drunk now on Rod's lap)* Let's have a toast. Eeeh! I don't know what was in that orange juice. To Sam!

A RAISING OF GLASSES AND UNEVEN CHORUS OF 'SAM!' WITH A
FEW MUMBLED 'YE JAMMY FUCKING BASTARD' AND 'GOOD
LUCKS' THROWN IN. SAM GRINS. DIONYSUS RAISES HIS THYRSUS
STAFF AND POINTS IT TOWARDS HIM. SPOTLIGHT ON SAM, WHO
STANDS AND SINGS, THOUGH APPARENTLY UNHEARD BY ALL
EXCEPT DIONYSUS.

SAM *(glass raised)*   To me. I'm reaching out for fame,
It's near enough to touch, my name

119

In lights. These canny people here
Mere index notes in my career.

HE ADDRESSES MAUREEN, SLUMPED SULLENLY IN HER CHAIR,
ARMS FOLDED, WATCHING HIM WITH LOATHING.

SAM   Yes my career! d'ye hear that, dear?
                        My glist'ning, shiny new career!

SPOTLIGHT SHIFTS TO MATT, NOW DESPERATE AND CONFUSED
ENOUGH TO SPEAK.

MATT   What are they all on about?
DIONYSUS   Uninitiated are you, boy?
MATT   See that's it! All these words, words,
                        words. I don't know what they mean.
                        And who are you when you're at
                        home?
DIONYSUS   At home or abroad, I'm God.
MATT   Oh aye? There you are then, got
                        another thing wrong. Thought that
                        Greg was the boss, like, but pleased to
                        meet ye all the same. Listen, I've got to
                        be honest with you, I'm never going to
                        fit in round here. I may as well gan
                        back to the Careers place. I cannet do
                        owt, man. Cannet dance, cannet sing,
                        cannet act...
DIONYSUS   Have some more wine.
MATT   I don't drink wine. I don't eat hearts.

	Why's everything so weird? I mean you were lying on the table, you cannet tell me that's normal…
DIONYSUS	*(pouring wine)* Drink, boy, drink. You're going to have a really good time, you'll see.
LYNETTE	*(leaping up)* Let's have a dance! Put on something good.

SHE, JENNY, ALICE AND JANE BEGIN TO DANCE TO 'THE WITCHQUEEN OF NEW ORLEANS'.

MATT	*(Drinking)* I never dance, me.
DIONYSUS	Maybe even a bit of fucking… *(He gets up and joins the girls dancing)*
MATT	*(Calls after him)* What are ye, like, some kind of pervert?
ROD	Who are you calling a pervert, man?
MATT	Talking to him.
ROD	Who? *(inhaling)* Have a puff on this. Put hairs on your chest. You're on next, you know. *(passes Matt the monster spliff, says in low voice)* Take a look at Jenny man, tongue practically hanging out…
MATT	Who's Jenny?
ROD	Cuff's wife. Way she's looking at Greg, he'd better watch hisself.
JENNY	*(dancing)* Fuck me sideways, Fuck me frontways, Fuck me anyways you please…

121

DIONYSUS	How about under trees?
JENNY	God! I wasn't speaking out loud was I?
DIONYSUS	No, I'm just your inner self. I do think you should go outside, though. Things happen in woods, under trees, you know.
JENNY	*(gyrating in the middle of the other girls)* I'm changing into something wild, Some bitch that longs to get with child, A cat with claws to scratch and tear, I'm coiling ivy in my hair…
NIC	*(shouts above drumming)* Let's go outside. Light the bonfire!
JANE	Or the woods.
LYNETTE	Yes! Jesmond Dene! In the dark! Ooh, I'll be so scared! Do you think it's haunted?

THE WOMEN STAMPEDE OFF STAGE, SCREAMING WITH EXCITEMENT, LEAVING THE MEN WATCHING AFTER THEM IN SOME CONFUSION. PAUSE.

ROD	I'll look after you, Lyn! *(he runs after them)*
HAM	I'm going too. Come on! *(he runs off followed by Greg, Stafford and Sam)*
MATT	Where's everyone going?

DIONYSUS LIGHTLY PUSHES A CONFUSED MATT OFF STAGE TOWARDS THE WOODS. FINALLY, CUFF FOLLOWS, WALKING SLOWLY AND THOUGHTFULLY. DIONYSUS, LEFT ALONE IN THE EMPTY ROOM APART FROM THE PRONE HARDLEY, FOLDS HIS ARMS IN SATISFACTION AND LAUGHS. CHORUS TIPTOES UP BEHIND HIM, AND RESTING HIS CHIN ON THE GOD'S SHOULDER, WHISPERS.

CHORUS

To the woods! To the woods!
To the woods they will go!
With the wine,

DIONYSUS

And the beer!
Anybody still here? *(he picks up Hardley's head from the table and lets it fall again. Shrugs)* Let's go!

BLACKOUT.

Scene 3

LIGHTS UP ON STAGE BARE EXCEPT FOR A SINGLE TREE PUSHED ON. THERE FOLLOWS A MIDSUMMER NIGHT'S DREAM-LIKE SCENE OF CONFUSION, WITH THE PLAYERS RUNNING ABOUT THE WOODS BEARING FLAMING TORCHES, SINGING. DEPENDING ON THE PERFORMANCE SPACE THEY COULD APPEAR AMONG THE AUDIENCE, ON STAGE, IN FRONT OF THE CURTAIN, ETC. ENTER ALICE AND MAUREEN, MAUREEN SOBBING AND SINGING.

MAUREEN

It should've been me!
Why Sam? Why not me?
Why not me, God?
It should've been me.

123

ALICE	Hey remember that Yvonne Fair song? The one about the woman in church watching her man marry someone else? 'It Should've Been Me?' Just reminded me then, you did. *(she starts clapping out the intro of the tune)* 'I saw my true love, walking down the aisle 'And when he passed he turned to me and gave me a smile.' *(Maureen wiping her eyes, begins to join in)*
MAUREEN	'Then the preacher, the preacher asked there be silence please 'If any objection to this marriage, speak now or forever hold your peace…*(they walk off together into the trees, singing)*
MAUREEN/ALICE	*(voices off)* 'And I stood up and shouted IT SHOULD HAVE BEEN ME!'

THEIR VOICES FADE. ENTER NIC, SHINING HER TORCH AROUND HER.

NIC	I feel so strange! This can't be me! *(she squeezes the nipple Dionysus had earlier squeezed)* I want to be suckled. Anyone want some milk? Am I mad? Come on. I know you're there. In the trees…

124

STAFFORD	*(calling from off stage)* Nic? Ni-ic?
NIC	*(whisper)* Oh no! Leave me alone why can't you? *(Nic runs off)*

ENTER STAFFORD, WHO SITS DOWN AND LIGHTS A CIGARETTE, BY THE LIGHT OF WHICH WE SEE HIS RUEFUL FACE.

STAFFORD	What the fuck's got into her? *(Greg, torch aloft, the zip of his jeans open, backs onto the stage, reversing into Stafford)* Oy! Watch where you're going!
GREG	God! What have I done? Who *was* that?
STAFFORD	*(looking him up and down)* Got lucky, did you?
GREG	*(looks down, zips himself)* No! I don't know! What was in that joint, you bastard?
MATT	*(running on)* Did you see it? Did you see that?
GREG	See who? A woman?
MATT	Nah man, a bull! The whacking great bull! Standing in the middle of the path right in front of me, swishing its tail. I swear it said me name. Then it ran at me, I thought 'this is it', but it upped and jumped right over me head. Like this, whooshsh-up! Came this way it did…amazing! Listen! It said it again! It's calling me name! *(exits running)* I'm coming!

125

JENNY	*(voice off)* Greg! Greg!
GREG	*(pulls Stafford up)* Stick beside me, okay? Don't let me do anything… strange.

STAFFORD SHAKES HIM OFF.

STAFFORD	Nah man. I'm just ganna sit here, smoke a joint and admire the scenery till Nic comes back.

GREG RUNS OFF. ENTER JENNY, DISHEVELLED, SHIRT HANGING LOOSELY REVEALING HER BRA, HAIR TANGLED WITH IVY. SHE SEES STAFFORD AND MAKES A VAGUE ATTEMPT TO STRAIGHTEN HER CLOTHES.

JENNY	Have you seen Greg?
STAFFORD	That way.

HE POINTS THE SPLIFF IN THE OPPOSITE DIRECTION TO WHICH GREG WENT. JENNY RUNS OFF. STAFFORD SITS DOWN WITH HIS BACK AGAINST A TREE AND LIGHTS UP. HE WATCHES, UNSEEN, AS TWO TORCHES AT OPPOSITE SIDES OF THE AUDITORIUM, GRADUALLY APPROACH EACH OTHER.

JANE	*(singing)* I have often walked down the street before, And the pavement always felt beneath my feet before,
HAM	People will say we're in love.

THEY STAND LOOKING AT EACH OTHER THEN HAM PUTS OUT HIS HAND AND JANE TAKES IT. THEY WALK OFF TOGETHER SPEAKING THE FOLLOWING.

HAM	I know a bank whereon the wild thyme blows
JANE	Where oxslips and the nodding violet grows
BOTH	All overcanopied with luscious woodbine
	With sweet musk roses and with eglantine. (*exit*)
STAFFORD	(*inhaling joint*) Bit of a turn-up.

SAM ENTERS THE CLEARING WITH A SERIES OF FORWARD FLIPS. AFTER EXECUTING THE FINAL ONE, HE STANDS AS IF ACKNOWLEDGING THE APPRECIATION OF THE CROWD. STAFFORD CLAPS.

SAM	(*not at all abashed*) Didn't see you there. (*sits down beside him. During the next few lines they smoke the spliff between them*) Funny evening, don't you think?
STAFFORD	I can't find Nic. Something strange with her tonight.
SAM	Something strange with everything. Something wonderful too.
STAFFORD	Good news about your TV thing.
SAM	It's like. It's like… I don't know. What's the best thing you can think of?

127

STAFFORD	*(ponders)* Getting a fox in your sights, gorgeous red, one paw raised, and killing it PAM with just one shot. *(pause while Sam digests this)* Shit. Bloody raining. *(he stands up)* Better go and try to find Nic. You can finish that.

SAM LEFT ALONE ON STAGE IN THE RAIN REACHES UP INTO THE TREE ABOVE HIS HEAD AND PULLS DOWN A FIRE-EATER'S TORCH. HE IGNITES IT WITH NO DIFFICULTY USING THE LAST OF THE SPLIFF AND PERFORMS AN EXCELLENT FIRE-EATING ROUTINE. THEN HE PLANTS HIS TORCH IN THE GROUND AND PERFORMS ANOTHER SERIES OF FORWARD FLIPS. HE TAKES A FEW BOWS, APPARENTLY TO AN ECSTATIC AUDIENCE. SNATCHING UP HIS TORCH, HE RUNS OFF, WAVING FAREWELL. BLACKOUT.

Scene 4

LIGHTS UP ON THE LIVING ROOM AN HOUR OR SO LATER. HARDLEY IS NOW LYING ON THE FLOOR, SNORING. NO CLEARING UP HAS BEEN DONE. TABLE IS PILED WITH LEFTOVER FOOD, BONES, HEARTS, ETC., BOTTLES, CANS AND SO ON. CUFF ENTERS FROM THE KITCHEN CARRYING A STEAMING MUG. HE SITS DOWN AT THE TABLE AND USING A TEASPOON SQUEEZES OUT A TEABAG. HE YAWNS, LOOKS AT HIS WATCH. DIONYSUS ENTERS.

CUFF	Hello.
DIONYSUS	You're the poet.
CUFF	Playwright.
DIONYSUS	I prefer poet.

128

CUFF	You're too kind. We haven't met. Are you something to do with the play?
DIONYSUS	No. I'm just a…groupie. They call me Di.
CUFF	Welsh I suppose? Can I make you a cup of tea?
DIONYSUS	No. *(picks up wine bottle and studies the label)* Bull's Blood. Sounds promising. *(he drinks, grimaces and sits down beside Cuff)* You stayed here, then?
CUFF	Oh no. I followed, for a little while, and then came back.
DIONYSUS	A mistake, if you don't mind me saying.
CUFF	What do you mean?
DIONYSUS	Well, you're the poet. *(pause)* How *is* the play going, by the way?
CUFF	Flat, to be honest. It isn't breathing yet. Greg says he can sort it out on the floor, but I'm not convinced—
DIONYSUS	On the floor or – *(he leans forward towards Cuff, gesturing towards the door to the garden with a wave of the near-empty bottle)* – in the woods? You have to make it *real.* Like out there. That breathes, doesn't it?
CUFF	Gasps and pants. Emotional chaos.
DIONYSUS	Emotional chaos? Keeping your distance aren't you? Call yourself a poet?

129

CUFF	*(almost to himself)* I should never have married her. She's hungry for life and…adventure.
DIONYSUS	Precisely. It's all here! What more do you want? Blood and family. Betrayal. Jealousy. Tragedy's basic ingredients.
CUFF	*(sipping his tea)* The pain of watching is. Quite excruciating. *(he drains the mug then stares into its empty interior)*
DIONYSUS	Where is she now, I wonder? Who is she with? Go on, torment yourself. It's a gift. If you *are* a poet.
CUFF	*(sets down mug with trembling hand)* The poet's eye, in a fine frenzy rolling, Doth glance from heaven to earth, from earth to heaven…
DIONYSUS	'Fine frenzy.' That's very *good*.
CUFF	Stolen, I'm afraid. Like most of the best lines.
DIONYSUS	I have to go. *(leaving, calls back)* Remember what I said. EXITS.

CUFF, NOW ALONE APART FROM SNORING HARDLEY, LOOKS THOUGHTFUL. PUSHING ASIDE DIRTY CROCKERY TO MAKE A SPACE ON THE TABLE, HE TAKES A NOTEBOOK FROM HIS TROUSER POCKET, EXTRACTS THE STUB OF A PENCIL FROM ITS SPINE, AND STARTS TO WRITE. LIGHTS DIM, INDICATING ELAPSING OF TIME.

ENTER JENNY, EVEN MORE DISHEVELLED, MUDDY KNEES, IVY FALLEN OVER ONE EYE, THE IMAGE OF A NAUGHTY CHILD.

JENNY	Oh Cuff. Have you been waiting here all this time? I'm sorry. I don't know what I've been doing. I don't know what came over me. *(she starts to cry as she walks over to him and perches on his knees)* I've been a bad girl—
CUFF	Never mind. Never mind. *(he starts disentangling the ivy from her hair. She leans into him, pushing her head into his shoulder)* It's my fault. It's all my fault. *(he pats her back comfortingly)* Shall we go home? *(gently, he dislodges her from his lap, stands up and takes her hand)* Did you have a coat? *(Jenny shakes her head)* You should have brought one. It's chilly now. *(he takes his battered leather jacket from the back of the chair and drapes it around her shoulders, before leading her out through the kitchen)*

SOUND OF BACK DOOR SHUTTING SETS THE DOGS UPSTAIRS BARKING. BARKING SUBSIDES, REPLACED BY OCCASIONAL WHINING. LIGHTS DIM. BLACKOUT.

Scene 5

A LITTLE LATER. IT'S RAINING. LIGHTS UP ON THE CLEARING IN JESMOND DENE. A SLIGHT GLOW, FROM THE TREE UNDER WHICH STAFFORD EARLIER SAT, REVEALS DIONYSUS IN THE TREE, HALF HIDDEN BY THE FOLIAGE. NIC SWIGS FROM A BOTTLE OF

WINE, WANDERS INTO THE CLEARING AND LIFTS HER FACE TO
THE RAIN. SHE WALKS OVER TO THE TREE AND EMBRACES IT,
CURLING ONE LEG PARTLY AROUND THE TRUNK. DIONYSUS
BEGINS TO CUP-HAND CLAP, BUILDING AN INSISTENT RHYTHM.
NIC PEELS AWAY FROM THE TREE AND STARTS TO DANCE IN TIME
WITH THE CLAPPING, LIFTING HER LONG SKIRT FLAMENCO
STYLE TO FREE HER LEGS. THE BEAT SEEMS TO PULSE THROUGH
DOWN THROUGH HER BODY TO INTO THE GROUND AND THERE
IS A WONDERFUL ABANDON ABOUT HER MOVEMENT. HER EYES
CLOSING IN SEMI-TRANCE, SHE TURNS FASTER AND FASTER.
DIONYSUS DROPS LIGHTLY OUT OF THE TREE. WITH THE
CLAPPING STOPPED, NIC COMES TO AN UNSTEADY, PANTING
STOP.

NIC	You.
DIONYSUS	I'm sorry I was so long. *(he takes a stride towards her but she sidesteps)* Don't you want me?
NIC	I might. On the other hand, I might not. You left me all alone for *hours*.
DIONYSUS	Yes. But wasn't I right to do that?
NIC	Right? *(she laughs)* I've decided. I don't want you *at all*.
DIONYSUS	You're wrong. But let's play a game. What is it will please you most?
NIC	You on your knees.
DIONYSUS	You are as beautiful as a goddess. But I can't go on my knees. Ask me anything else. Anything—
NIC	*(turning her back)* Goodbye then.

DIONYSUS	Wait! *(lowers himself on one knee, head bowed. She walks around him, touching his curls with the tips of her fingers. He shoots out a hand to grasp her but she jumps out of reach)*
NIC	Hands off! *(hugs herself and laughs again)* Now. Close your eyes and count.
DIONYSUS	*(keeping one eye open)* One! two!
NIC	No cheating! Shut your eyes! *(she unzips her dress and steps out of it, leaving it on the ground)* Now start counting! *(she darts away into the woods)*
DIONYSUS	One *(he stamps on the ground with one foot)* two *(stamps with other foot)* three *(he kicks earth behind him)* four *(more earth flies up. He transforms into a bull, raising his great head to release a tremendous bellow, before crashing through the trees in pursuit of Nic)* BLACKOUT.

Scene 6

FRENZIED BARKING. UPSTAIRS, STAFFORD'S DAD'S DOGS ARE HURLING THEMSELVES AT THE BEDROOM DOOR. DIONYSUS IN HUMAN FORM ONCE MORE ENTERS, EXULTANT.

DIONYSUS	Yes! A fine frenzy rolling! *(hears dogs yelping and points his thyrsus upstairs before exiting in a flash of fire)* I'll be back!

133

SOUND OF DOGS BURSTING THROUGH STAFFORD'S BEDROOM DOOR AND THUNDERING DOWNSTAIRS BARKING. THEY PAUSE TO SNIFF AT THE PRONE BODY OF HARDLEY AND THEN LEAP LIGHTLY ONTO THE TABLE WHERE THEY BEGIN TO FIGHT OVER THE REMAINS OF THE FOOD. LIGHTS DIM ON THEIR SLURPING, GROWLING FEAST. ENTER CHORUS, WHO TIPTOES DOWNSTAGE.

CHORUS   Ambition fed, Ambition thwarted,
                            Forbidden love, disaster courted,
                            Lust unrequited, jealousy's black hole.
                            All pains and pleasures of the soul…
                            Ah yes! We have a play! EXIT

ENTER MATT.

MATT   *(shouts)* Hello? I'm ready to do my turn now.

CURTAIN

I. 11

'Why is it, Mr Nicolson, in your country there is only one word for love? Only one idea for love? It is of no wonder everyone is divorced.'

The question drifted over to me as I leaned into the biggest chest freezer. I surfaced to reply, 'Not everybody gets divorced.'

It's the magazines Mr Khan's decided to sell that got him started on this topic, though there's nothing top shelf, just a few celebrity and women's titles. He waved a cover at me, 'Eros,' he said, and read, "*My Husband Loves my Brand New Body*". And this,' he brandished another. "*Rock Star Nights of Passion*". Eros again. All Eros. Nothing but Eros, Eros, bloody Eros.'

It caught me off guard. I couldn't think what a statue in Piccadilly had to do with *OK* and *Hello,* and the words came out, 'What do you mean, Eros?'

'So you are not familiar with the ancient Greek ideas of love?' He bore down on me with a little clipboard in one hand. 'Shall I tell you about it, while we complete the freezer exercise?' The freezer exercise. That's what he calls upending me in the ice to bring all the about-to-go-out-of-date stuff to the top. 'But first, Mr Nicolson, a question. How would *you* define your word love?'

I'd spent the last few days remembering Jane and trying to work out why I'd never got over her, so I felt I had a few things to say on that one. 'Well. It's desire, for one. Your heart beats faster, every touch is sort of electric—'

He held up his hand to silence me. 'Eros again, you see.

135

Greek word meaning love for the body, physical passion, taking sex from each other. It's all you Britons understand—'

'Hang on,' I said, but it still came out in an indignant stream:

'Sex sex sex never stopping sex what about eternal love?'

'There is here no *Agape* love for God, or God for us, or for a noble purpose, the best, the highest love of man for woman, or woman for man, not this rubbish of plastic flesh this me me me – come on Ham we must work while we talk.' He pointed downwards sharply with his index finger.

No *we* in it I thought, upside down, hacking packets of food out of the permafrost with a plastic spatula, where his voice still reached me like an oracle's from the depths of a cave.

'Then there is *Philia*. Love of friends and community – and love for spouse also but in the way of friendship – so you have three kinds of love to offer a woman and that is what is very present in my country and very missing in yours.'

A surge of anger brought me, and a load of individual chicken and mushroom pies, spluttering to the surface. 'I don't agree with that *at all*.'

He picked up a pie. 'But see. The proof! One of my best sellers! People eat alone here. They are not invited to partake of the plenty of others. Such a thing would never be seen in Herat.'

I said, 'There *is* love of community here.' The way he talks about it, you'd think it was all hunky dory back home, all peace and light and being kind to your mates in jolly old Afghanistan. He put on his glasses to peer at the date on the pie. Turned out to be two months past its sell-by so he added it to the little pile. Depending on how ancient the product is,

Mr Khan reduces the price or puts it aside for either him or me to take home. Most out-of-date stuff tastes fine. I wouldn't recommend three-year-old peas.

'In Afghanistan, young men and young women are chosen for each other very carefully, so that all these kinds of love are possible in one marriage. It is no good marrying simply because Eros is present. That is a menu for disaster.'

'Recipe,' I said.

'Eros-only love is the overwhelment of reason by brute passion.'

There was no bloody stopping him. 'I don't think there's such a word as overwhelment.' For a while he said nothing while he ticked off things on his clipboard, breathing in big angry huffs. 'So is that it, then? No other Greek words for love?'

He gave me one of his looks. 'When children arrive, there is *Storia*, the natural love parents feel for offspring. I hope my English is correct?' He paused and in the icy chill the idea of *Storia* hung between the childless pair of us. Then he looked down. 'I see something else there.'

'There isn't anything.'

'Yes. To the left.'

He was right, of course. I scraped the ice off a sticky toffee pudding at its best before January 2006.

'You want it?'

'Okay.'

'One pound to you. I will deduct it from your wages.'

'I'm not having it if I've got to pay for it.'

He huffed again, then said, 'In the spirit of *Philia*, you may take it as a gift.'

'Right then.'

He looked at me with his head on one side and I wondered if he was waiting for some kind of big thank you. Which I wasn't going to supply. He tucked the pen back in the pocket of his white coat and said, 'The ancient Greeks defined one other kind of love and that was *Xenia*...' but I was saved from xenia by the arrival of some people in the shop. Mr Khan went over to the till leaving me to refill the freezer.

I knew by the heavy slap of flip-flops on bare feet that it was my friend Fat Sue coming down the aisle; the raised voices meant she was with her partner, Egg and Chips. I call him that because it's his favourite meal. I get to hear a lot about their diet because they're always arguing about what to spend their few pounds on.

Fat Sue's voice had already reached warning levels. 'I'm havin' a dessert and that's it and all about it.'

'Worrabout me fuckin' cans ye fuckin' cow?'

Mr Khan shot over a worried look. They've come to fists more than once and it's shop policy to try and get them out before they cause any damage. Fat Sue came steaming round the corner just as I'd shovelled the last stuff back in the freezer.

'There ye are, Ham pet,' she panted. 'Have ye's got something nice for afters? Not more than two pound?'

Ahhh. There they were, on show as always, a couple of lovely big pink blancmanges like my Gran used to make, bulging out of Sue's lime coloured boob tube. You can't help liking a woman who gets them out in all weathers, come wind come snow, giving you just about your only remaining brush with sex. 'Do ye like sticky toffee puddin'?' I said.

Egg and Chips appeared. 'I've telled ye, ye greedy fucking

cow, I'm getting a drink. Fuck yer fuckin' pudding.' He stopped, followed my eyes. 'Fuck ye looking at?'

'Nothin'. I was just tellin' your Sue she can have this on the house.'

Sue put her head on one side and shivered her blancmanges at me. 'That's very kind of ye, pet.' Egg and Chips was snorting dangerously. I tore my eyes away and said 'We've got McEwans on offer.'

'Not drinking that shite.'

'Fair nuff. I divvent drink it mesel' come to that.'

'Fuck you trying to sell it to me for?'

'Good point ha ha. Ye've got me there, like.'

'Stupid fuckin' bastard,' he said. He smiled as he passed me, cheered up by a) seeing me admiring Sue's pair, b) exposing me as an idiot, c) showing what a hard man he was. 'Come on, lass.'

Sue rested them on the counter for Mr Khan, while Egg and Chips laboriously counted out the change. They left quite companionably. She even slipped her arm through his. But that didn't stop Mr Khan ranting on about them being the perfect example of a completely unsuited Eros-only couple, whose coming together tormented the whole community and if marriages were arranged, like they were back home, such unions would never happen.

I went back to packing the freezer, envying Egg and Chips his warm bed and slowly filling up with self pity as I mulled over my past life, wondering how it was I'd ended up on my own.

Not that I ever had loads of girlfriends, I thought, as I walked home through drifts of autumn leaves and polystyrene take-out trays. I'd realised by the age of 12 that I wasn't the stuff of young girls' dreams. I've never been great looking, more sandy and indistinct, and I'd not been the lusted-after type at school – more the distant observer of other lads' exploits around the back of the slag heap. My first close-up experience was Betty the Prostitute crapping on Cap'n Pike's face, so that probably put my development back a bit, too. Perhaps I never would have got going at all but for the fact of Justin Josephs going down with gastric 'flu two days before the Tech's production of *Romeo and Juliet* opened, forcing Adrian, the course tutor, to choose between promoting me (Benvolio) or Sam (Mercutio) to the main part. I won, a fact that threw me into the arms of Cindy Edwards, who played Juliet. There is a heightened intensity to rehearsing and performing love on stage that for a while gets mistaken for the real thing. I'm sure Thespis and his Greek actor mates had a word for the type of love you feel when the lines of the play get muddled into normal Eros-type desire, putting you in to this intense bubble of romance. Before you know it, you find yourself leaving the pub that follows the show hand-in-hand with your onstage love, walking along litter-strewn streets that are still the Forest of Arden, Verona or wherever.

I think the Greeks might have defined that better. Anyway, the fact that the Tech's *Romeo and Juliet* turned out a great success, much to Adrian's surprise, added to the magic of the Cindy relationship which lasted for a couple of months and, I reckon, 'normalised' me before it came down from its creative high, becoming a pretty boring relationship, involving many Saturday afternoon trips to Miss Selfridge, and we broke up.

I had a few other relationships like that, discovering soon

that once the fuel of the part and the shared creative excitement of the production is over, romance dwindles. But by then I'd learned that doing drama and being an actor has its pulling power with girls *outside* the business. I reckon it's still that creative thing. People want the fairy dust to rub off on them. I had plenty of short-term romances and then went out with a teacher called Margaret for a year before she decided acting wasn't the strongest foundation upon which to build a family and went off with some bloke in insurance. But by the time of Cuff's last play, Margaret had a couple of kids and I hadn't been out with anyone for two years; I'd even lost the appetite for one-nighters.

I put the key in the lock and let myself into the bedsit where I've been living for the past five years. Something to eat and then back to writing, I thought, stooping to pick up a manila envelope from the doormat. *The Department of Work and Pensions.* Everything conspired to remind me of unattainable Jane.

Our first kiss took place on the night of the Feast against the wire enclosure of the Children's Zoo in Jesmond Dene, in the presence of a strong smell of goat. A small kiss. Then we ran hand in hand along the path by the stream, excited, laughing, filled with that sense of speed and energy that you get being out in a breathing wood at night. We ran for ages, like kids, supercharged, superhuman kids high on home-grown ecstasy. At the end of the Dene we took to the roads, quiet in the dead of night, stopped running and started talking. Or rather talking, talking, talking, about what I can't remember, but as though we'd only just discovered language.

I'd loved her from afar for so long. That it was actually

happening seemed unbelievable to me. The most I hoped for was the occasional snatched half hour in Jane's company after rehearsals, or in the van, or on the odd time she'd come to the pub. Then everything went crazy. All that passion swirling around, I suppose, but it still seems hard to explain – unless there *was* a god on the loose.

We walked for miles, ending up outside the DHSS offices in Longbenton, its long rows of barrack-like huts stretching away from us under yellow lights. Sulphurous yellow is the colour I see now when I pass that way, but then the light seemed golden, the gates an entrance to a magical kingdom. I kissed her there for the second time and ever after, whenever I've received a manila envelope from Longbenton, about my benefit or pension, I've been reminded of the love of my life. That and the smell of goat.

A soft rain began to fall as we walked back to no. 12, coming through the door showering raindrops and gasping laughter. A last guttering candle showed us the ruins of the feast. Everything was silent. I grabbed the candle and led her upstairs to the top of the house, where Nic had her little den under the eaves. I knew the room contained a desk and a bed, made up by Nic for the designer who hadn't yet shown up.

It's hard to choose the right word for sex. 'Had sex' can work but it's much too uncaring; 'made love' sounds either too soppily romantic, or as if you'd been on a cunnilingus course. Could be some money in that. *Learn the arts of love in a rural setting, guided by renowned experts.* Couple. It seems the right word, remembering us lying there, a delicate moon curving its frail protection over us as we tentatively explored each other's bodies. Wood smoke and apples. Her skin and hair.

I must have gone to sleep because the next thing I remember is being woken by Nic's voice, harsh and breathless in the hallway, and the dogs going mad in the room beneath ours, flinging themselves at the door, growling and barking, Nic's voice shouting above it all, 'You've got me. So! What are you going to do about it? No! I said no *touching*. Oooh! I'm taking charge. Hear that. Hear that? Oooooooooh! Shhhh wait. I said wait! shh wait shwai shwai shwai...' and then the unmistakeable rhythm – amazing how it communicates through walls and floors – of big sex going on down on the living room floor.

That got me and Jane going again, really going the full Eros this time, so that the whole house must have been rocking until Nic shouted, 'Oh fuuuck! Oh GOOOOODDDDD!' so the whole house rang with it, and Jane whispered, 'Oh Ham.' We lay on our backs gazing up through the skylight at the fingernail-clipping of a moon, feeling the laughter in each other's bodies.

Anyone in love with someone already spoken for will know there are four words dreaded more than any others, though when Jane turned her head towards me the morning after and said 'I've got to go,' I hadn't yet learned that. It felt so right, being with her that I knew we were going to be together, that the problem of Gerry would disappear into *The Cherry Orchard* never to be seen again.

The microwave pinged and I got up to remove my individual chicken and mushroom pie. My lonesome, solitary, single pie. *Chef recommends: serve in front of TV with a small portion of chips.*

I. 12

In the ten-hour traffic of my shift, I usually find enough drama to keep me interested. There's a music to the day, a narrative build and decline that begins at 8 a.m. with the early rush for the *Sun*, cigarettes and sweets from those in work, declines to a dead calm for about an hour until just after the free bus passes become valid, and then in they come, the old ladies with their baskets on wheels. 'Mornin' Mr Nicolson,' they say, 'How are you keepin'?' and off they go down the aisles, inspecting, handling; they may never talk about consumer rights but they've been exercising them extensively all their adult lives.

I remember the butcher waiting respectfully as Mam took the big purse out of her massive handbag, counted out the coins slowly, and waited for the closing politenesses, enquiries after the family, the thanks that were her due. She was the kind of woman Alice and Maureen used to play, arms folded across her large bosom, 'What time do you call this?' She lorded it over the butcher, the baker, the timid grocer on the corner and most of all, the greengrocer, meekly offering his spuds and apples for inspection, 'These ones all right for you, Mrs Nicolson? Just in today. King Eddie's.'

Back then, she looked indestructible, standing proudly over her smudgeless front step. Oppressing rather than oppressed; Da handing over his wage packet and going quietly down the pub for a couple of pints. When she knotted a scarf over her perm and put on her housecoat she meant business. Dust surrendered, no stain could withstand the rasp of Vim or Ajax, no smelly toilet survived lethal doses of Sanilav, brushed well up under the rim. Carpets cringed as they hung over the washing line and waited for a thrashing.

There was a united front of mams, grans and aunties, always watching, ready to tell you off if you stepped out of line, reporting back using some mysterious backyard information link that worked via clothes lines, 'I've heard tales of you, our Ham…'

Alice and Maureen don't play them any more, because no one writes them. They're dying out. Shrunk and silenced, you see them creeping around supermarkets with their trolleys. They clock the brazen gum-chewing girls at the checkouts, or the older women who should be at home minding their bairns, but it's difficult to have their say when the conversation begins: 'Do you have a loyalty card?' and everybody behind them in the queue is getting impatient as they fumble for money. *No wonder there's all these discipline problems* they want to say, and they could go on but everyone is in too much of a hurry to listen.

That's why they prefer Mr Khan's shop and it's probably why I've got a job, because despite his politeness and willingness to help, Mr Khan's foreignness makes them uneasy. They love me. We talk about their childhoods in the war, rationing, Players' cigarettes, Mrs Dale's Diary – it all comes out like vanished music, a theme tune from the Home Service.

Sunlight Soap they ask for. We got that many requests, I looked into it. They only sell it in Africa, now. Mr Khan keeps Brasso in stock but I'm not sure how long that will last and we're down to our last tubes of grate blacking because the supplier's gone out of business. 'These spray-on things, I canna get used to them,' they say. 'Take all effort out of the job.' And I suppose it's hard to take pride in your laundry when it gets so white all by itself.

They miss counting money out of an envelope. 'Tell you to get it out of a hole in the wall!' they grumble, outraged, then, 'I'm not saying we're not better off. But it's so...' They tail off, and I cheer them up with a tin of Mansion polish. I've made them sound pathetic and pitiful, but we have a laugh. 'I had a lovely big chest, ye knaa. Could've made me fortune taking me clothes off.'

They'll disappear, as surely as the ships in the Tyne. Mams used to be battleships, cleaving a path through stormy seas, nosing out bargains, swabbing the decks, docking in tight spaces. But they've sold off the navy, broken up the battleships. I was at school with girls who just wanted to be like their mams. One choice it turned out they didn't have.

Alice and Maureen are still going strong, as it happens. But then, they were only acting. Maureen's half the size she was and plays a batty science teacher in a kids' TV series. Alice works for an estate agent. 'Viewin' homes,' she said, the last time we met, 'is a bit like curtain up.' Suspending her own disbelief, perhaps.

The old ladies are strictly daylight customers. They're not around much between 12.30 and 2.00 because that is, and always has been, dinner time. The shop's pretty quiet then except for a few pairs of workplace adulterers topping up their sex drives with high-energy drinks. Then the wheelie baskets are back for an hour or so before disappearing off the streets by 3.30 p.m. in order to avoid the school kids coming in for crisps and chocolate on their way home.

Now there's this fear of kids, when as a lad it was old people I was afraid of. Funny how that's changed isn't it? Most of the kids are fine, few too many on the fat side in my opinion, but not much trouble. Mr Khan gives me a nod when one or two he knows of old come in and I follow them to make sure they don't stuff things in their pockets. The sad ones are the lads with hoods up who come in for Rizlas and cigarettes so they can stay smashed out on skunk all evening in the park down the road. Thirteen upwards I'd say, but some of them may be younger. We shouldn't be selling them tabs but Mr Khan won't listen to me; he's even breaking up packs of Lambert & Butler so we can sell them separately for 40p each. He hasn't any sympathy. Sees them as 'weaklings with poor blood'.

There's one I've taken a bit of an interest in, trying to engage him in conversation – without much success, like. I asked him where he went to school and he shot me a Darth Vader look out of his hoodie. 'Why do you want to know?' I realised he thought I was about to challenge him on his age.

'Only askin',' I said.

He *is* still at school. I know because one night this woman came in at the same time and said hello to him. He just grunted and walked away with his hands pushed down into his pockets. She raised her eyebrows at me, 'I'll see you tomorrow in Citizenship, Matthew. Don't be late.' Then she noticed the stack of books by the till and exclaimed, 'Goodness me! Academic diaries! Just what I've been looking for!'

It gave me a shock when she said his name, because I realised then that's who he reminded me of: Matt. Here was Matt Mark 2, thirty years on. The same kind of hunched and aimless kid Matt was when he joined the company.

I suppose there's always been Matts, Mr Khan's weaklings with poor blood that the rest of us would probably call the underclass. There seem to be more and more of them, not so poor perhaps, a few more clothes to choose from courtesy of cheap Chinese exports, maybe a mobile phone, and (I hope, anyway) a bathroom in the house; but still as lost and hopeless. Back in the seventies, Matt Mark 2 would've been out of the classroom and on a scheme; now, for lack of a better idea, the government wants to keep him in school till he's 18. As she left the shop the teacher murmured to me, 'I've got a whole class of year 11 lads like him. Sad, isn't it? Don't know what they're for any more, do they?'

From Matt Mark 1's point of view, us Kicking Theatre lot must have been the biggest bunch of weirdos he'd ever come across. He probably didn't even know people like us existed. Sure, we sometimes went into schools, but plays usually got shown to the good kids in the higher streams, partly because the heads didn't want any embarrassing kid behaviour scenes, and the foul-mouthed toe-rag-likely-to-make-their-own-theatre types were usually in the lower sets. They got put there because they had big mouths; others got stuck in the D stream because they were the quiet *disappeared* kind of kid. Matt would have been one of those, struggling to understand the lessons though there was all hell going on, coming up against worn out, exasperated or just plain lazy-bastard teachers who never gave him any help.

So that was you, Matt, in 1978. You'd put up with the shite of high school for five years and then they gave you a careers interview and told you what your options were: the shipyards, the coke works, or the Davy Roll Company. Only there weren't any vacancies. The rowdy arseholes that stopped you being able to learn anything, pulled their fingers out at the last minute and bagged the best apprenticeships. No, you couldn't even train to be a lowly caulker burner, scraping weld off the great big sheets of metal they built ships with, using screaming machines that screamed into your ears all day – no, all the places were filled.

Instead, the careers man put your name down for a scheme. And you ended up on about the most embarrassing scheme possible, Matt, more shaming than you could ever have imagined, because in your head all work for men involved hitting or shaping things, making holes or filling them in, digging stuff out. The only time you'd ever *acted* you were a shepherd in the nativity play and the memory is painful as you were the only one who didn't bring a tea towel from home for your head. You didn't bring one because you couldn't find one, and your mam didn't know what you were on about. Shite though it was, school was a lot less shite than home.

And thirty years on, nothing's changed, except there's even less work out there, and almost nothing that makes you feel like a man. 'They don't know what they're for,' that teacher said, and she was right.

What Mr Khan can't understand is the lack of family love. He told me he lives next door to an old woman whose family hardly ever visit her. 'Sometimes I hear her crying at night.' Then her son came knocking at Mr Khan's door. 'He didn't want to see her, just to know she is alive, so I tell him. "She is alive. I hear her walking around. If that's all you want to know, she is alive."'

He told me this story after work, as we sat upstairs under

the picture of Herat. I'm beginning to find out about Mr Khan, but it comes out slowly. There's a Greek epic in there I'm sure – some spectacular odyssey from there to here.

'Another brandy?' He handed me the bottle.

'How come you drink alcohol then, Mr Khan?'

He sipped from his mug and smiled. 'A hit! A palpable hit! I have an Achilles' heel, Ham, learned in war. I try to indulge seldomly.'

Mr Khan would make a great character, and typing up stuff on my ancient word-processor after work, I keyed in Herat as *Heart*, which I suppose sums up what the place represents for him: home is where Herat is, in the north west of Afghanistan. He told me why he had to leave in 1979. The town mutinied against the Soviet occupation, and 20,000 people died before the Russians and their Afghan allies regained control.

'There was nothing left for me there, except death,' he said. 'Anyone with education or land was treated as the enemy.'

'Did people in your family get killed?'

'Of course. I was sick so the Red Cross helped me. I have only my wife, now. And she, I met here.'

I thought about him arriving alone and unwell in the cold northeast of England, finding himself among many other refugees, none speaking his language and all feeling equally lost, but he took one look at my face and waved away sympathy. 'Poof! I moped a bit, yes. Foolishly, I used to climb hills and look down on the people, trying to find those with black hair. None of you British have black hair! But there is only one life. I don't want pity!'

So there we have them: the full cast in the daily drama of shop life. Pathos with the old ladies, lust with the lunchtime adulterers and despair – despair in spades really, because the bulk of our customers are the terminally lost, the disappeared, the underclass – those who just about get it together to cash their giros next door and then stagger in for some overpriced microwave chips and bottles of cider. And presiding over all these we have a homesick exile, most of whose family were wiped out in a savage war.

I. 13

That first morning under the rusted skylight, Jane rolled away from me, got up and scrambled into her clothes. 'Ham, could you go down and check nobody's there? I don't want anyone to see. You know. It'll only cause trouble. Whistle if it's okay.' She had a hair slide between her teeth, one hand pushing back a mass of chestnut hair.

It was completely quiet in the living room. Then I heard a thump thump thump and saw Stafford's dad's black dog curled in an armchair, mouth leaking chilli-coloured drool, tail wagging by way of greeting. The crockery littering the floor was spotted with orangey vomit, and deeper pools lay on the carpet. Most of the plates, cutlery and leftover food had found its way onto the floor, The table, collapsed at one end but still covered in its splattered sheet, rose above the horror like a sagging tent at a particularly bloody medieval joust. I whistled. Jane came down.

'Oh my god.' She laughed, opening her eyes wide. We looked at each other. She squeezed my hand briefly by way of goodbye, and skipping lightly round the vomit, exited out of the back door.

Jane spirited herself away just in time because while I was standing among the debris, contemplating my bereft state, Hardley's voice penetrated. 'Bit of a mess.' He stood behind me, in paisley-patterned dressing gown and carpet slippers. 'What happened last night, Ham? I can't remember a thing.'

'You passed out early on. Stafford's spliff.'

'Ah.'

He shuffled into the kitchen and started to root around in the fridge. 'I couldn't have had very much to eat. I'm ravenous.' I joined him, more to get away from the dog puke than anything else, and hoping he wasn't going to eat anything disgusting. Hardley was a bit of an offal man. Clearing a space in the wreckage, he laid a breakfast tray with teapot, mug, milk, etc. and set about making scrambled eggs. Hardley had this ability to carve himself out an ordered place in the chaos that was Kicking Theatre and inhabit that space, ignoring the horror around him. He lined up three rounds of bread to toast under the grill, lighting it with a pack of Swans he took from his dressing-gown pocket. 'Fancy some toast?' he said. I thought about it. Felt the first twinge of digestive disturbance.

'Not hungry, thanks.'

While his toast browned he collected his *Observer* from the back door and made a pot of tea. He even had a toast rack. When all was ready, he took his tray back through the living room, paused for a moment, as if assessing the possibilities of breakfasting there, then proceeded up the stairs to his room.

With his dressing gown and his breakfast tray Hardley appeared like a square peg in a round hole, but in fact he fitted brilliantly into the company so far as the rest of us were concerned. He rightly supposed the childish nature of most actors (and *artistes* in general) meant they were incapable of doing anything – other than perform – themselves, and took it upon himself to look after us, even down to deducting money from our pay packets to cover tax bills at the end of the financial year. I suppose we mildly resented the apparent contempt in which we were held, but not enough to stop him sorting things out for us, and in a wider way for Kicking Theatre Co itself.

I didn't recognise it at the time but Hardley's assumption that none of us could be trusted to organise/remember/plan for the future, and his habits of doubt and questioning were his most invaluable contribution to the company. The rest of us couldn't be bothered to think about artistic policy beyond how big our parts were and when the reviewers were coming. When Greg described a huge and wonderful set, it was Hardley who raised an eyebrow and said, 'What about Biddick?' reminding him that all sets had to be small enough to get into the smallest venue: Biddick Farm Arts Centre in Washington New Town, where our tours usually ended.

'Fuck Biddick!' Greg would shout – but he and the designer went back to the drawing board.

I used to wonder when Hardley would come to his senses and leave Kicking for a job that paid better and didn't involve looking after a lot of egotistical overgrown children, but then in an unguarded moment he confessed he actually found performance magical. Underneath the paisley dressing gown beat the heart of a *fan*. Well, it helped to explain why he stayed in such an apparently thankless job. Not that we appreciated him. Hardley claimed that it was only his questions, his unpleasant practical interventions, that kept Kicking Theatre Co solvent, brought in the plays on budget, filled our pay packets each week and kept us all in employment. We disputed this hotly at the time. But he was right.

Come to think of it, I can only remember that one occasion when his vigilance failed. On that post-Feast morning, one day before rehearsals began, only Greg, Cuff, and, with an increasing sense of guilt, me, actually knew the next show was *not* going to be a jolly Geordie knees-up.

I watched Hardley's thin white ankles ascend and wondered what to do, wanting to stay in the vicinity of Jane, but not able to go round to her house. Though I didn't know it, that feeling of suspended animation was about to become a way of life for the next three months. I started half-heartedly on the washing up and then went back to bed.

The living room stayed in that condition until the evening, when it became clear to Stafford, me and Hardley that we might not be able to avoid doing something about it. 'Where's Nic?' Hardley said, gazing at a patch of dried dog puke.

'Don't know,' Stafford said. 'Must have gone out really early this morning.' He looked a bit worried.

'Greg?'

'No idea.'

We got stuck in and cleared up. I spent a second night under the skylight, still on cloud nine. Next day I'd see Jane. Have to. Because next day rehearsals started.

CUFF'S SHED, 4 A.M.

GREG	*(looks up from reading)* I see why you got me out here. You've re-written the whole second act.
CUFF	*(without looking at him)* Have you got a play or not?
GREG	You didn't have to do that. I'm sorry—
CUFF	No good then?

155

GREG	No. It's good. Very, very good. But it must have been difficult, I mean...
CUFF	I'll be taking myself to bed, then.

CUFF STANDS, STRETCHES, OPENS THE DOOR AND STEPS OUT OF THE SHED. GREG, CLUTCHING THE SCRIPT, FOLLOWS. HE TURNS OFF THE LIGHT AND THEY STAND TOGETHER THE GARDEN.

GREG	Gonna photocopy this first thing in the morning. *(pause)*
CUFF	Morning's here. *(he yawns)* See? 'In russet mantle clad.'
GREG	*Hamlet.* Something 'yon high eastward hill...' After they've seen the ghost.
CUFF	Spot on, laddie.
GREG	I'd better go. *(he doesn't move)*
CUFF	Funny. Just now I feel like a ghost. A ghost of myself.
GREG	Take me an hour to get back. Grab a couple of hours sleep—
CUFF	A shade. Something thin and insubstantial. I've written myself into a shade—
GREG	You need some sleep. Get some sleep, okay? *(he starts to walk quickly towards the gate, then turns and calls back)* Cuff?
CUFF	What?
GREG	Nothing. Nothing. I'll see you at the read-through. Okay?

We were called for ten. But it was only just seven when I woke up to a hammering on the bedroom door. Greg stood there, black hair standing on end, eyes bright with fatigue. 'I need you to come down to the Building.' He flourished a sheaf of papers at me.

'That the script?' I mumbled.

'Yep.'

'You been to bed?'

'No. Cuff finished it at four. Well, finished this draft. You gotta help me do the photocopies. Come on.'

'Right now?'

'Yep. Get dressed. I'll be in the kitchen.' He leapt down the stairs about five at a time, looked back, '*Now.*'

In a few minutes we were outside, the engine already running. 'Shit! We need the fucking keys to the building. Go up and get them from Hardley.'

Even Hardley didn't set his alarm before eight. When I finally got him to open the door, he eyed me suspiciously.

'Greg needs the keys to the Building,'

'Why?'

'Photocopy the script.'

'Ah.' He disappeared into the room in search of keys. It was a job that usually fell to Hardley himself, and I suppose he remembered this because he came back without them. 'Why's he doing them?'

I shrugged. 'Search me.' Greg honked the horn.

Reluctantly, Hardley handed over a large set of keys. 'Whatever you do, don't give them to Greg,' he said, and then laboriously explained where exactly I should leave the keys for him together with the procedure for the correct use of the photocopier. The honking of the horn became frenzied.

When we arrived, we found the postman had left several boxes at the entrance to the Building. 'Can you manage them, Ham?' Greg said, reaching out a hand for the keys. We went upstairs to the office, I dumped the boxes and we got on with the photocopying.

There's something very exciting about a new script, perhaps particularly a *secret* new script and I scanned the pages as I sorted them, hot and curled from the photocopier and Greg's hands, into nine piles on the floor. Greg, shouting to be heard above the groaning Rank Xerox, talked non-stop about his ideas for the show.

'We need choirs, Ham – a miners' choir would be good… I want lots of voices, got to give the impression of hundreds of people onstage…' I listened very happily until Hardley arrived at least half an hour earlier than usual, his anxieties perhaps having got the better of him. By that time we'd moved on to collating the scripts. Hardley inspected the photocopier, still working though extremely hot, made himself a cup of coffee and sat down at his desk to observe. We were nearly finished by then; Greg was barking out the lines on the top of the last few pages.

After a bit, Hardley said, 'Not exactly a laugh a minute, is it?'

Greg's eyes flicked uneasily in his direction. I thought he might confess, but he said nothing until we'd finished, when he looked at me. 'I've gotta meet the designer at Central Station. You take the scripts in the minibus to the rehearsal. Mark out the floor. Don't forget the tape measure. I'll see you later.'

'Keys.' Hardley held out his hand to Greg, now halfway down the stairs.

I went off in search of a tape measure. By the time I returned to the office a lost-looking Matt had arrived. 'Where am I supposed to be?'

I dumped a pile of scripts in his arms. 'May as well come with me.'

Hardley looked at us both over the top of a colourful leaflet. 'Off now? he enquired, brightly. He was always happy to share the building with a few technicians while all the thesps were safely occupied elsewhere. But it turned out to be more than that accounting for the smile on his face. 'Take a look at this,' he said, handing me the flier. 'What do you think?'

It's chaos in the Redpath household. Mam's lost her poss stick, Da's lost his job, Grandad still thinks he's fighting in the Crimea and young Lizzie's in love. It's also **Blaydon Races** *weekend.* **Kicking Theatre's** *new play takes an old song and brings it to stirring new life. You'll be laughing till you cry and then some more!*

I read it slowly, noting with sinking heart that it was glossier and more expensive than usual. I turned it over to find a long list of venues.

'Very nice,' I said, and then, as Hardley seemed to be waiting for more, I added, 'Biggish tour.'

'Biggest yet,' said Hardley, with pride. 'Found this one very easy to book. Our audiences love a bit of nostalgia.'

I struggled to find some hope in the situation. 'Is this an inspection copy?'

159

'No.' Hardley rubbed his hands and nodded over to the corner where I'd left the boxes. 'Arrived this morning. Good printers they are. I'll definitely use them again.'

It was time to leave.

Act II: Rehearsal

II. 1

Our Joe's given me a computer. Making room for his new model, but I'm dead pleased with it. I asked Matt Mark 2 if he could help me sort an internet connection. He looked a bit uneasy when I ushered him into my bed-sitting room, but sat down at the desk, willing enough, while I went to the kitchen to fetch him a drink.

'What password de ye's want, like?' he called over.

'I've written it down for you. On the right.' I opened a pack of chocolate biscuits.

'Oh aye. Worrever that means,' he said. He had his back to me, brown hoodie up, long fingers flying over the keys, and for a moment I was a kid again, face pressed against glass in the amusements arcade in Whitley Bay, watching the ghostly monk crouched over the organ slowly raise his head. Transfixed, even though I knew what was coming, that inside the cowl, reflected in the facing mirror, I'd see a grinning skull.

'This thing's dead old fashioned,' Matt 2 said, turning round to see me standing behind him, a glass of Coke in one hand and a Kit Kat Chunky in the other. I must have had a funny look on my face because he jumped up, said, 'It's working now. See yer around,' and clumped off down the stairs before I'd even had time to say thank you.

Seeing me loitering there with treats probably set the bells in his head, already tinkling following 'How about coming back to my place to get my computer working?' peal out a full-scale perve-alert. I listened to the door downstairs bang shut and thought the truth was even weirder. Rather than *I want to lay aged hands upon your young flesh*, it was *I seek a connection with Matt Mark 1 via you, Matt Mark 2.*

And then I sat down at the computer and realised he'd connected me to a whole lot more than that, connected me, in fact, to my whole world of yesteryear. Twenty-first-century ectoplasm, that's what the internet is, I reckon; a link to the past, the disappeared and the dead.

I was up till 3 a.m.. Started with Sam. A mere three-hundred-and-fifty-seven thousand entries. Moved on to Cuff and Cuff's plays (six hundred entries), Ham Nicolson (fifteen entries – all ancient cast lists). Finally, I typed in Jane's name. I sat back, expecting the same thing for her, but a website flashed up immediately. *Not the same Jane*, I thought, getting up to make my umpteenth cup of coffee. I stood drinking it in the darkness, my hands trembling with caffeine overload, that little luminescent square luring me back.

I opened the link. DRAMA WORKSHOPS TO SCHOOLS. Was *that* Jane, kneeling on the floor, gesturing and smiling, surrounded by kids apparently hanging on her every word? I groped for my reading glasses and peered at the face. Older, yes, but still *hers,* the cloud of hair fairer than I remembered. Active buttons in dayglo orange. *Workshops Jane offers. About Jane. Contact Jane.*

162

I shut down and stumbled across the room to my bed. But I couldn't sleep. *Contact Jane.*

Well that was a fucking stupid idea, nearly thirty years after the fact. If fact it ever was. Never a fact in the public domain because she was so scared of anyone finding out. In reality, being in love with Jane was fantastic for about ten per cent of the time and gut-wrenching for the other ninety. Jane was so paranoid she hardly spoke to me in rehearsals. I had to make do with little secret signals of intimacy when we were onstage together, and back at her place after the pub on the limited number of times she invited me.

I never knew what was coming next. One minute she'd be mine, her dark eyes over the top of her glass giving me that secret look, and the next she'd withdraw, say 'I've got to go,' excluding me even from the goodbye smile that encompassed every bugger else in the group. Screwed me up emotionally. Screwed up my digestion as well. People don't write about that aspect of love much, do they? Its intestinal repercussions.

Come to think of it, I don't think she ever asked me back to her place completely sober. The way to her heart went via the guilt-clouding effects of Guinness and blackcurrant. I'm not saying what we had was just drunken fucks because I know she felt too when we were together – that no one else has ever understood you so easily and so completely and that everything the other says illuminates your own soul. But I never knew when it would happen again; it was like being in an audition lasting all autumn – with frequent bog breaks.

The idea of autumn seems appropriate. It was the autumn of that particular company and the autumn of poor old Cuff, though he didn't know it. A harvesting, and not just by the grim reaper, because Cuff's last play fattened up a few careers; at the end of the run some plump fruit dropped into the baskets of other companies and television. It was also the autumn of Jane and me – or rather the spring, summer, autumn and winter – all packed in between September and Christmas while Gerry was away, doing Chekhov.

'Now then, Mr Nicolson, tell me about the rehearsal process.' Mr Khan, like most people I think, imagines rehearsals taking place in theatres, but the reality is theatres are too busy putting on shows to have redundant space for practising. Even the big companies rehearse anywhere with a floor big enough to mark out the dimensions of the acting space. The inexpensive venue Hardley had found for rehearsing *The Blaydon Races* was St Columba's Church Hall. Driving there with Matt I'd felt too nervous and excited to say much. Then he'd surprised me by speaking first. 'Weird party the other night.'

'Ye can say that again. Enjoy it?'

'Sort of.' A pause had opened up. 'Worram I going to be doing?'

'Bit of everything I expect.'

'Not acting, though?' Matt's eyes had met mine for a moment as I'd shoved open the heavy door. He had big sorrowful brown ones, like a spaniel's.

As a *set*, the hall comprised a bare wooden floor edged by stacks of chairs, dusty windows set high in the walls and a small stage at the back. Three *dramatis personae* were already present. Stafford sat on the edge of the stage rolling a cigarette;

164

Maureen, arms folded, stood in an open doorway to one side. From the middle of the room and while simultaneously juggling three red-and-white balls, Sam addressed them both.

I suppose Sam must have been wearing jeans and a wool jumper – Shetland probably, or maybe a checked shirt tucked in, in the style of back then, but I picture him dressed like Shakespeare's clown Will Kemp; velvet feathered cap, bright doublet, and hear him jingling with the bells he wore below the knee.

'Ham!' he tossed me a ball, which I failed to catch. 'How are you, me old mucker!'

I stooped to pick up the ball. 'Where'd you get that?'

'What?'

'Mucker.'

'London I s'pose. I was just telling them. Heard this fucking great joke.'

'Down London?'

'Divvent worry your little head Ham pet lamb hinny, this one's as Geordie as they come. Isn't it?' He looked at Stafford, now running his tongue along the edge of the cigarette paper.

'Oh aye,' Stafford said, and laughed. 'Gorra light, Ham?'

'So. As I was sayin', Geordie gans down the doctors to talk about him and his wife's little problem, like. And the doctor listens to Geordie and then he says, "Well now Geordie – ahem – one difficulty couples come up against is a lack of variety in their lovemaking. Ahem. So. De ye's always use the missionary position when ye have sex?"'

'Urn doesn't work,' Maureen interrupted.

'Never mind Pet, this joke will cheer you up. So anyways, "The missionary position? What's that like?" goes our Geordie.'

Alice came in. 'Urn's buggered,' Maureen called over. 'Bloody typical, Hardley not checking.'

'Shut up about the fucking urn,' Stafford said. 'Listen to this, Alice. Go on, Sam.'

I'm sure Maureen wanted a cup of tea but running underneath the complaint she had a Stanislavski type *objective* in the scene to stop all the status she usually enjoyed as senior actor bleeding away to Sam. But there was nothing she could do: his relaxed body language said it all. While the rest of us were all to some extent anxious about the play and wanting to get a good part, everything about him said *just this one last play and I'll be gone, swung aloft on fortune's wheel while you lot crane your heads skywards, your gaping mouths little black dots far below.*

That sounds bitter and I suppose, loaded as it is with hindsight, it is. But I don't think I saw him then through jealous eyes. Fact is he was my friend, then. I'd known him and liked him for ever.

'"Wae Geordie, that's when the man lies on top of his wife, like."

'"Oh aye. That's the way we do it."'

I gave Matt one end of the tape measure. 'Me and Matt have got work to do here,' I said, to beginning pay it out, 'Why don't you lot get up on the stage?'

Maureen turned her anger on Matt. 'What he can do if he wants to make himself useful is go and buy a kettle.'

Matt looked terrified. 'I don't know where the shops are,' he whispered.

'Need to get this done first,' I told Maureen, giving Matt the end of the tape measure.

166

'You'll not stick anything to that floor unless you sweep it first. Broom's out there.' She flicked her head towards the side room and Matt went off to fetch it. Satisfied, she climbed up on stage and joined the circle around Sam, now swelled by the simultaneous arrival of Lynette and Rod.

Still no Jane. Helping with the brush and dustpan I had one ear out for the door, and the other following Sam's joke.

'So the doctor says, "There's doggy fashion, for one."

'"Doggy fashion? What's that?" So the doctor explains and Geordie shakes his head. "I divvent think wor lass'll fancy that... Is there nowt else?"

'"Well there's the Sheriff of Nottingham."

'"The Sheriff of Nottingham? How de ye dae that?"'

Matt and I started taping the floor. Jane appeared. My stomach lurched. She had a knack of materialising out of thin air and the fact she wore a silvery grey top added to her ethereal quality. She gave me a fleeting smile, perhaps torn for a moment between talking to me or joining the others. 'You look busy,' she said.

'Jane!' Sam interrupted himself. 'Come up here!'

'Aw flaming hell fire you'll have to start again, now,' Stafford said.

'Okay Matt it's 17 feet this way.' I could hear the impatience in my voice. I wanted to get the chairs into a circle fast and then make sure when Greg arrived I got a place next to – or perhaps facing would be better – Jane.

'"Oh hec, Geordie," says Geordie's lass, "I divvent like the sound of *side saddle* and I'm certainly not going to try *tea for two*. Is there nowt else?" So back he gans to the doctor and the doctor scratches his head for a bit and finally says, "Wae

Geordie. I wouldn't normally tell one of my patients this but there is one other position my wife and I particularly enjoy…"'

Greg arrived. 'The Urn doesn't work,' Maureen shouted over to him.

He looked at her blankly. I reckon 'urn' unless possibly prefixed by 'Grecian' was not among the words in his vocabulary.

'No way of making *tea*,' I added.

'Ah.' He muttered to me, 'Least of our fucking problems.'

'How was the designer?'

'Wanker. Gone back to Birmingham.' I wondered if the designer had got the same surprise everyone else was in for. 'Stupid precious fucker. Missing a great opportunity with this play. Come on, let's get the scripts.'

'"The Wheelbarrow? How do you do that, like?"'

Greg clapped his hands and whistled. 'Right everyone. In the circle. *Now.*'

It says something for the allure of the new script now thudding on to the seat of each chair that everyone left Sam's joke hanging there to claim their sheaf of fresh white play.

'This is gonna be a little different to what you expect,' Greg said when we were all seated, scripts on our laps. 'It's Cuff's.' He let that sink in. 'It needs shaping, and a good read-through will help Cuff and me with that – but I think what we've got here is the makings of a great play.'

Rod spoke. 'Well? Who's reading who?'

I love those moments. Everyone sitting on the edge of their seats; if we were dogs our ears would be pricked, one paw raised, expectant. Waiting for the allocation of parts. Greg reeled off the list. '*Ham*, could you read Morris, Ally the Tote and First

168

Soldier; *Sam*, you read Harry and the priest; *Jane*, I want you to do Lizzie, Edith and the Insulting Woman, *Rod*…'

'Is this who we'll be playing?' Sam asked.

'Not sure at all yet. Let's get started.'

But even though he said that, life felt very good. I had the part I wanted. Jane had the part I wanted for her, and though it's not the done thing at read-throughs to leaf frantically through the script checking how much your character's on stage, from what I'd read during the photocopying I thought they were also the main parts.

But that assumption was dodgy. You can never tell just by looking because plays are never quite what they seem. They grow. Some of the most unpromising characters on the page blossom and the bombast of another fades into a shuffling supporting role. And Greg's 'the makings of' hadn't been lost on any of us either; this play was still being written and would undoubtedly change, so our roles within it were dynamic also. We'd evidently all be playing two or three parts anyway, from the number of characters.

Maureen looked up from scrutinising the list. 'Either we're a man short, or you've got plans for women to play men.'

Greg nodded. 'Man short, Yep. Cuff's working on it. May have to cut. Let's get started.'

Two hours of intense concentration followed. When we got to the end, a few moments' silence followed.

'Well!' Alice said. 'I *think* I like it. Wouldn't call it a comedy though.'

'Bit close to home, isn't it?' Rod sat forward in his chair and stared hard at Greg. 'Old husband. Young wife looking for a spot of action. Who's Morris based on, then?'

Greg flushed and stood up abruptly. 'Coffee break. We'll go again at 12.20.'

'Coffee? You'll be lucky,' Maureen snorted.

I looked around for Matt. There was no sign of him, but a faint grumbling sound issued from the side room. Then he appeared in the doorway, smiling from ear to ear and holding up a screwdriver. 'Coming up to boiling now. Only a wire loose.'

'Just what we need,' Greg said as he gulped hot coffee a few minutes later. 'Help in the lighting department.'

Cuff arrived and we read the play through again. Then he and Greg went out for a bit to talk about the casting. Back in the circle half an hour later, Greg said, 'I want to make one or two changes.' I crossed my fingers. Couldn't look at Jane. We waited. 'Sam. This time I want you to read the second soldier and Rod, you do the priest. Otherwise, everyone read the same parts.' He glanced at Cuff. 'That's how it'll stay.' Greg took a stopwatch out of his pocket and threw it to Matt. 'Need you to time this one. Okay, let's go.'

They say happiness is something you only feel looking back, but I remember thinking *this is the happiest day of my life* as rehearsals ended for the day. I drove the minibus back to the quayside and while Greg took Matt inside to talk to the technicians about the lights, we actors went for a drink, filled with the excitement of doing a good new play by Cuff – meaning possible reviews and probably transfers and then obviously *success* – all of this made even more intoxicating for me because I sat with Jane's thigh brushing mine. She looked over to Sam and said, 'What about the end of the joke, then, Sam?'

'Where did I get to?'

'The wheelbarrow.'

'Oh aye. "The wheelbarra?" Geordie gans to the doctor. "That sounds canny. How do ye do that?" So the doctor explains how Geordie's wife supports the top half of herself on her arms – "Like doing press ups, ye know," and Geordie stands between her legs and lifts her thighs like he were pushing a wheelbarrow. "That Geordie, is the position my lass likes best."

'"Sounds like sports' day," Geordie says. And thanking the doctor for his advice, off he gans back home to his wife. When he gets there, she's just rollin' out a bit of pastry, but she wipes her hands and makes him a cup of tea, sayin', "How did you come on at the doctor's, Geordie?" So Geordie explains what the doctor said and tells her about the wheelbarrow. And after he's explained, Geordie's lass gans quiet for a bit, thinking. Then she takes a big breath and says, "I tell you what, Geordie. We'll give that wheelbarra thing a try… Long as we don't go past me Mam's."'

I woke myself up shouting. Lay there for a bit with my eyes closed, willing myself back into the dream. I'd been so *there* in Jane's house, with its linoleum, its scumbled doors. She'd found three rolls of that Victorian wallpaper – by William Morris or some disciple of his – on a market stall, and we'd hung it one weekend during rehearsals. In my head I walked around Jane's house, picked up the tortoiseshell comb from the top of the tallboy in her bedroom, poked in her little pile of scarves and trinkets. She liked *old*. Cameo brooches, never mind the cracks; 1940s jackets with ration marks stitched into their crêpe linings; chenille, lots of chenille.

I turned on the computer, filling the room with a companionable hum, and sent a message. Then I ran away to work twenty minutes early.

I think I'd have told Mr Khan all about Jane if I'd found him in a better mood. Silence was all I got for greeting, not a murmur about me being so prompt, and when I finally broke it by referring to our last theatre argument, 'Three thousand people you could get in the *Globe,* which is not what I'd call a *small* audience.' He just snapped back, 'The rubbish needs burning.' *I want you to clear off* came over loud and clear. I was shocked at how upset I felt. Didn't trust myself to speak. Just took a box of matches from the shelf and went into the backyard.

Being a stingy bastard, Mr Khan refuses to pay the council extra for disposing of all the acres of cardboard and plastic packaging the shop generates, instead getting me to send toxic clouds into the ozone with twice-weekly illegal burning. The shop's in a dip and the yard surrounded by high walls – prison-like even on the brightest days. Now, with all the suddenness it happens in late September, the weather had turned cold. A sky the dull white of an old sheet stretched above my head.

I relieved my angry feelings by crushing boxes and shoving them in the incinerator, anxious to get a blaze going. But the air was so amazingly still, no wind at all, that I paused for a moment, crouching there with the matchbox. Everything that rose around me – the glass-toothed top of the back wall; the long brick terraces; the endless slate roofs, their darkened chimneys sprouting aerials and satellite dishes – were outlined against the clay sky as though someone had drawn around them with a sharpened pencil.

I struck a match and got ready to roast because, once it gets going, plastic burns hot. A wisp of smoke came out of the top of the incinerator, thickened, turned black, then climbed vertically into the sky. I'd never seen it go up so straight before. I blocked the chimney with a piece of cardboard, unblocked it, blocked it again…

What's Sioux for *thinking of you*?

Mr Khan appeared. 'Need any help?'

I wasn't having any of it. 'No,' I said, turning my back. I felt him stand there for a minute before going back into the shop and was glad. Didn't need him any more. Had my memories, not to mention his melting plastic, to keep me warm. And when I got home, I found I had something more than memories—

Re: A Kick up your past

Ham,

Just got your email. Of course I haven't forgotten you! Are
you still acting? On the road? Where are you living?
Jane.

I sat there, staring at the words, words Jane had sent to me.
Of course she hadn't forgotten me, how could she, after what
we'd shared? After who we'd shared? And then I thought how
right it was that the one to bring us together had been Matt
Mark 2.

One morning two weeks in to rehearsal, Matt didn't show up.
By the time we finished for the day, Greg sounded decidedly
jumpy. 'Someone will have to go look for him,' he said. 'Can't
do the lights without Matt.'

I caught the look in my direction. 'Why's it always me?'

Jane came in, 'You know North Shields better than the rest
of us, don't you? I'll keep you company if you like.'

'Who's got the keys?' I said.

Hardley had Matt's home address. I waited impatiently for
him to flick through his card index to find it. The street name
looked a bit familiar. I had a feeling it wasn't far from where I
used to walk Betty the Prostitute home with her bag of coal,
and on the way down the coast road I found myself telling
Jane about dirty Cap'n Pike. 'Ooh,' she said, dead intrigued.
'I've never heard of a real-life case of it till now.'

'What?'

'Coprophilia. What he had. Getting turned on by, you
know, shit.'

'Is that what you call it? It was a bit of a shock to me, to be honest. I was only seventeen.'

'Poor little Ham. I bet you were sweet,' she said. 'I wish I'd known you then.'

All too soon we turned into the maze of streets and alleys lit by yellowish street lights near where old Betty used to live. 'Amazing. I've never seen houses like these,' Jane said.

'Back-to-backs.'

'I didn't know there were any left.'

'Quite a few, round here.' I pulled into the kerb. 'You wait in the van. I'll try and find him.'

The cold surprised me, that kind of misty chill you get close to the sea, the yellow street lights and the crumbling warren of homes making it feel like I'd stepped on to the set of *Dr Jekyll and Mr Hyde* just prior to the enactment of a savage murder. A woman pushing a pram came towards me and I asked her the whereabouts of no. 17, my breath pluming into her thin face. I don't normally come across like Bela Lugosi, but she waved me down a narrow side alley clogged with overflowing dustbins, and ran off.

I found the door and knocked. Matt opened it, saw my face in the gloom, stepped outside and shut the door behind him. 'What do ye want?'

'I can hardly see you,' I said. 'You all right, Matt? We were just wondering why you didn't show up.'

He put his hands deeper in his pockets and looked at the ground. 'Never thought you'd come looking for me.'

'Need you, marra,' I said. 'Countin' on you, in fact.'

'It's mam,' he muttered.

'Is she ill?'

'Sort of.' He kicked at an uneven paving stone. 'Said she needs me here.'

Jane got out and came down the alley, hugging herself against the cold. 'Everything okay?'

'Is your mam in now, Matt?' she said. 'Would you like me to come and talk to her?'

A look of fear crossed his face.

'That's a good idea,' I backed Jane up. 'Can't do any harm, can it?'

'It's a mess,' Matt blurted out. 'I don't want ye's to come in.'

Jane touched his hunched shoulder. 'You should look at my kitchen. And you know what a state no. 12 gets into! Only it's important, isn't it? You like working with Kicking…and we need you.'

But I don't think Jane had ever seen a mess anything like Matt's mam's three rooms. I certainly hadn't. In Pity Me, just about everybody I knew lived in terraced houses, which were luxurious compared to back-to-backs, and though there were one or two families who'd maybe lost the plot a bit and my mother never let me go round theirs for tea, most of the homes I was familiar with were spotless. But as Matt pushed open the door and the foul smell wafted out, I had the feeling of stepping into some infested corner of the past, and a sudden desperate desire for a lavender nosegay.

We followed him into a sort of dark scullery, the floor sucking at the soles of our shoes. It seemed filled with buckets and clutter; shadowy nasties floated in the sink. For a minute I felt about to retch with the smell. Then a voice cried, 'Matty? That you? You got me tabs?'

The face illuminated by the flickering TV set could have been

176

any age between sixty and a hundred, though as we learned later, Matt's mam was fifty-two. An absence of teeth was partly to blame, but even if she'd had her dentures in, the sight of Sandy would still have chilled me to the marrow. She sat in a chair on a nest of newspapers as though she'd festered there for years.

'These your pals, Matty?' The words were a little slurred.

'From work. This is Jane.'

'Wae pleased to meet you. I'm Sandy.' She held out a mottled claw.

The smell was unbelievable: piss, rotten meat, rancid fat – it was all part of Sandy's rich aroma. Jane, taking courageous command of the situation, advanced and shook hands.

'And Ham.' Matt mumbled.

'Ham? Funny name, like.' I stood my ground on the sticky carpet, opening a palm in greeting.

Jane got chatting, while I forced the camera to pan out from the central horror and took in the rest of the small – I suppose you'd call it a living room. Evidently it was also Matt's bedroom, because to one side I saw a narrow bed on which lay a sleeping bag and a small pile of neatly folded clothes. Above the gas fire a thin pair of Y fronts and four socks hung over the piece of string serving as a washing line. Through the slightly open door on the far side of the room a bed could be glimpsed and another sinister-looking bucket. Looking at Matt I marvelled at how, coming from here, he kept himself so relatively neat and clean.

'Ye'll have to excuse the mess,' Sandy was saying. I noticed the floor around her throne was littered with empty beer bottles. 'I'm bad with me leg. If I'd have known ye were coming I'd have got Matty to spruce the place up a bit. Not that there's much ye can do wi' a place like this. Still waiting

177

for a bathroom off the council aren't we Pet? Did ye's put the kettle on for wor visitors?'

Picturing the space we'd just passed through I couldn't imagine how Matt would be able to achieve such a thing, but he went off to do as he was told. I just wanted to leave as fast as possible, didn't want to touch *anything*.

Jane said, 'Mind if I sit down, Sandy?' The bravery of it. I watched, overcome with admiration.

'Aye gan on, of course. Just shift that stuff onto the floor.'

'We were worried when Matt didn't turn up this morning for work.'

'Wae ye cannet call that work can you? I was telling him this morning, wasn't I Matty? I says ye wants to get yersel' on a proper scheme, not this acting rubbish.'

'It's not acting he's learning, you know. He's doing electrics and carpentry mostly. Really good skills for his future.'

Sandy must have felt the implied criticism because she returned to her leg. 'Oooh, I was taken that bad this morning… I said "I need you today."' She pulled up a stiff blue skirt to show the scaly red flesh of her legs and just above the knee, a putrid-looking sore.

'Ooh. That looks nasty,' Jane said.

'Chip fat burn,' Sandy sighed. 'Chippy was closed, y'see. I told him that pan was too heavy for me, but he will have his chips.' I supposed the injury proved she did occasionally get to her feet. She looked down at her rotting leg. 'Cannet hardly move.'

Matt appeared carrying two mugs of tea. He gave one to his mother and Jane took the other. 'Lovely,' Jane said. He turned to me.

'I'm all right, thanks.'

Sandy sucked tea into her withered cheeks. 'I need him here with me. He's me last one. All the rest have buggered off haven't they?' Her voice cracked. I thought of the wheedling old witch with the poisoned apple in Disney's *Snow White*. 'State of me leg.' She gestured downwards with a yellowish fingernail. 'Cannet even switch the tv on of a morning.'

'So the main problem's the leg?' Jane enquired, sweetly.

'Oh aye, that's it, like.'

Sandy might have regretted sounding quite so sure, because it was the cue that Jane needed to spring into action. Within half an hour we'd separated Sandy both from her chair and from the bits of the *Sun* newspaper that clung to her suspiciously damp backside and were all of us in the minibus on the way to casualty. Jane, in another amazing piece of heroism, sat in the front, pressed up against Sandy while I thanked god for the gears providing a separation between me and that skirt. Matt sat silently behind.

On the way we stopped at a corner shop where Jane bought a pack of 20 Embassy Regal for Sandy, cheering her up enormously, and after that the women laughed and joked together so that by the time we sat her in a hospital wheelchair and rolled her into *Accident and Emergency* anyone would have thought we were some lovely family unit with an oddly neglected-looking granny in our midst.

Sandy puffed away steadily throughout the two-hour wait and watching her out of her lair I thought she'd changed for the better, the hyena-like face, its little flickering self-seeking eyes softening into something recognisably human. She patted Jane's hand and told her she was a good lass. Finally, a nurse beckoned the two women in to a cubicle.

I think Jane must have had a word in someone-in-authority's ear, because the next thing we knew Sandy was admitted to hospital for a couple of days 'for observation'. Fumigation, more like.

We three watched as Sandy got wheeled away by a motherly looking nurse. She peered back anxiously, miming smoking gestures at Matt, and as we walked out of the bright lights to find the minibus, he said he'd have to take her in tabs the next day, and probably Guinness too, because she couldn't do without it. Jane said she'd go with him. He looked at her like she was an angel.

'Fancy a pint?' I said.

He'd been pretty well silent for three hours, but after necking down a couple of lagers as though he'd needed them very badly, words suddenly tumbled out of Matt's mouth. 'That nurse was canny wasn't she? They'll look after her in there. And it'll give me the chance to get the place cleaned up.'

'I'll give you a hand. How about Saturday? You'll help too, won't you Ham?'

'Course.' He looked at our faces – Jane's real commitment, my pretended commitment on account of her – with a kind of wonder, shaking his head as though it was hard to believe. 'Fancy another?' I said, gathering up the glasses and wondering where they sold lavender nosegays these days. He nodded wordlessly.

He was talking nineteen to the dozen by the time I got back. About the play. 'I like the bit when yous two are hand in hand and it seems like summer. There's going to be song, too, isn't there?'

'If Cuff gets round to writing one,' Jane replied.

'Is it real, the stuff in the play or is it pretend?'

"Well Cuff's tried to make it feel truthful but characters like mine and Ham's – he's made them up.'

I added, 'The war bit at the end. That was real. The Great War? Nineteen-fourteen to nineteen-eighteen? You'll have learned about that.' Matt looked blank. 'Did you not do any history at school?'

He shook his head. 'I didn't go much after me stepdad left. Mam needed us…'

'Two million soldiers killed.'

'Canny lot.'

'Some of them as young as sixteen. Anyway, I think there's this assumption, I mean the audience expects both the men Sam and me play to get killed, after the play's finished, like.'

He nodded slowly, taking it all in, then burst out, 'He's mad, that Greg, isn't he? I mean not really mad but weird, like. Nice. I like him. But weird. Talk about lights! I just thought it was switch on, switch off but he was going on to me about how you can make it all seasons. Spring is different colour to autumn and then there's the change depending on the time of day… In the play – when you're all off to the races – Greg wants a sort of white light to make it sunny like July and then later when you,' he looked at Jane, 'I mean when Lizzie runs off on her own looking for Morris,' he glanced at me, 'Greg says he wants it "Dusk in winter". I says "What's dusk, then?" and he goes "November, five o'clock," so I says "like when you hear the hometime hooter at the shipyard and the lanes are full of leaves gone to squidge," and he says, "Yep! You got it!" Says "yep" a lot doesn't he? I like that bit when yous are just outlines walking towards each other till you kind of join in one big shadow, and then it's the end of the first half.'

'You can make great silhouettes with lights,' Jane said.

'Aye! Silhouettes! That's the word.'

I watched Jane watching Matt, watched her nod and smile and laugh and encourage. I took the van keys out of my pocket. 'About time we were going.' Jane shook her head firmly. I don't think Matt heard me at all.

'S'funny how people change, isn't it? When they're acting like? That Maureen. In real life she's bossy and nebby – always asking questions – but when she's the woman selling flowers and asking for her son she's dead canny, like you'd trust her with your life and then I heard her sing. You'd never think looking at her she could sing like that.'

We sat around the table in that dump of a North Shields pub till closing, listening to Matt talk about the show and seeing the magic of theatre shining in his eyes. A kind of 'holy glimmer'. Don't know why I just thought of that. It's in that Wilfred Owen poem about all the young lads dying in WWI.

After dropping him home, we drove to Newcastle along a Coast Road sparkling with frost. 'The poor lad,' Jane said. 'He's had no chance. And he's got potential, you can see that.'

'You were dead good with him.'

'You were good too, in the pub.'

'You were fantastic with Sandy.'

'I'll need a bath, I think.'

And we rose together, her hand over mine on the gear stick, to the ranks of angels, our love elevated by something special, something holy. Project Matt. I pulled in at her place and she leaned over and brushed my cheek with a kiss of soft hair. 'Do you want to stay?' she whispered.

182

II. 3

After burning day we didn't talk for a while. Suited me fine; gave me plenty of headroom for reliving the past prior to writing it all up in the evenings. Mr Khan wasn't happy, though. Tried to get a few conversations going and when I didn't respond, kept creeping up on me to see what I was doing. I'd turn around and there he'd be, watching me, so I actually found it quite hard to stay in my own mental world, as you would with a buffalo huffing down your neck. Got quite sharp with him. 'Everything all right, is it? Stacking the soap powder to your satisfaction?'

'Yes, yes,' he said, 'very satisfactory.' He turned to go and then turned back, thrusting his hands deep into the pockets of his white coat. 'Always, I try to be civil. But I am sometimes boorish.'

'Oh aye?'

He cleared his throat. 'If I have been so to you, Mr Nicolson, I apologise.'

I stood there, a giant packet of Daz clamped to my chest, quite taken by surprise. He looked at me. 'Apology accepted,' I said.

Thinking about it afterwards, I realised there's a pattern to Mr Khan's behaviour. Grumpy in the mornings, he gets friendlier as the day goes on, almost as if it takes him a while to accept the fact that he's a shopkeeper. Or maybe there's unhappiness at home? I've never met his wife but she phones occasionally, and he takes the receiver into the back to murmur into it for a while before coming back looking depressed. Or maybe it's more of a case of the closer he is to 'the News', since things are so bad in Afghanistan. Endless fighting and shortages of just about everything. He's always packing up parcels of paracetamol and embrocation to send to relations, says the only pharmaceutical stuff on sale at home comes from Pakistan and none of it works.

Anyway, we sealed our renewed friendship one evening last week with another session about the Greeks. Plato. Before I got lost I gathered Plato liked things to be static rather than moving about, which made me think how my world used to move a lot more than it does now.

Take theatre. I remember how we longed for the Building to get finished so we could stop being in a state of constant movement, heaving rostra in and out of places and lurching around in the truck, getting back at 3 a.m. Oh, the elegance of leaving the set just where it was and coming back the next night to perform in the same place. But static hasn't turned out to be healthy. The Building, which has been up, if not in my opinion exactly running, for more than 20 years, just seems to suck a lot of people in to work administrating it.

I've lost count of the staff it takes to keep projects going and do you know what the irony is? Where we used to tour six new plays a year in Greg's day, they now do one. One. The building gets used for exhibitions and conferences most of the time. There's virtually no work for actors, just 'enablers' – enabling the Building to carry on being pretty well completely unproductive in my opinion. Staying in one place doesn't seem a healthy idea for theatre, at least not in Kicking's case, and when I come to think of it not in many cases. Think of the height of theatre in the days of Elizabeth I; literally thousands of plays being written and performed in what were pretty temporary structures, and in pubs and great houses around the country. Actors on the move. Perhaps that's why the Building didn't work. Tried to contain a bad tempered, noisy but sometimes beautiful wild animal in a box and succeeded in attracting a lot of keepers looking after a muzzled, tamed beast.

They've got eight people doing what Hardley used to do on his own. There's Marketing, Programming, Finance, Project Management – all with assistants of course; and that's before we come to Greg's job – the actual *Art*. Whole load more employed on that side, basically to not produce plays. I suppose there's no money left after all their pay's gone out. I could be very bitter.

After this extended whinge it must be obvious I *am* bitter. I've entered old git territory, fallen out of love with the present day, and feel nostalgic for the movement of youth. No. 12, Jarvis Grove, where Greg, Hardley and Stafford, together with the lovely Nic, lived, and I unofficially lodged, was all about movement. I picture Greg thundering down the stairs or Stafford dad's dogs hurling themselves at the door, or beautiful Nic surfacing in the bath, even Hardley's pigs' trotters come to horrible life in the compost bag. Up in the morning, off to the pub...ah...I don't remember watching the telly then. Or anyone spending any more time than absolutely necessary on the house itself. Just a shelter it was, a scene in which *action* was set.

We all alighted at no. 12 briefly, like migrating birds, did a bit of mating, feeding and preening and then flew off. I was winging my way somewhere hot, I thought, keeping airborne for a while, finding some good resting places, and then looking around a bit more desperately as the wings got wearier and wearier. Where I was going, it turned out, wasn't that exotic after all. Mr Khan's shop.

Not that I came entirely clean about my present circumstances to Jane.

Re re: A Kick up your past
Hi Jane
Back in Newcastle just at the moment as it happens! Still acting but focusing more on writing these days. How about you?
Ham

From my own *deeply static* perspective, I did not like the sound of Plato. 'Look. I get Dionysus, Mr Khan, but can we leave Plato out of things for now?' It was getting late. We'd got through six packs of *Hula Hoops* and almost a whole bottle of something called *grape spirit*.

He raised his finger. 'Please! First name terms! You prefer to talk of theatre, I suppose? I could say you have one-road mind…'

I decided to be honest and tell him why I wasn't that keen on talking about staying in one place. He listened, nodding.

'You feel trapped,' he said. But it is the human condition to feel this. Our escape is through thought, philosophy, conversation. It *does* nothing, yet it is a consolation.'

There was no way I could say I wanted to go home after that. 'I liked talking about Archimedes,' I offered.

'Because of the theatre connection I suppose?'

'Is there a connection?'

'Of course there is my dear Ham. Cranes! *Deus ex machina!*'

I'd always understood the term to mean the kind of unlikely plot resolution you get in rubbish plays, father-comes-back-from-the-dead, or fairy-godmother-appears-with-magic-wand kind of stuff; it took Mr Khan to actually translate the words for me.

'God from a machine,' he said. 'The crane lowers a god onto the stage to resolve the plot.'

'Oh I get it. Like in *Medea*,' I said, remembering. 'She flies off in a chariot provided by the gods. After killing her kids! But you can't tell me that's the right ending!'

'What has right got to do with it? All this fair play, fair play – such a British saying! But there is never fair play, least of all from the British.' I let that one pass. 'When all is anarchy it is perfectly real to have a god descend and decide what happens.'

'I don't know about that…' But through the oily haze of *grape spirit* I began to see a bit of logic in his words, or rather the illogical truth. Things do happen out of the blue. They'd been happening like that all my life. Taking the *success* idea, was there any inner logic as to why, of all of us, only Sam had enjoyed fame and fortune? What explanation – other than that he *was* favoured by the gods – explained it? And hadn't I seen death suddenly claim those whom, according to the demands of a realistic narrative, should still be happily alive? 'You might have a point. Mr Khan.'

'Please, please! No more Mr Khan.'

'Okay, sorry. What does Najib mean, like?'

That started us talking about names till it got time for locking up. We went through his rigorous security routine;

screwing down all the window locks, bolting the back door, padlocking the grilles. Then I waited, shifting from one foot to the other in the cold wind, while he locked up the front: top, middle, bottom. He held out his hand. 'Goodnight Ham. Thank you for your company.'

I wanted to get home fast and thought for a moment of taking the short way, by the river. But then Noah got in the way.

I'd thought Najib would have found my name as foreign as I found his, but apparently Noah's in the Koran. He's called Nuh. Ham's Ham, seemingly, Shem Shem and Japhet Japhet, but there's another son, who refuses to come on the Ark with the rest of the family. Poor old Nuh tries to save him and begs Allah to forgive the son for his unrighteous behaviour. Allah just says *nuh*. The son climbs a mountain to escape, but the waters rise above the top and swallow him up.

I opted for the longer route. Walking quickly down the empty streets, I tried to concentrate on the cruelty of gods rather than water and drowning. I suppose you could say Noah's son had it coming, but other people I could think of did nothing to deserve their fates. Arguments against *deus ex machina* plot resolutions seemed less and less valid when you thought about the cruel and premature deaths in real life.

I put the key in the lock and shut the door against the wind at last. The streetlight showed me another letter for Alexander Spong – whoever the fuck he is – lying on the mat. Nothing for me. I stood for minute staring at the floor. Someone had kindly posted a few empty crisp packets through the letterbox.

Contrary to Najib's idea, I felt more depressed by our conversation than consoled. He'd told me that my namesake,

Ham, because he saw his father naked, was cursed and made the father of all the black peasants or slaves of those more fortunate descendants of Shem and Japhet. I don't think Mam could have been paying attention in chapel.

Najib means of noble descent. 'So better than Ham, like?' I'd said, and as I stumped slowly up the stairs the thought came to me. Not only am I an out-of-work actor. I am, in fact, Mr Najib Khan's slave.

II. 4

Rehearsal finished at 12 on the Saturday, so we picked up Jane's vacuum cleaner plus scrubbing brushes, disinfectant, bleach, etc. and drove over to North Shields to clean up Matt's place. Jane's purposefulness had me almost convinced we could do it, but standing knee-deep in shit in the living room I completely lost heart. 'Never going to get this sorted.'

'Course we are,' Jane said. 'Get us a cup of tea, Matt, while we make a plan.'

It's a pity Hercules wasn't on hand to redirect the Tyne a bit to the right and give the place a good swilling out, because Jane's Hoover certainly wasn't up to it. Gunked up almost immediately. While Matt unscrewed plates to try and fix it, Jane pulled on her rubber gloves and went down on her hands and knees with a bucket of bleach. I got the easy job of getting rid of the crap, I mean rubbish, no, I mean crap, already bagged up.

Nowadays, you can never find a litterbin when you want one, hence I suppose all the cans and bottles lurking in every gutter, and the sheets of plastic billowing out from motorway embankments like veils discarded by runaway brides. Back then, you could still find big metal litter baskets on just about every street corner. I took the van and over the next hour filled North Shields's handy repositories with Sandy's nasty debris.

Thinking now about the poor bloke who had to empty them I feel a bit sorry for him, but only a bit. Dustmen got paid well, and the council hadn't invented the sort of uniquely humiliating jobs on the cleaning front they've come up with now.

Take the poor bastard I met a decade or so later during a lunchtime session in a South London pub. After a few increasingly companionable pints, he invited me to a discreet corner of the car park to show me his *Pooper Scooter*. We stood there, swaying slightly no doubt, staring at the monstrous thing. It had a hose attached, for sucking the dog turds off the streets of Lewisham into two big tanks, one on either side of the back wheel. There was a choice of hose nozzle to use – depending on the breed of turd, I suppose – and brushes to scrub the pavement after removal.

'It only does twenty miles an hour,' the bloke said, finally. 'There's no getting away from the abuse at that speed.' We stared at it a bit longer. It was very shiny and covered with slogans like *Working for a Better Lewisham*; then we went back in the pub.

'What do they call the job, then?' I said as he ordered me another pint.

He took a long swig and sighed. 'Canine Waste Warden.'

'Better go easy or you'll be drunk in charge of a shitmobile.'

'That's the plan,' he said. 'Only way out. Can't stand it any longer. I'll ram the bloody thing into a police car if I have to.'

I found Jane still on her hands and knees. She sat back on her heels, pushed the hair out of her eyes with the back of a Marigold-yellow hand, and, with a little frown, finally recognised me for the fastidious coward I am. 'Matt's sorted this stuff to wash,' she said. Why don't you take it to the laundrette?' She reached behind her for a pack of detergent.

Luckily a big-sized washing machine was vacant. I untied the bag and tipped in the contents, slamming the door shut as fast I could. But the smell still escaped, wrinkling up the noses of a little row of women who seemed to be there for the social, rather than the washing side of things. 'Phoorargh!' a big woman with a red face exploded. 'Where have ye been living, pet?' They all wafted their hands in front of their faces and shook with laughter.

It's the kind of situation where improvisation skills can come in handy. 'Industrial rags,' I said, tipping half the box of detergent into the drawer. 'Ye want to try it. Paying ten pound a ton at the minute. But it has to be clean, like.'

I perched on the edge of the bench where they were sitting and watched Sandy's things, periodically identifiable amid the grey foam, churn past the porthole. 'A corset?' one of them said,

'Good silk that is. Use it for polishin' watches.'

'Havin' us on.'

I folded my hands over my chest. 'Would I lie to ye, flower?'

'Wae course ye would, wouldn't he, Susan? Ye're a man aren't ye?'

After that we had a good banter. A couple of them helped me unload Sandy's stuff into a basket, a few things disintegrating in my hands before I could stuff them in the tumble drier. Grime must have been the only thing holding them together. 'Like gold dust, this stuff,' I said. By the finish, I think they believed me.

Anyway, that was my minimal role in the cleaning campaign. Jane and Matt did the lion's share and a couple of days later we picked Sandy up from the hospital to take her back to her transformed three rooms, sparkling clean, new sheets on the bed, thoroughly vacuumed and scrubbed and smelling eye-wateringly of bleach.

Sandy sat beside her bed at the far end of the ward, equally transformed. Matt must have found her teeth somewhere during the clean up, because her cheeks were plumped, her washed hair white and fluffy. She still looked like an old woman, just a nice, clean old woman wearing a pink blouse with a little frill round the neck and slippers with pom-poms on. And being a nice little old lady she should have smiled at the sight of us three walking down the ward towards her. Instead of scowled, that is.

The words hit Matt at fifty paces. 'Where were you when you were wanted? They've nicked me clothes!'

He picked up the plastic bag lying on top of the bed. 'Isn't this them?'

'They're not mine! Ye should have been here! What have they done with my blue skirt? Where's me good clobber?'

Matt sat on the bed and grinned at her. 'I think you look dead nice, Mam.'

'Yes, that colour really suits you, Sandy,' Jane said, giving her a pack of 20. Sandy sniffed. 'I just want what's mine.' Remembering the shredding effect of washing on Sandy's things, I thought I knew what had happened.

A nurse arrived to bathe us all in her big, moony smile. 'Arrr. That's nice for you, Sandra, your grandson coming to fetch you.'

'It's me son, ye daft cow. What's happened to me clothes?'

The practised smile switched off. The practised *wary* look switched on. 'No need to be rude, Sandra. I'll go and ask.' She addressed Matt. 'You'll find dressings for your mother's leg in the bag.'

We finally got out of the hospital, Sandy grimly clutching the plastic bag on her knees as we wheeled her towards the exit. 'Canna wait to get home,' she said. 'Scrub, scrub, scrub, it's a wonder I've gorrany skin left.'

Matt whizzed her down the corridor at top speed. It was the first time I'd seen him look his age. 'You wait till we get home, Mam!'

In the car park, Sandy announced she wanted to take the wheelchair home with her. 'One good thing we could have from all this hassle,' she said to Matt, 'Ye could wheel me to the shops…'

'Didn't the nurse say you're all right to walk?' Jane chipped in. 'In fact it would do you good to take some daily exercise?'

'Fat lot *she* knows.' Sandy rose on her spindle legs and tottered a step forward. 'See? Purrit in the van.'

I looked around. Nobody seemed to be watching, so I collapsed the chair and chucked it in the back.

Stealing from the NHS definitely cheered Sandy up. She chatted away on the drive home and up the narrow alleyway – going by chair, of course. But once through the door she fell completely silent. We passed through the scullery, emerging into the light of the living room. Sandy blinked at the clean glass, the whitened nets, the open curtains… In my simple-minded way I waited for her to take in the huge amount of work Matt and Jane had done, and to be pleased. To be grateful.

'What's happened?' she said, turning to look at Matt, her mouth quivering.

'I tidied up a bit, Mam. Don't you like it? Jane and Ham helped.'

Sandy said nothing. We watched as she slowly stood up and began to shuffle about the room, opening cupboards and drawers, running her fingers along surfaces, her nose twitching like some tiny mammal released into an alien burrow. Finally she perched forlornly on the edge of her old chair. 'Put me to bed, Matty.'

Matt looked about to cry.

Jane said, 'Why don't you have a cup of tea first? Shall I make one for you?'

The little beady eyes turned on Jane. 'Ye've stolen me things,' she panted. 'I've been in hospital and ye've stolen them. Poor old woman like me ye've picked on.'

Since we'd spent about thirty quid kitting out the bloody place, I said, 'No one's stolen anything. The place was in such a state we had to throw some of your stuff away and replace it. Your home was a health hazard, no other word for it.'

Matt and Jane looked at me as though I'd just stamped on a gerbil. Big tears began pouring down Sandy's cheeks. 'I want me bed,' she blubbered.

'Go and get some chips,' Jane hissed, pushing me backwards out of the door, but before she shut it in my face I could see Sandy in the bedroom, fingering the new sheets.

By the time I got back, the atmosphere had improved a bit. At least, the air was full of cigarette smoke, the curtains were drawn and the telly jabbered away in the corner. Sandy sat in her old chair with a beer in one hand and a No. Six in the other. I added to the homely bouquet by sharing out the chips.

She seemed dead pleased with the wheelchair. Had us try it

in a few spots before she was satisfied. 'Looks nice by the window,' she said, waving us goodbye. I still didn't get it, still felt indignant as we drove back. Jane understood, and amazingly to me, reproached herself.

'I should have thought,' she said. 'The way she crept around, trembling all over, it was as if we'd pulled her old skin off her and given it back smelling of someone else. I think it's a primitive thing, you know with your own bed, your own smells...'

'Like your own farts?'

She laughed. 'Yes, I suppose. Frightened. That's what she was. If you've got very little, like Sandy, if you never go anywhere, that animal thing we've all got must be stronger. Most of us only get back to it occasionally, like when someone dies and all we want to do is smell them again, keep burying our heads in the wardrobe snuffing what's left of them out of their hats and coats... It's bad enough taking a loved one away. Imagine if you take a person away from herself. That's what it must have felt like for Sandy. I should've realised.'

'God Jane, you did your best. We had to clear up, didn't we, for Matt?'

'I know. Poor old Matt.'

'I still think she could have said "thanks".'

'Have you been listening to a word I've been saying?'

I must have been listening, or I wouldn't be able to remember what she said all these years on. But I listened with only half an ear because I was thick then; she definitely knew a lot more than I did. Part of her attraction was that sort of compassionate wisdom she had. Well, compassionate to everyone else except me. I expect on that journey back my main thoughts were on whether we'd sleep together that night, because (just to confound the theory, like) Jane and Gerry's bed was a place I felt utterly and completely at home.

II. 5

Me and Fat Sue were at our special place, the big freezer. She leaned in, supporting her huge breasts on folded arms. Pair like that, I thought, wonder how much they weigh?

'I'm looking for something special... She glanced at me, grinned and pointed downwards with one finger, 'In here, like.'

'Sorry.'

'What d'ye think of me new top?'

'Very nice, aye.'

'Pink's all right on me?'

'Aye, champion. Gans with your eyes.'

She stared at me for a moment before gurgling a laugh. 'Eeeeh. Havin' me on. I've got blue eyes! Two quid in the pound shop, it was. We told them it should have been one pound – like what the fuck's it called a pound shop for? He, you know, my partner, said mebbes we could go back next week for a different colour.' While she talked, one chubby hand played idly among the frosted boxes, lifted one out. 'This fish? He likes fish.' She handed it to me. 'Glad I got that diary off you, Ham, cos I worked it out. It's wor anniversary tomorrow. Been together a whole year! So I want to cook something that bit different to celebrate. '

For the next few minutes, I lined up the gourmet possibilities for Sue's consideration, while she lounged in dreamy fashion against the freezer. 'Read that bit again, Ham, pet.'

'Made with one hundred per cent white fish from sustainable fish stocks in the North Atlantic and rich in vitamins D, A and—'

From behind the till, Najib growled. 'Mr Nicolson has much important work to do.'

Sue hissed spearminty words in to my ear, 'Eeh, worra cheek! He's dead nasty, him. Don't know how you stand it.' But the intervention finally decided her against the fish fingers. 'I'll take them cod ball thingies.' She peered into her furry purse, counting under her breath and from time to time glancing over at Najib. 'He likes to make you feel dead small,' she said, a little louder. Then she straightened her back, pushed out her chest and turned the volume up high, 'Wish it was your bloody shop, Ham, not his.'

Slap, slap, slap, Sue marched towards the till.

The shop went quiet after she left. Najib signalled our lunch break by selecting two ripe tomatoes from the fruit and veg section and putting one in my hand. 'Thanks,' I said. 'I was thinkin'. She'd make a great character.'

He polished his tomato with a large white handkerchief. 'Who?'

'Sue.'

'She has a worthless character,' he said, opening the tin he brings from home and releasing a delicious, spicy smell.

'I meant for an actor, she'd be a good character to play.'

Najib frowned into his selection of foil-wrapped delicacies. 'What would be the point of portraying such a woman?'

That got me. 'So it's only kings and queens, the powerful, like, who should be in plays?'

'Only those who are *worthy* should be in plays, not just kings and queens, of course not.' Najib looked at my sad cheese sandwich and took pity. 'Please. Have one.'

I accepted one of his lovely lamb pasty things and we ate in silence for a while. Then he said, 'How do those who can teach us nothing, who cannot edify, belong on the boards?' He took a little ivory-handled penknife from his pocket and began peeling and quartering an apple. 'People like her are a disgrace to humanity.'

He was beginning to make me angry. 'What about shopkeepers? They make good enough characters?'

He speared a piece of apple and shot me a look. 'A shopkeeper can be a worthy man.'

'So, in a play about this shop, there'd be a part for you, but not Sue—'

'Not she, certainly not she.' He paused, reflecting. 'Or, I regret to say – any other of my customers.' He liked the idea of a play featuring himself in the one and only part. *An Audience with Najib Khan!* Probably be quite entertaining.

'Pretty borin' play, like.'

'I remind you, Ham. This play is your idea.'

'But it could be good, you and Sue. A two-hander. Cheap, too.'

'Two hands?'

'Only two actors in it. You and Sue.'

'A most horrible thought,' he said, sweeping up the peel and standing to drop it in the waste basket. 'And it is impossible to make such a person of interest to anyone. She has no value. She is merely a worthless lump.'

Some of the men from the building site up the road came in, so lunch and the conversation ended there. A new game: *Fat Sue and How to Play Her* occupied my otherwise tedious afternoon. For a while I thought about who could do her well – Jane? Or maybe Maureen? – and then I began imagining

200

playing her myself. It was just the kind of acting challenge I needed; I'd never done a big juicy female role – and I'd have to write her, too, who else would? Best of all, it gave me a chance to show Najib that someone like Sue had as much complexity and depth to her as any of his favourite princes. Playing the role, I decided grandly, would be a vivid illustration, a vindication, of the whole idea behind Kicking Theatre, that *all* human life is the stuff of art. After seeing me as Fat Sue, Najib would be silenced.

As I lugged Lucozades from the back to restock the drinks' shelves, I thought about the gender problem. I'd learned a few female impersonation skills playing *Handmaiden to the Queen,* not to mention *Woman in Bus Queue* and *Toothless Fishwife,* and physically, Fat Sue was quite straightforward because of her tits. Because of the way she used them, thrusting them at you as if to clear a path through the world, or perhaps to cushion herself against its sharp edges. 'Hell-ow, pet. Any special offers?'

But her tits were just a good starting point. There'd be a lot more to it than that. I remembered the way she mouthed the words when trying to read, that uncertain pause before she laughed.

It's a ritual, preparing a role; you remember something said, observe a mannerism, imagine an event and it's like these are all in little bottles labelled 'drink me'. You swallow the magic potions and slowly become the character. I gave myself three days.

Role: Fat Sue

An actor prepares…

Ground level is a good a place to start. Footwear. Flip-flops, always flip-flops. The walk. A rhythm to it. Two beats, then a

201

pause. *Slap, slap, pause.* I listen from the other side of the stack and, peering round the end, see her turning things over in one of the special offer baskets.

She moves on. Slap, slap, pause. Slap, slap, prolonged pause and inspection. Make it last. There's no hurry. No appointments to get to. Nowhere to go except back to Egg and Chips. Slap, slap… Women walk differently from men, leading with the hips rather than the chest. Following her, I try a couple of steps. She brushes the edge of the shelf with her fingers as she walks, as if liking the contact, stops, selects a plastic bottle and looks round – to find me behind her. 'Oh there you are, Ham, pet.'

I bow low. 'At your service, ma'am.'

She giggles. 'Fuckin' mad you are. I'm not your mam! I wanted to ask – these spray things. What they for?'

'Erm. I think they're for keeping bacteria off your kitchen surfaces.'

'Ah.' She moves slowly on. 'I haven't got any of them. Have you?'

'Bacteria? Loads, I expect.'

'What are they, like?'

'Germ things.'

'Ah. Got anything else new in to show us?'

She turns the corner, taking up the pace a little as she approaches the freezers. Slap, slap, slap, slap. Under the cushion of fat, muscular calves show, mottled pink and white from the cold. I remember she once said, 'Used to run canny fast, me.' Move from the hips…

'What's the matter? You done something to your leg?'

'No no. Just a bit stiff. You know.'

202

I used to run canny fast. Lying on the bed, I dream a few scenes in Sue's life. At nine, her dark plaits flying, little Sue flat-chests the tape in first place and turns a gap-toothed smile towards the line of chairs where the parents sit. Other kids' parents, that is. *I've always had a sweet tooth, me.* Sue at thirteen, suddenly a lust object, going up for seconds of treacle sponge…

Jane got into a character with *things*. She'd go around looking for bits and pieces her character would like – a book, a brooch, a child's rattle, a photograph – and from these constructed little shrines. It's an individual thing with actors; we all have our own ways of absorbing the spirits of our characters. I do the dreaming bit and then find someone – a real person – to build on. Then I observe, listen, try to move like they do, get the rhythms of their speech. Lots and lots of that. But this would be the first time I'd actually played a real, living person, never mind the first time I'd have to write, direct and stage manage – as well as act – the show. Some challenge I'd set myself.

Greg said going on stage the first night was like being a lone soldier fighting in a jungle. You're on your own against an unseen enemy, so need an incredible amount of skill and technique, but you also must be ready to abandon everything you've prepared and act on instinct. Understand your terrain, have all your gear in perfect order, be at a peak of fitness; all are incredibly important for actors in my view, but perhaps the rarer skill is the ability to abandon all plans and go with the situation if that's the way to survive. I've always reckoned I have that skill.

Or *had* that skill. Sitting in the flat the *Playing Fat Sue* thing now looks like a terrible idea. The unseen enemy ready to stake me to the ground with bamboo and fill my underpants with huge, red, man-eating ants, is Najib. How can I defeat *him*? I'll never be able to get the moves right. My bayoneting sucks! Where is my bayonet anyway? And my ammo? Fuck, I don't even have any foot powder! A lingering and humiliating death of trenchfoot awaits me. There's a reason, you know. A reason for that phrase *dying on stage*.

The fear gets me going. At the back of the wardrobe, the rubber near perished and still gritty with sand from some long-forgotten trip to the seaside, I find a pair of flip-flops. And then I look in Mam's box. The box I inherited, along with the unwanted pans and utensils, on the grounds that 'Ham likes dressing up', and from which I now select an all-the-rage-in-the-1960s-synthetic wig, a vast pink elasticated undergarment with suspenders dangling off the bottom and a lime-green cardie.

Some of my Leichner sticks have dried out but I manage to get a bit of tan on my face and dark round the eyes. The wig's the wrong colour but it'll do and under streetlights I'll pass. The boobs. I don't have any good fillers like beans or rice, but since I seem to remember the human body is ninety-odd per cent water I fill and tie off two strong plastic bags to approximate double E cup, and with the help of a linking piece of string, hang them round my neck. A couple of goldfish and I'd be a walking fairground attraction. Waterboobs wedged in position with the corset, I step into a pullover – knotting the arms over my bum by way of a miniskirt – and top it all off with the cardigan.

I do (usually) like dressing up. On Greg's orders I've spent whole nights *in role,* right up to last orders, but even he wouldn't have expected me to subject my Sue to pub-level scrutiny. I set myself the task of surviving ten minutes in the bus queue, plus the walk there and back.

Chest out, lead from the hips. The first problem is staying upright on the icy pavement in flip flops, especially since my top half's on the unstable side. The tits weigh a ton and the string cuts into my neck something fierce. And it's freezing. Still, I make it to the bus stop and even at 50 paces, in dim street light and under a giant cardie, my whoppers get the male gaze all right.

Four women huddle in the queue. None of them appears to notice my arrival, which I suppose is a victory of sorts, but I need to get some reaction. I try a bit of Sue out on the old lady next in line. 'Fuckin' hell. When's it fuckin' coming?'

She stares sternly at me out of her headscarf. Looks me up and down. Clamps her lips together in a vice of disapproval.

A triumph! I can go home! But on the way back, a drunk weaves across the street, hands stretched out ready to grope my beauties. 'Hello darlin'. Gie us a feel.' Hurrying to outpace him I slip on a patch of ice. Down I go, hitting the deck side-on, unseating Mam's hairpiece and puncturing both tits. 'You all right?' The drunk squints down at me.

'Fine.' I get up and jam the wig back on my head. Water runs down my legs and splashes onto the pavement. He blinks.

'Never mind, hinny,' he says. 'Cancer, was it?'

Act III: The Show

III. 1

I was all set. I'd written and learned my lines, knew all the *I wants*, paced the ground on which I was to perform, practised my moves and checked my gear over and over again – and yet I delayed, filled with the nauseous conviction the mission was doomed and Najib would tear me apart. *Give it up, Ham,* I thought. *Desert!*

It was the arrival of the dolls that sent me into the jungle. Flamenco dolls, some job lot Najib had found, a bit faded and crumpled, but which he thought he could sell as 'Ideal Xmas Gifts'. The moment I saw them, it seemed a sign. 'Got something to show you tonight after work, Najib.'

'Oh yes?'

'A performance. I want to act for you.'

'Very good, Ham! I will look forward. Some Shakespeare I hope?'

The Performance
One hour. This is your one-hour call

Once I'd told Najib and set the whole thing in motion I was hardly aware of anything happening in the shop. I kept going to the back to check all the props were in the right place, murmuring lines as I went. The Cup-a-Soup I'd had for lunch resurfaced a few times in my mouth. Suddenly, I knew the costume would be an encumbrance. I'd not be able to move freely, or improvise, and it wouldn't stop the bullets. So I ditched it. All but the flip-flops.

Five minutes to curtain up. Five-minute call

I'm too bloody tense. I lie down on the floor in the back room and work from the toes up. Clench, relax. It works except for my right calf, which I rub until it eases. Sue's muscular calf. Now I'm just a body. I breathe. I send commands to my limbs, my voice. An intricate acting machine. I hear myself say, 'Go and sit in the back Najib, where you did when you interviewed me. There's a stool there for you. Don't move it. And don't touch anything. Okay?'

BREATHE IN, BREATHE OUT. TURN OFF LIGHTS. WALK. SLAP SLAP SLAP. PART BEAD CURTAINS, TURN ON LIGHT.

HAM	Ooh. Never been in here before. What you hidin' then? *(chest out. Move from the hips. Touch, inspect, replace. Where is it? Where is it? Spray air freshener. Sniff)* That's a lovely aroma. *(replace. Leave cap off)*
NAJIB	You have her! You have her exact!
HAM	*(steady. Breathe. Sit. Cross legs, pull one knee high. Lean back. Chest out)* See?

Get the idea? Instead of sitting there all stern at the till like a teacher or something putting people *off* you want to give me a job. You stay in the back, put Ham on the till, and leave the selling to me. Cos I've got what it takes. Nice smile. *(show teeth. Pause. Cup breasts)* And *these…*

NAJIB   Naughty!

HAM   *(he likes it)* Don't make out you haven't noticed. *(use the pole! Get up. Hold pole. Lean back. Najib upside down. Roll tongue. Tweak nipple. Again)* God gave us these when I was thirteen. *(pull up. Wrap leg round)* That was the best year of me life. *(flop. Be little Sue. What's the line? What's the line? Swing. Chew nail)* I was in this place – Care they called it, couldn't care less more like. Nobody gave a toss about me, you know? *(look at chest)* And then these came and everyone started to give me things. Lovely things. Took me shopping. Bought me dresses. One man took me to Fenwicks. We had tea there. Cream cakes. *(walk. Pick up pack of biscuits from shelf, put down)* Loads of chocolates. Not just Mars Bars, I mean posh chocolates, like those Belgian thingies you see on telly. Always had a

sweet tooth, me. *(turn. At Najib)* You
don't have enough nice things. *(louder.
Lean in)* You don't have enough nice
things. *(pause. Breathe. Sit. Wriggle)* Like
I say, I could do selling. I'm not so thick
as you think. I've been practising. *(take
deep breath)* Special purchase for you
today exclusive super value you know it
makes sense every little bit helps
because you're worth it… *(pause)*
Forgotten the rest. *(pause. Up pitch)* Or
I could cook stuff on one of those single
burner things and do tastings! So long
as I had the right clothes, like some sort
of shiny top, low cut you know, but
with one of them shrugs on top so I'd
look classy and shoes, proper shoes with
high heels and jewellery – people look
at your hands when you're cooking…
(getting samey. Hurry) You should sell
jewellery. I could do that for you an' all.
(drop hand in front of Najib) Look at
the colour! Look at the cut! *(look at
hand. Pause. Nibble nail. Spread fingers,
hand at arm's length)* He said he'd buy
me a ring. We saw this lovely one on
Rocks 4 U and he's going to save up.
(pause) He bought me a thong for my
birthday. *(use pole again. Soft porn)* It's
not fair. *(grind crotch)* I could have

209

made money. Like on Babestation.
(hold breasts) Don't think some of them
on there are even real… We play the
game, me and him. Real or not real.
Mine are 100 per cent real. Tits like
yours, he says, should have made you a
fortune. *(nod)* Yes. A fortune. *(long
pause. To shelves. Run fingers. See basket
of dolls. Pick up doll. Smooth dress)* She's
beautiful. She's really beautiful. *(turn.
Accuse)* What's she doing here upside
down in a basket with her skirt up over
her head? It's a crime that is. Who's
looking after her I'd like to know? *(little
Sue. Love doll)* Don't worry pet. I'll see
you right. *(dance doll)* She can ride like
a princess in a carriage. Live in a palace
all pink and white and blue… *(sit doll.
Adjust)* Comfy? Make it smell nice for
you, pet. *(spray. Pause. Breathe. Whisper)*
You spray this stuff, but underneath the
flowers.
You know the stink's still here. I never
had nowt white, or pure, or clean.
(look up. Big eyes) What happened to
the angels? *(change. Louder)*
I don't want seconds, or smudged or
ripped, I don't want DHSS *(look
Najib)* I want what you've got and she's
got and they've got

210

(pick up remote. Point at Najib) I want to have the credit and press buy *(louder. Get a crack in voice. Press)* I want to change the channel *(press)*, get a makeover *(press)*, Hire a personal trainer to make me new. *(look down)* I want nice things! I want to be nice. *(press, press, press)*
(louder) I don't like cheap! I don't like hard! *(throw remote on floor)* Where's the special stuff to make me soft? *(grab tube of cream. Smear cream on face. Lots of it. More. Najib is mirror. Try chant)*
I want to gleam and glimmer
I want to shine and shimmer
I want that inner healthy glow
(straighten. Keep staring at him. Pause, two, three, four)
Don't give me that look. I know
When you look down your nose like that what you think
(five, six, seven) I know. *(turn. Slap slap slap slap. Back straight)* EXIT. *(one, two, three, four,. Head back through curtain)*
And another thing. *(five, six, seven)*
Loyalty points. I want loyalty points, so's I can get something I want free at Christmas. Understand? BLACKOUT.
ENDS.

In darkness, among silent cabbages and potatoes, I panted, exultant. There's nothing in the world to me as good as the rush you get from having pulled off a performance. I'd come through the trees, ducked, dived and survived. Not just survived, but triumphed, because I knew the gods had been with me, even before Najib's voice boomed through the curtain, 'Ham! Your bow!'

I turned on the light, swished through the beads and curtseyed low. Najib smacked his great hands together. 'Bravo! My hat off to you. I could not have believed it possible.'

'Ta very much.'

'How did you do it? Your research! You must tell of your research, Ham.'

'Well… I talked to her of course, and I watched her, and I watched a lot of television: the shopping channels and the sex stuff and Big Brother, because that's what she does.'

'She told you that?'

'We talk about telly, yeah.'

'And she had no love from her father or mother or brothers or sisters? No family love?' He sounded dead empathetic. Fat Sue's back story came pouring out.

'That's right. She got put into care when she was 12 because her mam didn't like the attention she was getting from her – the mam's – new man, and then, the next year, she developed like and got the breasts and she sees being 13 as kind of a golden time because she got spoiled by men, bought loads of presents, you know, in exchange for sexual favours and somehow that's led to her feeling now that breasts are all she's got to offer. That's why she's got no kids. Spoils your breasts, she thinks. So she's had a few abortions and when she was 18

212

one kid got adopted. A boy. Never seen him since. And then there's the front she puts up… *Front* – I should have used that! Seems confident but scratch the surface and she's dead scared most of the time.'

'She told you all this?'

It sounded like a compliment and I was too pleased with myself to be on my guard. 'Know some of it, dreamed the rest. That's the actor's job, filling in the gaps.'

'Aha! So this you have performed is not *she* but *you*, sentimental Ham! This woman, this pitiful child you wish me to indulge, is not real at all!'

'She is real! You talk to her. She's real!'

Najib folded his arms and gave me the sort of look he gives Fat Sue.

'You've seen it yourself! She's scared of you – that's why she sticks out her chest when she comes towards you, sort of warding you off – *I've got these please be nice to me*. She's a child! A victim of crap consumerism! Watch her next time! She's real!'

'Ham!' He raised a finger to silence me. 'This evening has been significant. I am happy to boast that I have in my employ a thespian of rare talent. This…creation you performed was indeed pitiful and, though of no importance, gave a little pull at the strings of the heart. But please. Do not tell me what I must think about my customers.'

'Hang on— ' I couldn't find the words. That *thespian of rare talent* came so sweet on the ear I lost all will to argue.

'You remember once you told me to be an actor was to play, what did you call it? Some game – for a living?'

'Make-believe.'

'Precisely. Play make-believe for a living. Well, for my living

I am proprietor of a real shop with many dishonourable customers and you will not make me believe otherwise.'

'All right. All right.'

'Time for a brandy? To celebrate your creation?'

We had a drink. Thing was, any noble principles behind *An Evening with Fat Sue* were much less important to me than the feeling of being on stage again, and the confidence boost I'd got from having it go so well. I'd improvised really successfully with the pole, a piece of timber holding up the shelf units, and it made me feel I could still do it, could still embody a character and think in his or her head, *be* somebody else.

Actually, my Fat Sue did shift Najib's views a bit. He's tried to be nicer to her, offering yesterday to help count out her money; and he's introduced loyalty cards. Though his efforts backfired with Sue, who's now convinced he's out to cheat her, the loyalty scheme is a great hit. He devised it himself. They're not exactly cards. Each customer gets a little sheet with spaces on for stickers, just like getting stars in primary school. Once you've filled a sheet, you get a free gift. The sheets are filling up fast. The gift, as I was instructed to write on all the sheets, is to be 'at the whim of the proprietor at such time as the conditions of the scheme are met'.

I wouldn't call our customers dishonourable, but those free gifts better be good.

III. 2

After four weeks of rehearsal, the play opened on a Thursday night, in Wallsend. Good audience for an opening night, too, including quite a few pensioners lured in by Hardley's publicity and expecting a jolly bit of *Geordierama*. Bar the title, though, the posters bore no relation whatever to Cuff's finished play. And I say 'finished', but the end was subjected to more tweakings than I can remember for any other production. We were rehearsing Cuff's rewrites or Greg's new bits of stage business right up to the last night.

You never know for sure if a piece is good until the final player, the audience, gets in on the act. For the first twenty minutes in Wallsend I thought, 'This isn't going to work.' People shifted in their seats, unwrapped toffees, coughed, uneasy-verging-on-the-resentful. Then, they settled.

The main plot involves Harry (played by Sam), his wife Lizzie (Jane) and his friend Morris (me). Harry's a teacher in his forties who's only been married to Lizzie for a few years. She's much younger than he is and so is Morris, a lad more or less brought up by Harry, because his own father died young. The start of Lizzie and Morris's affair after a day at the Blaydon Races in 1913 ends the first half of the play. By that time on the opening night, I felt we'd won the audience over.

The finale is a family get-together a year later. Loads of jokes, then in walks Harry. In uniform. He's volunteered. At that point conscription hadn't begun and there's general shock, especially with him being so old. Turns out he's lied about his age, which apparently happened with older men enlisting to fight in World War I, though you only hear about the teenagers. Meanwhile back at the plot, the family party breaks up, and, at the very end, Harry and Morris are alone together. Harry reveals he's found out about the affair. He tells Morris he can have Rose, the house, everything – he's going off to war and doesn't plan to come back. We know Harry adores his wife; he's sacrificing himself because he thinks it's what she wants. All Morris has to promise in exchange is to look after Rose, which is where the problem comes because Morris wants to join up, too; all his mates are joining, if he doesn't do it now he'll miss his chance because it will be 'all over by Christmas' and he'll look like a coward.

So Harry says, you've got a choice: Lizzie or the war. At that point, Lizzie comes in, looks at them both, and then, blackout.

We knew from the confused audience reaction there was something missing. The *is that the end?* moment lasted too long, too slowly people started to clap. Finally, the reception was warm, but we actors felt the end needed work. In rehearsal, Greg had talked about how the audience would know there was no real choice, since all men of fighting age would shortly be called up and neither Harry nor Morris would be likely to survive the megadeath that followed. In that way, he'd argued, the audience consciousness itself would complete the play. But it wasn't happening yet.

The audience had gone and the clatter and shouts of the get out went on around me as I crouched behind a rostrum, untangling cable. Unaware of my proximity, writer and director sat together a couple of metres away. 'I don't think we can leave it there,' Greg said. 'I didn't think so before, and tonight convinced me.'

I nearly popped my head up and put in my two penn'orth to support Greg. But something stopped me, perhaps the tautness of the atmosphere penetrating through the wood to me. I imagined Cuff adjusting his glasses on his nose, tilting his chair back. 'Aah. But I like it left in the air. The choice not made.'

Greg's counter-argument poured out. 'Why not let it go where it wants to? If Morris chooses war, I think Harry would kill him. It's in his mind. That kind of betrayal demands retribution. This is the most important – the closest relationship in the play – Harry's taught Morris everything he knows, he's like a son to him, and he gets betrayed. It's beyond Greek—'

'If you— If you were Morris, what would you choose?' Greg's river of words hit Cuff's dam and its underlying message, *I want to make this personal.*

Behind the rostrum, I held my breath. Then I heard Greg murmur, 'It's that male thing, the attraction of war.'

'You'd choose war, then?'

Another pause. 'Yes.'

'Even though it would break her heart?'

'She doesn't love *him*. It's just an infatuation. She loves her husband.'

'If she loves her husband, why does she cry herself to sleep every night?'

Greg made a sort of trapped animal noise. The conversation wasn't about the play any more. 'Harry gives Morris the choice. Morris chooses war. Harry shoots Morris. That's what should happen.' *I want you to know how guilty I feel, how sorry I am.*

'Then shoots himself.'

'Why?'

'Because he's to blame as well, isn't he? The vanity of a middle-aged man trapping a young girl. Vanity and pride, are they not tragic flaws deserving of punishment?'

'What about *her* guilt?'

'It's not her fault.'

'What? Just because she was young when they married? She's older now. Has to carry her share of the blame. *So* Harry kills Morris, kills Rose, then kills himself. That makes a good bloodbath to end with.' I felt movement, pictured Greg standing, desperate to end the conversation.

'I don't want that. Too tidy, all that blood.'

'What *do* you want then?'

'I want the *mess*. The uncertainty. She wants *you*. Have her. Have her as often as you like. Only don't take her away from me.'

There was a very long silence. I'd been holding my breath so long I felt giddy. I don't think there was a thing Greg could say in response without making things worse, the unspoken *I want* being *I want our friendship, our partnership, above everything. All I care about is you. Okay I fucked your wife but I don't want her. It was a mistake! I don't know how it happened!* and saying that would be just as damaging as the fact of the night-of-the-feast betrayal, which I assumed Jenny had confessed to – and which had now become the force behind the play.

Greg exhaled noisily. I joined in. He said, 'So you want to leave the end as it is?'

'Yes.'

'Okay. I'll have a think about the visuals. How we can make the message clearer. I've gotta help load the truck now.'

FOUR A.M. EARLY MORNING OVER THE TYNE, MIST RISING FROM THE RIVER IN SMOKY WISPS. THE DARK OUTLINE OF A HUGE CRANE DROOPS IN THE EMPTY MORNING. A PALLET SUSPENDED FROM ITS MASSIVE CABLES HANGS IN STILLED FLIGHT. SILENCE. THE PALLET SHUDDERS, AS IF MOVED BY A WIND, OR THE ARRIVAL OF A LOAD.

VOICE OF DIONYSUS   Knock, knock.

VOICE OF CHORUS   Who's there?

DIONYSUS   Euripides.

CHORUS   Euripides who?

DIONYSUS   *You rippa dees trousas and you buy me anudda pair!*

THE ARM OF THE CRANE DESCENDS AND DIONYSUS ALIGHTS FROM THE PALLET, A MASK IN ONE HAND, A GLASS OF WINE IN THE OTHER.

DIONYSUS   Euripides! *There* was a poet who knew how to end a play; bring a god down to sort everything out. Simple! *(Dionysus drinks, looks around)* Now. Where am I? What does it matter? Any field will do.
An odeum, a wooden O, a stage,
An empty space, or in this case – a page—

219

(he drinks, then lowers the glass slightly,
his eyes blazing above the rim)
Wherein I warn you mortals to take
care—
Remind you foolish players to beware!
That place you lose yourselves and are
as one,
That place you *find* yourselves amidst
the fun—
(he drinks again, snorts derisively then
roars)
Is dangerous! Finding out that place to
'be'
Means, stupid mortals, that you
summon me!
(the god again seems to grow huge, then
shrinks back, to his frilly-shirted self. He
wags a finger)
Pour libations for me. *(he sits on the*
arm of the crane, which starts to rise)
Make sacrifice for me. BLACKOUT.

III. 3

Playing Fat Sue must've done the trick, somehow. I've got an audition. Fishbone, Murderer & Stab called me at the shop while I was hanging the new multicoloured bead curtains Najib had ordered specially from Pakistan. Ironically, I'd just come up with a couple of lines for my gravestone:

Beneath this sod a foolish actor lieth,

Bereft of work, no matter how he trieth

and was pondering another two to include *unloved by women* and *without a groat,* when Najib's big dark shape appeared. 'Someone on the telephone for you,' he said, offering the phone at arm's length to register disapproval.

'Hello?'

'Bit of good news, Mr Nicolson. Director wants to see you for a play he's doing.' Angie spanned the octave, adding a touch of vibrato on the word 'director'.

'Oh aye,' I said, trying to sound offhand. 'What's the part?'

She told me. When I'd recovered from the shock I asked for the details. Didn't have a pen, of course. Najib, huffing beside me, took one out of his top pocket. I scribbled the time and location on a piece of *Splash!* packaging (inferior corner-shop product masquerading as *Flash!*) and put the phone down. 'My agent,' I said, trying to forestall him.

'When, if I may be permitted to enquire, did you give your agent the telephone number of my premises?'

'Sorry, Najib,' I said, handing him the phone. 'It was when my mobile was out of action.' He grunted, but made no move to go back to the shop. 'Nearly finished here,' I said.

'What did your agent say?'

'I've got an audition.'

'For a play of Shakespeare?'

'No. Play I've done before, though.'

'A tragedy?'

'Mmm, yeah. You could say it's a tragedy. A tragedy and a comedy.' I couldn't get over it. The play I'd been thinking about, the play I'd been *writing* about and here it was. Kicking were doing a revival. Directed by their new artistic director, apparently a great admirer of Cuff.

'And what of your work commitments here?' His eyes gleamed angrily at me, the half-hung bead curtains draped over his head and neck making him a dead spit for Sitting Bull. 'Your conduct in this has not been honourable,' he said, and withdrew.

'I probably won't get it!' I called after him, but thinking, *of course* I'll bloody get it. They wouldn't audition me, would they, if they weren't going to give me the part? A very quiet voice in my head murmured *yes, they would*, but excitement at the news all but drowned it out. The old guy. The betrayed husband, that's what I'd be up for. In the original I'd played the younger, Jane the wife I fall for. Jane! They might audition Jane, too. Ought to, by rights, and there would be a part for her, too – the Maureen role.

I was pretty sure I had a copy of the script somewhere, which was a good thing because as far as I knew *The Blaydon Races* never got published, partly because in the aftermath no one ever got that sorted out. And the bad memories associated with the production made everyone involved steer clear of it, no matter how good a play it was. Time for a reappraisal, I thought.

Ever since I told him about the audition, Najib's been making sure I don't get to do anything I enjoy. After four days of being stuck in the back I complained on health and safety grounds.

'I'm going to get deficient in vitamin D,' I said, 'on account of being deprived of natural light. I'll go all white and get weaker and weaker and one day you'll find me curled up in the foetal position, dead.'

He glowered at me. 'I thought it was *limelight* you felt deprived of.' So I was surprised when, later on, Najib shouted for me to come and relieve him on the till. A salesman had arrived. 'My talented assistant will take over while we discuss this, upstairs,' he said, making me sound like the girl in spangles who gets sawn in two by the magician. The salesman was one of the old fashioned kind – he had a big suitcase of stuff with him. 'Do we have to go up here?' I heard him ask.

'Yes.' Najib said. 'This is where I discuss possible purchases, *in camera.*'

Quite a few customers came in and when the salesman left an hour or so later, I tried to get back on good terms. 'Must have taken sixty pounds while you've been gone.'

Najib grunted. 'Since I may lose you to fame and fortune soon, will you stay late this evening?'

'All right.'

I thought what he had in mind was cleaning the floor of the shop, but it turned out to be debate he wanted, so after locking up, we went upstairs. Najib made himself comfortable among his embroidered cushions. 'Sit,' he said, and then, once I was down at his level, 'Since our last conversation on the play I have read again *Hamlet.*'

'Oh yes?'

'"To be or not to be, that is the question." One might say, the *only* question in life. What is it you call this way he writes?'

'Blank verse.'

He snorted. 'Foolish name. It is obviously not blank but brim full with ideas.'

'Blank just means not rhyming, I think.'

'Ah Mr Actor, you only *think*? Why do you not *know*?'

'All right. I know.'

'But some lines rhyme do they not?'

'Yeah all right, at the ends of speeches, or when he wants to be, you know, more important sounding or romantic, or make a point, sort of a moral lesson.'

'Give me an example.'

Couldn't think for a moment, then this came to me:

'Integrity of life is fame's best friend,
'Which nobly, beyond death, shall crown the end.'

'Speak the lines again.'

I repeated them. Najib's brow furrowed. I thought I should explain. 'It means your name will live on after you die not because you were rich, but because of your good deeds in life.'

'I understand! Do you think me an idiot?' He said the lines once more. 'It sounds like this writer was a failure in life. But Shakespeare had success.'

'It isn't Shakespeare. It's a writer called Webster.'

'Ah.' He pursed up his lips and looked at me rather too meaningfully. I suppose it *was* a bit significant me remembering that line so well.

'I'm parched.'

224

'One of your strange expressions meaning you require a drink. But there is more I wish to know first. This blank verse was used by others?'

'Oh yes.' I ended up telling him all about arriving at the RSC with very little idea of anything *old*. My only previous experience of Shakespeare was the Romeo I played at college, under the none-too-brilliant guidance of Adrian, and his only note on verse was 'Extract the beauty!', repeated many times during rehearsals. The RSC took me on to do a big part in a Northern play and I actually thought that's all I'd have to do, but pretty well as soon as I arrived I got small parts in three Shakespeares. Terrified me. Most of the actors there seemed to have been born spouting lines of verse and in trying to copy them I got it completely wrong. Declaiming in a received-pronunciation accent with unmistakeable traces of Geordie just made everyone laugh.

They sent me off to a fantastic voice coach who first of all explained RP didn't exist in Shakespeare's time and the sort of accent he had in mind as he sounded the lines in his head was probably a mixture of Devonshire, Yorkshire, American and Irish accents, with rich vowels and hard consonants. The coach made me feel much better by saying we lose loads of meaning using posh accents. When I told Najib this, he looked very sceptical. 'You are telling me Laurence Olivier delivers Shakespeare's lines incorrectly?'

'Yes, well, sort of. Anyway, the other thing she told me was that blank verse, which is lines of what you call iambic pentameter, is actually very close to the normal rhythms of speech in English.'

'A brandy is it?'

'No thanks. I've got a few things to do when I get home. I'll have a cup of tea if that's okay. There! See?'

'What should I see?'

'I'll *have* a *cup* of *tea* if *that's* o*kay*. Perfect line of blank verse! Or... A *plate* of *fish* and *chips* is *what* I *want*. Another one!'

Najib couldn't quite conceal his interest, despite being so resentful about the audition and we went on for a while about stressed and unstressed syllables. He seemed to find it difficult, hitting the rhythm, and I remembered there'd been a few times Najib had offended customers just by the different way, I suppose the Afghan way, he stressed words. He'd say something like, 'That will be *five pounds* and *fifty-five pence* if you *please*' and they'd look at him thinking 'aggressive git', grab their change and stomp out, muttering.

Anyway, he seemed determined to test out what he called my 'theory of verse', taking up his copy of *Hamlet* while I went downstairs to put the kettle on.

When I got back with my tea he read out triumphantly: '"Let me not think on't – Frailty, thy name is woman!" Hardly de dum de dum de dum de dum de dum, is it oh noble actor Ham? More dum dum dum...'

'Ah yes! But Hamlet's upset isn't he? About his mam. So the verse goes a bit wrong – to show it.'

'You are saying Shakespeare does it deliberately?'

A loud banging on the door interrupted us. We waited for it to stop but it carried on. Najib got up and started unscrewing the security locks on the window. The banging got louder. At last, we leaned out into the cold night air and looked down.

It was Egg and Chips, his face greenish under the streetlight. 'Open up ye Paki bastard. I want some beer!'

'You are intoxicated,' Najib bellowed. 'Go home.' Egg and Chips started to kick the door.

I said, 'I'll just pass him out the cans. He'll never leave us in peace otherwise.'

Najib nodded and I went down to the shop and fetched a four-pack of lager. Egg and Chips's mouth was clamped to the reinforced glass of the door like the underside of a gigantic slug. One eye rolled towards me as I started on the locks, and he began rapping a 50 pence piece against the pane.

I turned the last bolt and opened the door. Denied its support he stood there, swaying. 'How much have you got?' I said.

He gave me the 50p and thrust in a pocket for some more, nearly falling over sideways with the effort, his voice rising and falling as he ranted, 'Who does he think he is talking down to *me*? Fuckin' bastard not like ye Ham fuckin' Pakis make me fuckin' mad come here to our country taking wor money least they could do is stay open 24 hours for us…' Finally he collected enough change for two cans and I handed them over. He stood there for moment, hugging them to his chest as though they could warm him up; then moved slowly off.

'Mr Khan isn't a Pakistani as it happens,' I informed his back. 'He's from Afghanistan.'

Najib stood in the shadows just inside the door. I didn't want to look in his face. 'Don't bother to lock. Time to go.'

Home in bed I thought about that line in *Hamlet. Frail.* Not a word I'd use to describe the women I've known. Certainly not Mam. In the play what he means is women not being able to stick to one man and that got me back to Jane, betraying

Gerry and then betraying me – though remaining kind of virtuous throughout it all. Could never imagine anyone calling Jane a slag.

So many times I'd thought, 'if only I'd said this or done that, things might have worked out,' but I've never known how to manipulate women, and in that I think I must take after Da.

I can only remember one conversation I ever had with my father about relationships. It took place on our only holiday, that fortnight in Lyme Regis just after he'd retired – so a year before he died.

I remember breeze and brightness, the roar and suck of the sea and Da's chuntering chest as he and I slowly walked the foot of the cliff, looking for fossils. Clear out of the blue, gull-wheeling sky he said, 'We've been all right, your mam and me.'

'I know,' I said, not knowing.

'What you've got to be careful to do, son…' He paused to inspect a golden ammonite I'd found and summon the breath to carry on. 'That's a corker, that is. What was I saying? Oh aye, ye divvent want to find yourself…downwind of them, like. Especially when they get together.'

We looked back up the shingly beach at Mam's head and flowery shoulders rising above the stripy windbreak. 'Good woman, your mother, but when she was young…her and her sisters out on a Friday night in Consett…make mincemeat, they would, of a lad they didn't like.' He squatted down to turn over a big stone and delicately sift through the shingle with his darkened fingers. 'It's their lymphatic systems at work… Ye know,' he weighted the word as he dropped a little conical whorl into my bucket: 'glands'.

In those days, only girls had glands and, at fifteen, I'd already gathered they were to blame for a host of problems including blood loss, bad temper and fatness. When glands got really inflamed women disappeared, whispered to be suffering from 'nervous breakdowns'. Even now, when I hear of someone suffering from glandular fever I conjure up crying fits and breast-like swellings breaking out all over the body.

That word – *girlpower* – it's not new. Da knew about it all right and according to what I've been reading it's something really ancient. It was girlpower old Dionysus liberated in his mad revels in the woods, and men that got torn apart as sacrifices. Go out on any Saturday night in Newcastle and storming down the Bigg Market you'll find girls walking six abreast or more, bare fleshed, tanked up, fucking raving mad; looking more than ready to tear some chap limb from limb. Which is what's behind my latest idea for a play: a Geordie *Bacchae* set in the Bigg Market on a Saturday night. I've sent off a letter already.

III. 4

In one week's time I'm going to see Jane. She'll be here. Eating. In my flat. I still can't believe it. And in a way I should thank Najib, because it was our conversation about Shakespeare that gave me the idea for the email.

Sonofnoah@yahoo.co.uk
Dear Jane,
Been talking about verse-speaking lately and came up with this – any use with your Shakespeare workshops?
    While at the Ah! Ess! See! I learned to speak in verse.
    There's nothing to it; five iambs to a line
    And when your character's on form it flows
    Like claret down the throat: when things go wrong –
    When someone's mad; or sad; or drunk, it stops;
    And starts. A bit like this. Conveying thus
    By fracture, a fractured state of mind.
Sincerely
Ham

Good eh? A helpful idea that also reminded her of my former success. But as it turned out fate also took a hand.

J.davidson@btinternet.com
Ham – That's really great! Thanks a lot. Glad you emailed because the director of Kicking got in touch today and asked me to come for an audition. They're reviving Cuff's last play!

*Living over here, I'm pretty out of the loop. What do you
know about it?*
Best
Jane

Best?

Sonofnoah@yahoo.co.uk
Dear Jane.
*Not a lot. I know the director wants to cast it before Christmas
and rehearsals start 2nd January. I'm auditioning, too. If it's
the same day perhaps we could meet up?*
All the best
Ham

J.davidson@btinternet.com
Mine's Tuesday 17th. Afternoon. J

Sonofnoah@yahoo.co.uk
*Same here. Why not come back to mine for tea? There's
trains back to Carlisle every hour, I think. H*

J.davidson@btinternet.com
*Lovely. I remember your cooking! Really looking forward to
catching up. Jx*

A kiss!
My cooking?
A picture came in to my mind. Strangely, it looked like an
advertisement from the *Good Housekeeping Christmas Issue*

1963, the sort of thing Mam would pore over in the doctor's waiting room. 'Ooh Ham, isn't that beautiful! That's cerise, that is. I'm going to knit one like that for you.'

Jane and I sit in comfortable fireside chairs with trays on our laps. Between us and in front of a blazing coal fire lies a cream fur rug that on closer inspection proves to be a luxuriant labrador. There's a warm light on Jane's ungreyed hair. I'm wearing glasses, an elegant, close-fitting red pullover and what used be called casual slacks. The fact that both of us have our feet tucked into velvety slippers makes us obviously middle-aged, but the flickering firelight flatters our faces into youthful contours. Jane hasn't changed a bit.

The camera catches us glancing into each other's eyes and smiling. We're obviously enjoying our meal. Dim, shining shapes in the background suggest polished furniture. The mantel above the fireplace is decorated with red-berried branches of holly. The caption reads, *Take it easy this Christmas with Smethers Best Pork Luncheon Meat.*

That's the kind of stuff we used to eat in the Sixties, you know. If only I could open a tin of corned beef and plonk a jar of pickled beetroot on the table, but food's changed.

I went back to the computer to re-read the emails and look up some recipes on the internet. *Braised lamb shank with raspberry and mint jus* sounded good. I studied the list of ingredients and the method for a bit, then ambled across to the part of my accommodation dedicated to the culinary arts.

It was then that I had a *Lights up on Ham's Flat* moment.

The only cupboard in the tiny kitchen area is a relic of the 1960s. It stands lopsidedly next to the single-ring burner. *The single-ring burner. Say it out loud, Ham, and it might sink in. Strange as it may sound, you do not possess an oven.*

I glanced at the ancient microwave, but Mam's voice spoke from above, 'Ye cannet cook a decent meal in one of them things.' A dish for which an oven is not essential, then? I dredged up that disused word, *casserole*. Perhaps I'd cooked casseroles for Jane before? But I had no memory at all of that and nobody else had ever said anything nice about my cooking. Was she being ironic?

I opened the cupboard by pulling down a flap – the sort on which beaming housewives in checkered aprons may once have rolled out pastry – and stared at my collection of kitchen utensils. Most people accrue *things*, you know, *useful* things over fifty-odd years in the world, but somehow all I'd ended up with were three old saucepans and a large ceramic pudding basin. I closed the flap and pulled out the drawer underneath. A bit of cutlery, two tea strainers, a fish slice, and a slightly charred wooden spoon. This curious collection represented my inheritance from Mam, or rather what was left of my inheritance after my two sisters-in-law got their mitts on the useful stuff. Most of this never got exercised. I'd been a tea-bag squeezer for years and the poor old fish slice, having once enjoyed weekly polishings on account of being silver plate, was now brown with neglect.

I'm not saying I've never owned things, but my only really serious attempt to play house happened when I finished at the RSC and moved to a rented flat in West London. I bought all the clobber, then, and, with regular work for a couple of years in adverts and small TV roles, I cooked and invited people round. Parts got scarcer in the early 1990s. I know now I should have weathered it, stayed in London, but when I got offered a season at Pitlochry I decided to give up the flat and sell most of my cooking gear to my housemate, a saxophonist called Tony. It was Le Creuset stuff – looks good, costs a fortune, weighs a ton.

It's still a badge of success, having those pans. Didn't do Tony any harm anyway because he's done quite well; should think he's bought a new set by now. Jane's probably got them too; she was already well set up in the *things* stakes when I knew her, having married young. I couldn't see her being very impressed with Mam's warped aluminium specials with best bakelite handles.

Face it, Ham, I said to myself, she's not going to be impressed with *anything*, least of all your faded self. Now, if I'd had a decent mirror I could have accompanied that thought with a despairing glance into it, but my own spotted shard was positioned on the windowsill to reflect head and shoulders only from a kneeling-on-the-carpet position.

As though shining a 5000-watt super-trouper on the room, I saw it with the disbelieving eyes of other fifty-somethings, rich in surplus possessions they plan one day to take to a car-boot sale, but which until then stay crammed in the loft or the garage – unless some loser of a relation happens by.

My relocation, or, more accurately, my retreat, to Tyneside a few years ago had given my least favourite sister-in-law, Frances (married to Joe, née Japhet), a chance for a 'bit of a clear out' as she'd said, which was when the single bed and chest of drawers, both adorned with SuperTed stickers and once the property of nephew, Phil (now 6'5"), came my way.

Spotlight for an instant on single bed. See it through Jane's eyes. A single bed. A three-dimensional admission of defeat.

I'd also been gifted a saggy sofa and nest of glass-topped occasional tables, one of which was in regular use as a nesting place for whatever out-of-date freebie from Najib I chose to eat. You don't need a plate. Tinfoil or plastic is thoughtfully provided.

But I do have plates. Three actually, survivors of a Habitat Six I bought my own self during my second Pitlochry season. So Jane would have a plate, a knife and fork, and a little table. And me. The Ham she wanted a chance to 'catch up with'. Bit of an unfortunate metaphor, but hope rekindled just a little. I went back to the cupboard. I still had Mam's pudding basin and I discovered it fitted a treat into the largest heirloom saucepan. That gave me an idea.

Food problem solved, at least theoretically, I allowed myself to dream about the play. Jane and me, together again, in *The Blaydon Races*. I picked up the papers I'd dug out of my old tin trunk and began to read them over for the third time. I say papers, because as well as a wodge that might be termed a script, there were loads of loose sheets of rewrites. Fitting them all in the right places had taken me a few hours, but now as I read my head filled with long runs, West End transfers, film options – all the usual suspects. It really was a good play, the sort that *grows* during the tour, until by the last night it's, well, more than good and somehow all the better because it's ephemeral: that production with that cast on that particular night can never be recaptured.

The emotions coursing through the company – Maureen's jealousy of Sam, Greg's guilt, Cuff's misery, my love for Jane, Jane's… Jane's what? Jane's mysterious, unexpressed feelings for me – had intensified over the tour. With hindsight, there were bound to be explosions on the last night, not least because among the packed house it seemed *everyone* was going to be there. Gerry, for one, emerging from *The Cherry Orchard* just in time; Jenny, Cuff... The stage was definitely set for something, but other, wildly optimistic expectations stopped me thinking about it. An agent from London, the RSC director due to direct Cuff's next play, and (Lynette breathlessly confided) a West End Producer, would, rumour had it, all be sitting in the front row.

'Mam says she wants to come,' Matt said in the pub the night before the performance. 'So long as she can get a lift.'

Jane stared distractedly into her beer. I said, 'I'll ask if I can get the van to pick her up. What do you think, Jane? We could get Sandy – so long as she doesn't mind getting there a while before the play. We're called for 5.'

Jane looked up and smiled at Matt. 'That's a good idea. Why's the call so early, anyway?'

'Greg says he wants to rehearse some changes in the second half.'

She laughed. 'What, now? Bit late for that.'

In the end, Jane didn't come with me to collect Sandy. Told me at the last minute she'd see me at the call. Came as a jolt. I didn't say anything, didn't challenge her. Scared of hearing her tell me, 'Gerry's back. *It's over.*'

Matt and I drove down to North Shields together on a cold, clear afternoon. I noticed Christmas had crept up on us while we'd been preoccupied with the play. There were lights and decorations everywhere. I'd imagined spending it with Jane. Could it really be true I'd be with my brother Joe, as usual? If

I hadn't been so preoccupied by *The Tragedy of Ham and Jane* I might have noticed how much happier Matt seemed. 'Greg says I've gorra be there at 5, too,' he said. What's he plannin'?'

'Haven't a clue.'

'I think he's right to do something different. The end's canny but I don't think it's canny enough. It's like the middle's the best bit now – and that's wrong isn't it?'

I glanced at him. He looked me right in the eye, something he'd never done before, waiting for my words of wisdom. 'You're right,' I said. 'Biggest climax should be at the finish.'

We drove along the river a little way before turning off, the wind whipping up grey furrows in the water. 'Mam's never seen a play.'

'Looking forward to it?'

'Oh aye. I've told her all about it, like.'

I turned up the blower. 'Need some heat out of this thing.'

'They said on telly it might snow.'

'Too cold for that now.'

We wound our way down the mean streets, quiet in the afternoon, and pulled in to the kerb. 'I love it when it snows,' Matt said.

'Getting your sledge out, I know.'

He turned, almost embarrassed. 'Never had a sledge. I like the way it cleans everything up, though. And the light… You get a different light with snow.' He opened the passenger door and hurried off down the alley.

I waited. Could it really be the end of me and Jane? It did seem a crisis point; she'd have to choose between us. She loved me, didn't she? Though she'd never actually said the words?

She couldn't love Gerry, surely? After tonight things could be a lot better. Or then again, unimaginably worse.

O meddle not with wives of other men
Lest ye in meddling lose your hearts to them.

Not that I put my feelings into quite those words.

Eventually, Matt wheeled Sandy down the alley and we hoisted her into the van. There was no evidence of her having dressed for the occasion and from the wafts she brought with her, she'd obviously already had a drink. On the plus side she beamed and greeted me cheerfully, 'All reet Ham?' she said. 'Let's gan to the play!'

III. 5

LIGHTS UP ON THE AUDITORIUM AT HEATON ARTS CENTRE, LATE
AFTERNOON. THE CALL IS STILL A HALF AN HOUR AWAY. **GREG** SITS
ON THE EDGE OF THE STAGE, GOING THROUGH A LITTLE SHEAF OF
PAPERS — CUFF'S LATEST REWRITES. BEHIND HIM IS THE SET,
PLAYING AREAS AT VARIOUS HEIGHTS, RAKED SLIGHTLY FORWARD.
STAGE FURNITURE, INCLUDING A LOPSIDED IRON BEDSTEAD WITH
CRUMPLED SHEETS IS ON ONE LEVEL, AND A GAS LAMP ON
ANOTHER INDICATING AN EXTERIOR. GREG PACES THE SET,
DROPPING THE PAPERS ON THE BED AS HE DOES SO, THEN SITS ON
THE EDGE OF THE STAGE, OBVIOUSLY DEEP IN THOUGHT.
DIONYSUS ENTERS. HE IS WEARING A WHITE SHIRT OPEN AT THE
NECK AND CLOSE-FITTING RED VELVET TROUSERS. HE APPROACHES
NOISELESSLY DOWN THE SIDE AISLE AND HOPS NIMBLY ON TO THE
STAGE. COMPARED TO GREG, HE'S ALMOST ETHEREAL.

GREG   *(standing up quickly)* Shit! I didn't hear
              you coming. *(he holds out his right
              hand)* You the guy from the *Chronicle*?
              *(Dionysus ignores the gesture and moves
              about the stage delightedly, exploring it.
              Greg watches, puzzled)* You got a
              background in the military? That silent
              approach thing?

DIONYSUS   Mmmm. Sort of. I know about yours,
              of course. The Kingdom of the
              Hong… A place of great beauty. A
              matriarchy…

GREG	Well, yes. Kind of an odd way of putting it. Never known the *Chronicle* so hot on research—
DIONYSUS	I like it here. *(he hops up a level and stretches out provocatively on the bed)* Ooh! nice and bouncy. *(he picks up the pages of script and begins to flick through, Then drops the rewrites on the floor with exaggerated sigh)* Oh dear.
GREG	What?
DIONYSUS	Your poet. Let you down again hasn't he? Still no vengeance. So now it's up to you.
GREG	Look. Let's cut to the chase shall we? I've only got five minutes to give you.
DIONYSUS	Ah, the chase! Never more alive than within touching distance of death. *(he advances across the stage like a hunter creeping up on prey)* Closer and closer until blade to blade, or better still, hand to hand, the real thing! *(he clicks his fingers and a shining blade appears in the air)*
GREG	*(stares at the knife, hypnotised, murmurs)* Is this a—?
DIONYSUS	Yes, yes, it is a dagger you see before you. To kill the adulterer with.
GREG	It's Cuff's play, not mine. I can't…
DIONYSUS	You've taken the coward's way. Not faced up to what's in the play. Guilt.

You know what I mean. *(Greg clenches his fists and rushes at Dionysus, who skips lightly out of the way)* I saw you, you know, you and your friend's young wife…

GREG   *(puts hands over ears, howls)* I only fucked her once!

DIONYSUS   *(lies down on the bed again, head propped on elbow, whispers)* Once is quite enough. My friend. The husband would kill his friend. His treacherous friend…

GREG   I could hurt you badly. I could kill you. I haven't forgotten— *(he lunges at Dionysus, jabbing first and index finger forward)*

DIONYSUS   *(laughs and rolls swiftly off the bed and to his feet. They face each other across the bed, Greg panting)* Of course you haven't.

DIONYSUS   I brought this for you. *(holds up a vial of blood, shakes it, opens it, peers in)* Beautiful stuff. Thick. Crimson. Nearly as good as the real thing. *(he sniffs it, wrinkles up his nose)* But the smell is wrong. *(he circles the still figure of Greg, whispers)* You know what has to be done. BLACKOUT.

That's what I saw when I arrived for the call, Greg on the stage, with several bottles of the best and most expensive stage blood that money could buy, German stuff. 'Going to kill someone?' He didn't seem to hear me. 'Splashed out, have you?' But he didn't laugh, just paced around, waiting for everyone else to appear.

By ten past five, all the cast had arrived. Greg looked at me. 'Cuff's changed a couple of Morris's lines. Have a look.' He thrust the rewrites at me. 'Otherwise, we'll go with the marching at the end, but we'll use the pit – so you march offstage into the pit, which should suggest marching to the trenches and then I want the set to *bleed*. We can do this because it's the last night and the set's gonna get bust up anyway. Don't have to clean it up for tomorrow. Matt, I want the blood to seep downstage and slowly soak the white rug, needs to come from different angles – and then we need to rig some very small lights at stage level to skim the surface. Things we can clip on – what can you sort out?'

'I could stick bulbs in tin cans and then cut into the metal to barn-door them.'

'We've got two hours – think you can do it?'

'Canny bit of work,' Rod said.

'Be worth it though, won't it?' Matt said. 'For the picture.'

LATER. THE BAR IN THE THEATRE SHORTLY BEFORE THE PERFORMANCE. **NIC,** LOOKING BORED, IS LEANING AGAINST A WALL, HER FINGERS CURLED ROUND A GIN AND TONIC. **DIONYSUS** MATERIALISES BESIDE HER, CLICKS HIS FINGERS.

NIC   Have we met before?

DIONYSUS   Don't you remember me?

NIC   Where was it, then?

DIONYSUS   The woods.

NIC	The woods! I do seem to remember something. Was it at pets' corner? I'm always there now. They let me have their surplus, you know, the little furries they can't keep. For my snake.
DIONYSUS	Wonderful! You have a snake?
NIC	Most people think it's really bizarre… But it's *wonderful*. I love him. He's a royal python. I've called him Boris.
DIONYSUS	You seem a lot happier than when we met before.
NIC	Hmm. Yeah. I am happier. Odd thing though, things aren't going well with Stafford – especially about Boris, as it happens – but I can't make myself care any more. I used to try so hard to make the relationship work. Now it's as though it's not important any more, as though I've moved on… God knows why I'm telling you all this. You don't mind? I've given up my job, too. Haven't told him yet. No more listening to people banging on about their problems, writing reports, going to bloody conferences. In meetings I kept wanting to shout, 'Get outside! Have a glass of wine! Buy a snake! Have a rampant fuck! Stop whingeing!' Most women are out of touch with themselves. You know what I mean? I

243

think you do. You're very good
looking. I don't know why I can't
exactly place you. Oh look, we've got
to go in. Where are you sitting?
Shame. Will I see you afterwards? *(she
blows him a kiss and goes into the
theatre)*

It seemed to work. The lights. The blood. At least, the *is that
the end?* moment only went on for a second before the
applause kicked in. Afterwards, I felt on an incredible high.
My scenes with Jane had never gone better. When she'd looked
into my eyes I'd *known* she loved me. Hadn't seen her to talk
to since the curtain call, but then everyone was working full-
speed to dismantle the set so we could get to the pub as soon
as possible. I'd see her then. We'd sort it out. It would be all
right.

Beside me, Stafford tore long strips of gaffer tape from the
rostra. He shouted across to Matt. 'You don't have to be that
careful now. Run's over. Just chuck everything in the truck and
we're away to the pub. Guaranteed lock-in.'

'You coming for a drink, Matt?' I said, as I wound electric
cable. 'You and your mam?'

He grinned. 'That'd be good.'

'Get the other end of this, would you? Meant to say, marra,
you did really well on the lights. Everyone said the end looked
great.'

Act IV: After the Show

IV. 1

Frailty, thy name is Jane. Three hours later I'm bar-stooled, fractured, fucking racked – and wrecked – watching the woman I love showing she doesn't love me back.

Home counties vowels intrude. 'It's Ham isn't it? I wanted to thank you for your performance tonight.' Fella in a trenchcoat, collar turned up.

'Ah.'

'Can I get you a drink?'

'Aye, why not? It's number eight I'm on – or could be nine.'

He laughs. Orders me a pint. 'You certainly know how to put it away up here. Cheers.'

'Aye! Here's to us, the whole shebang.' I wave my glass at the company behind us, 'Suppin' our fill at the City Vaults by way of…celebration.' I pour it down my throat. 'Whoops. Did I say us? Mishtake. Shlip of the tongue. She's with her husband, over there, see? I'm with meself.'

'Oh dear. Sorry to hear that. Anyway… Great show.'

'I should *do* something, shouldn't I? Shout her name across the room. What do you reckon?'

'Well. Maybe not. Could be counterproductive.'

'See that scarf she's wearing? I gave her that… A blue that turns her lovely eyes sea green.'

'Nice line of blank verse.'

245

'You what?'

'I've never been to a last night party quite like this before. There seems…rather a lot of emotional disturbance in the air. I mean… Look at Cuff…'

I turn my head, try to focus. There. Cuff sits, alone. A few yards to his right, Greg, stone-faced, plays the one-armed bandit. Jenny beside him, face blotched, mouth stretched open, shouts something against the music. There's Maureen, shooting red-hot bolts from her eyes across the room at Sam, mid-joke, surrounded by the TV people up from London. And Sandy. Well away. Beaming and waving her glass to the beat. Next to her, Matt. What'd he got to be so miserable about?

'I couldn't believe it when Cuff told me Ham's your real name. Run in the family does it?'

'Noooo. Son of Noah.'

'Ah. Well I just wanted to say you made a lot out of that part and give you my card. If you're interested in working together, give me a call.'

'They're leaving. Look. He's helping her on with her coat!'

'I've written my home number on the back.'

'Got to go after them.'

'It's none of my business, Ham, but mightn't you be better off staying here?'

'I'm all right. You'll see.' And I launch myself off the bar stool and start across the room, only a bit unsteady, till someone grabs me by the shoulder.

Matt's face, right up against mine, his spit on my cheek. 'Did *ye* know? About the scheme ending, like. About me being out of a job?'

'What the fuck you doing Matt? Nearly pulled me over.'

'Did you *know*?'

'Look, I've got to go. Haven't a clue what you're on about.'

'He said. That Hardley. He said there's just another week. Then I'm out. Fucking hell, just like that. Did ye know? I mean. Why didn't you tell us?'

I see the door closing behind Jane and Gerry and shrug Matt off. 'Listen. I'll see ye's later. Got to go.'

And out into the roaring night I crash, obsessed with finding her, with what idea in my head god only knows, something along the lines of *making* her speak.

Gerry! Jane's got something to tell you.

Oh yes, pet, nearly forgot. I'm in love with Ham so if it's all the same to you I'll not be coming home tonight.

In the clattering, rubbish-dancing streets lads go arm in arm, heads ducked down against the wind, singing. I want to run but I'm on the deck of a ship in a swell. The surge and suck of the waves tilt the street and I'm falling into people, sliding sideways, and the big rollers are breaking over me and I can't get my head above them. 'Jaaaane!' I call and in my ears my voice goes loud and soft, loud and soft, 'Jaaaaaane!' I'm doing front-crawl now, fighting my way up the street when suddenly I'm sucked into a whirlpool of girls, all clattering high heels and squeals, all breasts and mouths and hair and teeth. 'Have ye's seen a lad?'

'A beautiful lad with curly hair?'

'Answer us! Have ye's seen him?'

'Come on! Leave this stupid fucker! Down here!'

And they skitter away, screaming in excitement, leaving me spinning in their wake. I blink, reach out to steady myself against a lamppost. *Lasses on the rampage.* A terrifying sight, like Da had said. I blink again. Look down. There are diamonds in the pavement. Oh! Beautiful! The whole street is studded with diamonds! I bend down, try to pick one up for Jane. Ohhh! A wave is rushing up from my belly, an unstoppable rush of tea, vodka and lager fills my throat, my mouth, my nose, bursts through the barriers and surges, foaming, down the street, 'Jaaaaaaaaa—'

SAME NIGHT. 2.45 A.M. LIGHTS UP ON PART OF STRUCTURE OF THE TYNE BRIDGE. THE GROUP OF YOUNG FEMALE REVELLERS HAM GLIMPSED EARLIER RUNS UNSTEADILY ALONG THE PAVEMENT, HOLDING THEIR SHORT SKIRTS DOWN, LAUGHING, PANTING, GASPING.

FIRST REVELLER	There he is! Look! Come on!
SECOND REVELLER	He's not. There's nobody. *(Wails)* Why doesn't he come back?
THIRD REVELLER	It was me he liked, anyway. The rest of yous scared him away.
FOURTH REVELLER	Why would he like you, Lardy Bum? He said he loved me, whispered it, like, when we were dancing.
THIRD REVELLER	Eee. I can still feel his tongue in my ear. I just wanted to lie down right there and give meself to him.
FOURTH REVELLER	That's nowt. *(pulls down her top. reveals large red lovebite)* See that? Said he was going to mark me as chosen. So's he could find me again.

248

FIFTH REVELLER	*(lifts her skirt and sobbing shouts into the air)* I don't care. Yous can have us all, one after another, if you please, please come back.
FIRST REVELLER	*(sees Matt standing behind a girder, whispers)* He's right there! Look!
THIRD REVELLER	That's not him ye daft cow. Oy! Ye! What do you think you're doing hiding there? Oy! I'm talking to ye!
MATT	Not hiding.
THIRD REVELLER	Yes ye are. Hiding and listening in to girls. That's perverted, that is. Fucking little perve. Come into the light where we can see you better. Look at the clip of it! And ye thought it was *him*.
FIRST REVELLER	I must be drunk. *(starts laughing wildly. Others join in)*
THIRD REVELLER	Ye'd need to be drunk. Ye'd need to be out of your fuckin' head to dance wi' *him*. Let's see what's under the hat.
MATT	*(protecting his hat)* Leave us alone. Not doing any harm. *(he is now surrounded by the girls)*
FIRST REVELLER	Just minding your own business weren't ye, pet?
THIRD REVELLER	Just minding *our* business more like. That the way you get your thrills is it? Dirty bastard.

249

SECOND REVELLER	Bet he's never had a girlfriend.
FIRST REVELLER	Eeh worra disgusting thought! *(they start circling Matt and pushing him against the barrier)*
THIRD REVELLER	You're the type likes looking through keyholes—
SECOND REVELLER	Takes girls' knickers off washing lines—
THIRD REVELLER	Want to see me knickers do you? Want to touch my tits? *(she pulls up her top, shimmies into Matt who covers his ears)*
MATT	Leave us alone!
FIFTH REVELLER	Come on. Let's go.
THIRD REVELLER	No! We need to punish him.
FIRST REVELLER	For being ugly.
SECOND REVELLER	For listening to our private thoughts.
THIRD REVELLER	Let's take his trousers. *(she makes a grab for Matt who hoists himself quickly into the structure of the bridge, out of their reach. Third Reveller makes an attempt to follow but falls back onto the pavement, shouts up)* Stupid bastard. I'll get me father on to you.
FIFTH REVELLER	*(pulling Third Rev to her feet)* Come on. Leave the lad alone. *(she shouts up)* Don't you bloody fall, right? We're going now.

250

THEY MOVE OFF ACROSS THE BRIDGE, PERIODICALLY LOOKING
BACK AND SHOUTING UNTIL THE SOUNDS FADE, AND FOR A
MOMENT ALL THAT CAN BE HEARD IS THE WIND. THEN, FROM
OFFSTAGE, THE STRONG VOICE OF CHORUS BEGINS TO SPEAK.

VOICE OF CHORUS   And while Ham pours his libation of
vomit into the gutter, a slight figure no
one sees climbs from the world of flesh
into cold steel. His thin shirt balloons
in the wind as he plants a scuffed boot
on a rivet and reaches up, and up
again, into a gigantic cat's cradle of
girders, criss-crossing the Tyne. He's
halfway up, one hundred and fifty feet
above the water, when first he looks
down on the ramped tumble of
Newcastle, pouring its light upon the
great river. Beneath him, a silver
battleship lies moored; downstream, a
forest of cranes raise yellow arms in
salute; on the desolate Gateshead bank
a solitary grain elevator blinks a blue
shimmer on the water, *Rank Hovis.*
Rank Hovis.
Up in the cat's cradle the wind is
singing history. Listen for the bass
notes of the bridge builders, welders of
metal in empty space, *'Pass it us.'*
'Steady.' 'All right Charlie?' 'I divvent
like this breeze…' and for others, siren

251

voices calling down, *'Come on, come up. Stand where I stood…'*

MATT CLIMBS ONTO A GIRDER AND SITS. DIONYSUS JOINS HIM

MATT	I thought you were in me head.
DIONYSUS	I am – and I'm not.
MATT	I remember—
DIONYSUS	*(waggles his index fingers on either side of his head like horns)* Yes. When this all began. I'm sorry about the girls. They were looking for me and chanced on you. Women can be cruel.
MATT	Like being back in the playground. Always like that.
DIONYSUS	Let's go higher.
MATT	*She* laughed, you know, when I told her. Said she knew how it'd turn out. Said I was stupid. Good for nowt. *(he climbs and for a while all that can be heard is his rasping breaths)* The lights on the blood. I did that. It was *good.* It looked great! Really great! All that and then I'm finished *(his voice breaks)*, there's nothing for me. Scheme's over. It's fuckin over.
DIONYSUS	Rest for a minute. Catch your breath.
MATT	Felt I belonged. *(he wipes his nose with his sleeve)* Like I'd found somewhere.
VOICE OF CHORUS	And on up he goes. A tiny spider in a

252

	gigantic metal web. No one sees him, now so nearly at the top.
DIONYSUS	Take my hand. There. What a view, eh?
MATT	Never been this high. Never been higher than the big wheel at Whitley Bay. Thought that was canny high. But this. *(he pauses)* My knees…
DIONYSUS	Stand tall. The wind has dropped. There's nothing to fear.
CHORUS	It's not too late to go back, to climb down now and go home.
MATT	*(Matt shivers)* Not many people been here. Me head just seemed to go click, 'bing' for first time. I'd see how it'd look in pictures, and I'd work out how to do it all at the same time… I can do *this*. Make it look—
DIONYSUS	What do you need?
MATT	More light over there. On Gateshead. For balance.
DIONYSUS	Reach up! Punch a hand through the clouds and let the moon shine through. There!
MATT	Yes. Everything bright and still.
DIONYSUS	The stage is set.
MATT	Stop. Wait. Not yet. Need lights on the ship—
DIONYSUS	Save that.

MATT	Wait! (*pause*) Please. Do I have to? *(he sobs, then breathes in sharply)* I want *them* to see it.
DIONYSUS	They'll never forget it, I promise.
MATT	It's hard though.
DIONYSUS	I'm here with you.
MATT	What's my cue? I need a cue!
DIONYSUS	You have to decide.
MATT	I'll say – I'll say – 'Let go me hand'
DIONYSUS	Perfect.
CHORUS	And as Matt hesitates, a sailor walking on the quayside far below looks up at last. He sees the matchstick figure standing on the apex of the bridge and starts to run, to shout, to wave his arms. The grain elevator blinks its blue shimmer on the water, *Rank Hovis. Rank Hovis.* And all along the silver battleship, a row of brightly coloured lights go on.
MATT	Let go me hand.

IV. 2

Stafford blew out his cheeks, rested his chin on his hands and told me: 'He was looking for you.'

'How do you know?'

'I said to him, "Where are you off to?" Saw he was drunk, like. And he says, "Going to find Ham."' Stafford sighed. 'Know what I said then?'

I shook my head.

Stafford looked at me and his eyes filled. 'I said, "Mind how you go."'

So there was no avoiding the fact Matt came after me, joining the absurd game of tag going on that night in Newcastle's windy streets.

What do I remember of that night? I remember the wind, the crazed girls. I remember throwing up. After that, I remember sitting in a shop entrance for a while, recovering, and then, quest abandoned and with the beginnings of a hangover, wandering aimlessly in the emptying streets until I found myself walking down the hill towards the river.

I wanted quiet, so my first reaction to the kerfuffle going on at the quayside, where people were shouting and running to and fro in the headless-chicken way they have when things have gone seriously wrong, was irritation, followed by mild curiosity. But when I got to the water's edge there was nothing to see, just a lot of jabbering about a lad jumping. One woman had got to the stage of rehearsing the drama. 'Just a few minutes ago. Just on three. I looked up. Ooh! I saw him. I did. I saw him.'

My head was thumping. *Nothing to do with me*, I thought, and almost left, but then a show of sorts began. The river police appeared in a boat, shining a light on the water and a breathless chill got to me, a sort of ice-cold conviction that this *was* something to do with me, a feeling that grew as I listened to the witnesses and the onlookers and watched the boat coming towards us, one of the policemen carrying something small and dripping in his hand. He climbed onto the quay and wrung it out, shook it into a semblance of its former self. 'All we found,' he said... Matt's woolly hat.

For all its insecurities, vanity and bullshit, there's nothing better than playing make-believe for a living. We invited Matt into our enchanted garden, shared with him our lovely toys, told him he was one of us. Then we shoved him back into the dark, dirty cupboard under the stairs and locked it from the outside.

'The scheme ends in a couple of weeks. What are you going to do then, Matthew?' Hardley's question after the show, after Matt's triumph with the lights, had slid between his ribs like a knife. And I'd heard it go in, saw Matt's eyes widen with shock and said nothing – because I was too busy concentrating on my own torments.

John Hardleman. Murderer. It doesn't sound right. John Hardleman – insensitive-bastard-fixated-on-balancing-the-books – yes. Hardley could have added, 'We'll look into work for you outside the scheme,' or 'You've been brilliant – you'll get an excellent reference.' But he didn't. Hardley didn't go in for effusions or sensitivity. He couldn't know the impact of his words and I've never enlightened him because it wouldn't be fair; he's not to blame.

I should have stepped in, told Matt we weren't going to let him go, that something would be found for him, because that's exactly what *would* have happened, and how most of us had got into the company in the first place. But I said nothing. Then later, when Matt appealed to me directly, I pushed past him and walked away.

'It's all my fault,' Jane said, over and over again. 'I shouldn't have gone home early. I should have talked to him more. Of course he could have stayed on. We could have found a way.'

'It was *our* fault,' I told her, unable to prevent myself using poor, drowned Matt in a squalid play for togetherness. And his death did unite us – briefly. Then divided us for ever.

Nobody mentioned murder at the police station. Suicide they considered, and then dismissed. Eventually it was *'a prank gone wrong'*, *'alcoholic intoxication'*, *'high winds'* that dominated the inquest and prompted the verdict: death by misadventure. That word – misadventure – still brings a lump to my throat.

'All we said was, "Ye gave us a fright,"' insisted the biggest and nastiest girl at the inquest, but I doubted that. When the smallest and nicest later came to the funeral and cried all the way through, I knew they must have been cruel.

It seemed Matt came after me, and, not finding me, went to the bridge. The taunts from the girls started him climbing, and the higher he climbed, the less he wanted to carry on living and the more logical it seemed to jump.

I see him starting up the cold metal fretwork of the bridge, the wind invading every inch of him, shirt and trousers flapping against his thin body. I see him clambering higher and higher, finding the rivets with his feet; see him reach the top. See him stand there for a minute.

He screamed as he fell. Everybody does, I was told. A sailor who saw Matt jump said he'd held his arms out wide as he did it and rotated his legs as though riding an invisible bike. I've had that picture – and the sound – in my head ever since.

Twenty people a year chuck themselves off the Tyne Bridge, many, like Matt, having climbed right to the apex. It's a certain death from that height; unlike popping a few pills there's no pumping that great, deep river out of your system.

All of them scream as they fall. One of the policemen told me that. He also said the number of jumpers goes up around Christmas. Matt was their first of that year's festive season. A couple of years ago, two decades too late for him, a notice appeared on the bridge with a phone number, encouraging suicides to think again and call the Samaritans.

Landing in the middle of the river Matt was caught by the Tyne's undertow, so that instead of moving downriver he drifted slowly upstream, finally surfacing and coming ashore a fortnight later on mudflats by the Scotswood Bridge. The day after they found him, Jane insisted we drove to the place. She took two poinsettias, those plants with red leaves you see in people's windows round Christmas, and dug them into the mud with her hands. Then we waited, watching the little red flags fluttering until submerged in the swirling brown water. We hardly spoke. Jane cried while I stood there, unable even to put my arm around her, thinking I'd never loved anyone as much. I knew it was all over, and in some unconfessed way knew Jane felt his death was a punishment for our adultery. I didn't share that view, but had no better explanation to offer, and I certainly shared her sense of guilt. We both knew we'd looked away at the wrong moment. We'd failed him. Me much more than Jane, of course.

I realised the other day the Tyne Bridge looks like the top half of the Wheel of Fortune. That place we struggle all our lives to get to, he conquered in one night and then *chose* to jump off. For a moment I envied him that glory, then saw that particular moment of *enlightenment* as yet another pathetic attempt to shuffle off a bit of guilt.

I've started to tie that production and Matt's death together, seeing him as some kind of sacrifice. There was so much destructive emotion on the loose: lust, betrayal, jealousy, ambition; the tragic denouement not half bloody enough. The real play ended that night with a real body, another one to come by way of an epilogue, and a good number of walking wounded.

It was five a.m. by the time the police had finished with me. I climbed away from the quayside, leaving a little cluster of people still talking, energised by their brush with death. I left Sandy, still more angry with Matt for going off than aware he was dead, in the care of a policewoman who promised to contact her other kids and get her home.

Night rubbed against day as I walked towards no. 12, the city's quiet pierced only by the occasional scream of an engine, or a haunting human cry. Across the street, wires torn down by the winds hung in thick loops. An empty bin rested against the kerb. I came across its strewn guts as I walked: crisp packets, cans, bottles, sodden chips – the remains of a Saturday night out. The people who'd stuffed their faces with chips were alive, snoring in their beds and Matt was dead, mouth and lungs filled with the muddy water of the Tyne. How could that be? Even in the dark I could feel the sky thickening above my head, muffling the world in a thick blanket, and sure enough, just as the road levelled out by the breakers' yard, and I looked across the piles of ghostly vehicles to the humped terraces beyond, I felt a cold fizz on my cheek, then on my lips, as the first flakes of snow began to fall.

IV. 3

The show went on. A Christmas show, made up of sketches written by Cuff and a couple of other writers, slammed together in a week to tour old people's homes from mid-December to the end of January. It only involved four of us: me, Alice, Stafford and Lynette – and as gigs go was an easy one, no set to speak of, and most performances matinées.

I found out at the inquest that Matt's funeral was to be held on the morning of the 22nd of December. Hardley managed to swap dates so that we had a booking nearby in North Shields that afternoon. Everyone in the company went to the service, Sam even making the trip up from London especially.

As far as *catharsis* goes, I suppose you could say Matt's death purged the company of some of its more destructive emotions. The collective shock seemed to bring us together; Maureen actually offered to collect Sam from the station.

Stafford drove those of us in the cast, plus Hardley and Greg, in the van. It took a while to find the crematorium and I remember circling the same municipal Christmas tree several times before we located the turning. As we drew up I was surprised and pleased to see Cuff getting out of his rusty Datsun. 'Didn't know you were coming,' I said, as we went through the gate together.

'Well I wanted to. And since I'm seeing the show this afternoon it seemed a good idea.'

'Thought you were in London with the RSC gadgie.'

'I was. Doing rewrites. Came back yesterday.' He glanced

at Greg striding ahead of us up the path. 'These directors always want their pound of flesh, don't they?'

'How's Jenny?'

'Fine. Well, not really fine. She's had enough of coping on her own.' Cuff sneezed. 'And our house is full of cold at the moment.'

Tyneside as a whole was full of cold. The heavy snowfall on the night of Matt's death survived three weeks as a grimy crust edging the tarmac path. We climbed some steps and entered a red-carpeted foyer, where Sandy's empty wheelchair confirmed we were in the right place.

In the chill hush of the chapel itself, Kicking already filled a pew. I noticed Jane, without Gerry, sitting in the shadow of Maureen's huge hat. Actors tend to dress for funerals, our shiny feathery selves making a stark contrast to the other defeated-looking people present. All four of them; Sandy, and beside her a thin, gingery man, plus two women who might have been Matt's older sisters.

Appreciating a good funeral is obviously a critical faculty you develop with age, but I can say now – with a good few ceremonies behind me – Matt's was the worst I've ever attended.

I'd never been to a crematorium service before, never been to a funeral anywhere except Pity Me Methodist chapel, where Mam would take me, quite often it seemed, to 'pay my respects'. She'd often pass judgement on our way home as to how well the departed had been sent off, 'Eeh, Ham, worra lovely service that was', and even at the age of eight or nine the thespian in me understood completely what she meant, because a good funeral is basically a moving piece of theatre.

My parents' funerals were conducted by a minister who knew them well, and packed out with people who either liked or loved them. The priest who took Matt's service had never met him and, as it became obvious, knew very little about him. Though we were five minutes early, he paced impatiently as we shuffled into the pew already occupied by Maureen and Jane. I watched as Sandy said something to him and he inclined his head once, very slightly, as though reluctant to talk to her. Behind the altar Matt's coffin was visible, draped in a dark-blue velvet cloth.

From somewhere or other piped music began and we stumbled through a hymn. The door opened once again and I saw the girl from the inquest slip into a pew at the back. Then the priest, or vicar, or whatever he was, took a small card from his pocket and cleared his throat. There was a very empty feeling in that chapel and I think we were all willing him to say something to breathe a bit of warmth into our memories of Matt. I don't know if it was the bastard couldn't be arsed or, more charitably, Sandy had given him nothing to go on, but the end result was terrible. He began:

'Matthew attended All Saints Primary School and St Cuthbert's High School leaving at the age of 16 with a CSE in metalwork.'

He did better than that, I thought. I heard Matt's voice in my head. 'She was canny, the art teacher. She didn't bawl at yous all the time. I used to go to her room dinner times. I made this mask of a dog. I got a CSE grade 1.'

'That's canny good for a school like yours.'

'Aye. There was only two of we got the top grade, like.'

'Matthew was the youngest of Sandra's five children. As the youngest child, he stayed in his mother's care the longest.'

Got that the wrong way about, I thought.

'His favourite meal was a Sunday roast.'

Jane's reddened eyes met mine.

Like most young men, Matthew enjoyed a tipple. Unfortunately, it was indulging this habit that led to his untimely death. When he died, Matthew had a temporary job in a theatre company. However, his mother tells me that as a small child he loved to watch the boats in the Tyne and it was his life's ambition to work in the shipyards. Sadly, this wish will not now be fulfilled.'

I could picture him as a child, strapped into some scruffy pushchair outside a pub, watching the ships in the river while Sandy sank her Guinness. Other than that, I couldn't see or feel anything of Matt. I wish now I'd stood up, gone to the front and said some things – the things that made him special. But you don't, do you? You don't do what you should, don't say the things that need to be said.

Once Matt had been reduced to metalwork CSE and a longing to work in Swan Hunter's, the priest rattled through the rest of the burial service at the rate of knots. I wished he'd said nothing, left it all up to the Book of Common Prayer, because that at least had words suited to the occasion. *'Man that is born of woman hath but a short time to live, and is full of misery. He cometh up, and is cut down, like a flower.'*

Matt's long fall finally ended when the coffin shunted forward and slid out of sight behind a curtain, bound for the fire.

Outside, the women who might have been Matt's sisters got into a funeral car and left without saying anything to anyone. The young girl from the inquest hurried down the road, nose buried in a tissue. Restored to her chair, Sandy introduced her ginger companion as Dave. Dave nodded at me and looked away as she sucked on a tab and confided, 'Don't know what I would have done without him. He's sorting out sickness benefit for me, with me leg, like, and he's got me at the top of the list for a new flat. Because of my trouble.' She blinked away a tear. 'I need someone to look after us,' she said. 'You know what I mean, Ham. Are yous coming to the pub? Get that Jane, too.'

So Matt had gone, and Dave, probably attracted by the economics of the situation, had replaced him.

In the end we all went to the pub. There was nothing laid on, no food at all – I don't think the bar even supplied crisps. I thought again of Pity Me funerals and the mountains of sandwiches Mam and the other women of the village made; the times I got my hand slapped away from a lovely golden sponge or plate of flapjacks because all this wonderful stuff was destined for someone's 'funeral tea'.

Sam got a round in. No one even sat down; we stood around looking very out of place in one of Shields's most basic pubs, complete with brown walls, girly calendar, and two old soaks studying the racing form between glancing over at us with unfriendly eyes. After about twenty minutes Maureen took Sam, Jane and those who weren't going to the show back to Newcastle. Sam patted my shoulder as he left. 'I'll miss you, marra,' he said. 'Don't take it too hard.' I think he meant Matt. Since it turned out Sandy and Dave had no means of getting home, they came to the gig with us.

Sometimes, audiences in residential homes can be pretty well completely catatonic. You go through the routines watched by rows of blank faces. Now I come to think of it, it's

265

not unlike performing Shakespeare to Japanese tourists on a summer afternoon in Stratford. As it happened, though, this home was better run and the audience pretty lively and responsive. You got the impression the staff talked to the residents a lot and brought in regular outside stimulation to keep their brains going.

Though not all the details are clear in my memory, I know we did a good show. Lynette's snot-nosed kid in the Anderson shelter went down a treat among other World War I and II nostalgia and lots of song and dance. I suppose we're sure to have done the *ticking crocodile* finale, because we used the crocodile, a fabulous costume relic of a long ago *Peter Pan*, in all our OAP shows until it finally fell to bits. I usually got to inhabit its very thick, and very hot, skin, but can't remember if I did so then, though other things remain vivid. Like Sandy and her ginger Dave, sitting in the front row, drinking and smoking throughout.

Though she must have been at least twenty years younger than most of the residents, Sandy seemed in her element, conducting me on the tin whistle, laughing at all the jokes, and, in the short interval, chatting to Cuff in the next seat. I see now Sandy was one of those people who just can't rise to the demands of youth and middle age. She was born to be old.

We hung out the washing on the Siegfried Line, trudged to Tipperary – and, in between, performed some very funny sketches written by Cuff. Afterwards, the home laid on heaped plates of egg and cress, cheese and tomato and salmon paste sandwiches, followed by loads of home-made cakes. Mam would have approved. I wonder if that place is still going? Should book myself in.

Cuff came over to me, his cold apparently worse after sitting in the freezing chapel. He sneezed into a big check handkerchief. 'You don't sound too well,' I said.

'Just a wee bit tired.'

'Where's Greg?'

Cuff shrugged. 'If I didn't know better, I'd think he's avoiding me.'

'Guilty about working you too hard, I should think.' Cuff didn't reply. Then I saw Greg hovering near the entrance, obviously desperate for some way to escape the alien British ritual of afternoon tea. 'There he is,' I said.

'He'll be looking for a one-armed bandit.' Cuff's chortle turned into another violent sneeze.

'If you were so busy with the RSC and that, why didn't you say no to doing this show?'

'Never turn down work. Went down well too, didn't it?'

'Great success. Good writing.'

Cuff polished his nose and stuffed the handkerchief in the pocket of his corduroy jacket, 'So-oo, Ham,' he said, 'people tell me you knew this poor lad well?'

Ginger Dave had wheeled Sandy off for a look round the place by this time, so I could talk freely. 'Better than most of us, I suppose. Except Jane.' My tongue stuck on her name and he looked at me sharply, eyes glinting behind his specs.

'What do you think happened?'

I told him what I thought. Blathered on for a long time, while he nodded, sniffed, nodded, sneezed, and occasionally slipped in a question to keep me going right up to the end of the inquest. Finally, he said, 'The poor lad deserved a better send off.'

But if the service was terrible, you could say Matt got a decent wake, thanks to that old people's home.

Matt was a hero. He struggled against odds that would have defeated the rest of us. From the age of 12 he looked after Sandy alone; he put up with bullying and rejection at school every day because of where he lived and who his mother was, yet he never stopped caring for her – loving her. He shopped for and prepared the food they ate, and without even a bathroom he kept himself clean and tidy and didn't lose hope. I never heard him say a harsh word to her or about her. He was always kind, good humoured and patient.

Matt had very little confidence but he should have had a lot more because he had real talent. At Kicking, he learned quickly how to create lighting effects. He had the potential to make an artist, or an architect, or a theatre designer. His good eye was complemented by imagination, a practical ability to put ideas into action and a willingness to work hard. He recognised beauty when he saw it, which is not a common thing.

On a personal level he was never cruel but loyal and affectionate. Though let down very often in life, he trusted others.

That's what I should have said – at the funeral. Should have stood up.

Jane would have added, 'He had beautiful eyes and a great soul.'

Thinking back to that conversation with Cuff I realise why he kept asking me all those questions. The writer in him thought Matt's story would make a good play.

IV. 4

My unusual purchases of suet, flour, herbs, carrots and greaseproof paper aroused Najib's curiosity. 'What dish are you planning?' he enquired.

'Steak and kidney pudding,' I told him. 'It's a famous British repast.'

He wrinkled up his nose. 'Kidneys? It will not be appetising.'

I bought the meat during my lunch break and started cooking when I got home. The first problem I encountered was the bluntness of Mam's old knives. Where was the knife-sharpener when needed? A human knife-sharpener. They used to come round every couple of months when I was a lad. I remember one in particular used to set up his grinder at the end of the lane and sing out, so all the mams would bring him their scissors and knives. Armed and dangerous they looked, running up the back lane in their flowery pinnies and gathering in a tight little circle around him.

The knife man was a very dark and good-looking Romany and, I see now, all the mams fancied him. Even mine went strangely girly as he put a shining edge on her carver, all the while murmuring things to her out of the side of his mouth. I remember her screaming with laughter as she and the other women, followed by me and other baffled kids, made their way back home.

I struggled on with one of the knives he'd once ground razor-sharp, trying to cut the fatty cores out of the kidneys. I'd forgotten how much they smell of piss. Utilising my handy pull-down flap, I *lightly tossed* the cubes of meat in flour and placed them in the pudding basin along with some onions (fried in a little oil until *transparent*), herbes des Provence and a *soupçon* of water. Then I *popped on* the suet crust I'd made earlier, pressing it to the sides of the bowl so as to *create a good seal*. I cut out a little circle of greaseproof paper to rest on the top.

I'd sacrificed an old shirt for the pudding cloth. When I was little, Mam never even had a bowl. Suet puddings got boiled tied up in a piece of fabric. Only later did she acquire state-of-the-art 1960s cooking equipment in the form of the basin. I secured my cloth around it with a piece of string, put it in a saucepan half filled with cold water, and left it overnight.

As a child I spent hours in the kitchen with Mam, and because I was the youngest, she used to take me everywhere with her, treating me like the girl she'd obviously wanted. I mean, cerise pullovers? On Saturdays, for instance, if the weather was fine, Mam would take me to join the ladies outside the chapel, assessing the brides. They were a very critical audience, Mam among the most judgemental of the poor girls emerging from the safety of the porch.

'Hev ye seen the clip of it? I wouldn't boil a puddin' in that dress.'

The audition being at 2 p.m., and my traditional dish being one that benefited from a very long, very slow, cook, I set the burner on *low*, topped up the water in the saucepan, and went to work for the morning shift.

'Ah Ham!' Najib looked up from emptying bags of change into the till. 'I see you're coming rather late.'

I looked at the clock above his head. 'I'm early.' I said.

Najib raised his index finger 'Listen! I am not finished!' He cleared his throat. 'How cruel of you to make me stand and wait. Ha ha! See! I can do it. A rhyming couplet of iambs. Very easy when you get the hang of it. The more I try, the less awe I feel when talking of the bard.'

'Hmm. You could say his were better than yours.'

He silenced me again with that finger while rummaging underneath the counter; then held something aloft and chanted, 'These antlers have I bought for you to wear…'

'Oh no.'

'You are an actor are you not? I have given you a seasonal part – as a reindeer. A jolly reindeer. And I am to wear this. See?' He put on white wig and beard. The snowy curls against dark skin made him a pretty sinister-looking Santa. Lifting a large box onto the counter, he announced. 'This year, the shop will be decorated for Christmas.'

'I didn't think you believed in it. As a Moslem, like.'

He waved the objection away. 'Poof! I am Moslem, yes, but first and foremost I am a businessman! So. You are to decorate the shop.'

'Isn't it a bit late for that now?'

'As you British say, better late than never. There is a tree in the back for you to erect and garnish.'

So all morning I draped tinsel and hung lights while Najib manned the till. He was serving one of the more lost and bewildered among our customers when the time came for me to leave.

'I suppose I must wish you good luck,' he boomed. Then announced to the old wife, 'My assistant is attending an audition,' putting such stress on 'tend' she dropped her purse in fright. He leaned over the counter as she scrabbled on the floor and gave her another blast, 'For a part in a dramatic production.'

'Eh?' She looked over. 'Why's he shoutin'? What hev I done?'

I decided to walk to the quayside. A cold morning had turned into a cold afternoon, the pavements along the quieter streets slithery with brownish slush. As I started down the long hill I got a call on the mobile from my brother Joe. *The* call, I could say, because I knew what was coming next. Poor old Joe. At Christmas, like Snout in *A Midsummer Night's Dream* I take the part of *Wall*, or *Buffer*, perhaps, a human barrier between him and his wife, Frances. Around the same time every year Joe gets worried I might not show up.

'All right for Christmas as usual?' he said. 'It'll be just the three of us this year.'

Made it sound like an attraction, instead of the deterrent it undoubtedly was. 'Don't worry, I'll be there,' I said, thinking *I'll have an acting job by then. Something to shut her up.* By the time I'd convinced him, and we'd exchanged a bit of news, I could see the river in front of me. I started to feel nervous. 'See you Christmas Eve, Joe,' I said, and rang off.

It's daft, but the shining glass glory the quayside's become always takes me by surprise, as though I'm expecting it to have shuffled back to its 1970s dereliction since my last visit. Instead the place glittered more than ever, teeming with the prosperously employed hurrying towards a spot of Christmas cheer in the many wine bars and restaurants.

They relocated the courts down here some years ago, the legal firms followed and on the quayside now you see suited rich people who look like barristers and solicitors everywhere. I surged along with them, trying to breathe their air of confidence, telling myself an acting job lay just one left turn and another hundred yards up the road.

I used to virtually live at Kicking Theatre, but when it got to the point I no longer knew anyone there, and they didn't appear to know me, I stopped going. Without consciously avoiding the place, I'd kept away since, so it had been a very long time since I'd turned this particular corner. Now, standing looking up at the Building, it affected me so much I actually had to steady myself by putting a hand out to the wall.

Nerves, was it? Or perhaps pride at the place, once so much *my* place (and maybe about to be that again), being *here*, part of all this wealth and success. And looking so at ease, its period brick so buffed up, its paintwork so fresh. Some other feeling gnawed at me, but I shoved it down and wiped my feet on it as I crossed the threshold. A girl rang through from the box office to let the director know I'd arrived, inviting me to take a seat while I waited. I looked around. Leather chairs. Heavy darkened-glass tables. Piped Miles Davis. The sort of place that would've made Mam brush an imaginary crumb from her cardigan, lean forward and whisper 'posh'.

There were framed posters lining the walls. Large, glossy posters of plays I hadn't been in. But on the way to the gents I found Hardley's cheapo commissions lurking – lots of them, in fact – charting the history of the company. God, the number of plays we'd done! You could see how the six plays a year the company performed in the 1970s had dwindled to two by 1997 and then to one. This year it would be *The Blaydon Races*. There'd be a really big shiny poster. With my name on it…

Another young girl appeared. 'Sophie says she'll be about fifteen minutes. Can I get you a coffee while you're waiting?'

Well, it beat hell out of Hardley's 'What do *you* want?' office manner, I thought, watching the girl's bare feet disappear up the polished wood stairs. Little ankle chain, she had.

While drinking the coffee I read a leaflet on Kicking's joint venture with a German company called Wangen Theater Kunst and a glossy brochure publicising the Theatre Redevelopment Plan. According to this, *financing is almost entirely in place for a new five-hundred-seat theatre in the company's quayside location.'* The coffee tasted good. The future looked good. A play, a future back with Kicking – and Jane. Dinner with Jane. You bugger… when was the last day I'd had as brilliant as this?

The girl came back. 'You can come through now,' she said. We climbed the pale wood stairs, once wet and slippery stone, to the top floor rehearsal room. I'd forgotten how high the building was. Got quite out of breath. 'So you worked with the great Sam…?' she enquired.

'Yep.'

'He was up here last week,' she said. 'He's really sweet, isn't he?'

'Oh aye. Top man.'

'And so funny!' We reached the third floor and she opened a door into my past. I stood outside for a moment, looking in. The shape of the room remained the same, though the old bare walls had been plastered over and painted cream. The double doors in the exterior wall and the old hoist mechanism survived too, relics of the Building's former life as a warehouse, when sacks of spices were hauled up and swung in from the quay. I sniffed the air. It was still there; that faint smell of cinnamon.

Then I stepped into the biggest surprise of all; it felt *warm*. Three pullovers and fucking freezing all year, I remembered, as I followed the girl across the room and past the strange sight of a big pile of clippie mats to where Sophie Shuttleworth, the Artistic Director, sat frowning into a script. 'Ham Nicolson, Sophie,' the girl said, as though afraid of interrupting her.

The director looked up, stood and stretched out a bare, shapely arm. Some men might have described tall, slim and athletic-looking Sophie, as a babe, but I doubt they'd say it to her face. She smiled, tossed back her dark hair and invited me to sit down. 'I am *so* pleased to meet you, Ham – I hope I may call you that? I know of course all about your excellent work for the company.'

That sounded nice. It's standard in theatre to dish out compliments by way of greeting, but it still felt good. I waited for her to ask me what speech I planned to do, but instead she tucked one black-legginged limb under her bum and looked at me for a bit, tapping the end of her pen against her teeth.

I felt expected to fill the gap. 'I remember rehearsing up here. Looks a bit different. Still got the hoist I see.'

She looked over and sighed. 'Gets in the way a bit. But it's listed…' She looked at me, her head on one side.

'Had its uses of course,' I babbled on. 'I remember once we lowered a piece of set down to the street because it was too big to go by the stairs.' A picture of Stafford hanging in the air astride the carousel horse – 'just for the hell of it, like' – came into my mind.

'Really?' Sophie smiled.

'And the German company thing… and the new theatre, of course, I've been reading about it all…'

'Oh yes! And they go hand in hand you know! We're so *excited* about Wangen. I've just got back from a month over there. They've got incredible facilities. I came back with loads of ideas to feed into our redevelopment here. And their rehearsal practices! Fascinating. But this play, Ham. Can you give me a bit of background?' I didn't know what to say. 'Very powerful play of course. That's why I'm so passionate about doing it – but I wondered… the genesis of it?'

'Well,' I began, 'it was initially going to be a comedy written by someone else.'

From the expression on her face that made nothing clearer. 'That writer turned in a terrible script so Cuff got called in to write us out of trouble pretty well at the last moment… Thing was all the publicity had gone out so we were stuck with the same title which people thought a bit weird, because *The Blaydon Races* sounds like a jolly knees up and it's quite a tragic play.'

I think I thought she'd laugh. Her eyes opened wide. 'Extraordinary,' she breathed.

I didn't want to tell her anything else. 'I was wondering about the clippie mats,' I said.

She glanced over to the corner. 'We use them for warm-ups. I like to think it keeps us in touch with our roots in the community. Well, we're talking about Kicking's roots now aren't we…?'

'Sort of like yoga mats?'

'Yes. But Ham you must tell me more about the play.'

I didn't want to tell her. On the other hand, I really wanted a job. I took a breath and launched in. 'The play's got a lot in it about…what was going on in the company at the time.' I paused.

'Oh yes?'

'I don't know, like betrayal, jealousy and ambition… And a couple of people were in love.'

Sophie uncoiled her leg and leaned forward. 'How fascinating.' She did allow herself a little laugh then, and I reacted.

'Those things happened because the actors in the company were together so much. Kicking was a kind of living thing – you know, *alive and kicking* – where the name came from. We did six plays a year in the seventies.'

'Oh yes, I can see the problem.'

'Wasn't really a problem.'

'But six plays? Ridiculous pressure.'

'Shakespeare's company did 30 a year. Forty-three, one year.'

Sophie started to look very stern. 'Possibly. And rather rough and ready I expect a 21st-century audience would find them. My policy at Kicking is to create one *substantial* and *significant* highly *polished* production per year.'

We were on the verge of an argument. *You fucking idiot, Ham*, I thought. 'Really good policy, like,' I said.

'So Ham. What have you been doing lately?'

'Writing, mostly.'

'Oh yes? Anything that might be suitable for us?'

'I sent you one a couple of months ago.'

'Ah. I do have two first-rate script vets in the new writing team. Possibly they haven't got to yours, yet. What I'm looking for is topical, hard-hitting stuff, not necessarily regional. I want to get away from that.'

I wasn't quite so stupid as to pursue the first script – which one of the script vets had probably already put out of its misery. 'I'm working on something about Afghanistan,' I said. 'Done a lot of research in the Afghan community.'

'Well! That sounds very promising. Do send that one in, won't you?' Now, to business. I am very embarrassed to say I have never seen your work, but you come highly recommended.' I must have looked puzzled because she added, 'By Sam… Who I am delighted to say has agreed to do the show. Northern Arts wanted us to do our bit to mark the anniversary of Cuff's death and Sam suggested *The Blaydon Races*.

A vehicle for Sam. That explained it. Still, what did I care? I wanted a part.

'So what are you going to do for me, Ham?'

Then it hit me. 'Is Sam playing Harry?' She looked puzzled. 'The husband?'

'Yes.'

Shit. 'More the right age for it now.'

'I think that's what attracted him to the piece.'

If Sam was playing Harry, I couldn't see where my part was coming from. I racked my brains. The recruiting officer? But that was only such a small part. 'I did Morris, you know, in the original.'

'Yes.'

'Bit old for him now.'

She laughed. 'I don't think even you, youthful-looking as you are, would *quite* get away with nineteen.'

'Well, I've prepared a bit of Harry. So I'll stick with it, I think.'

'When you're ready.'

I'd learned Harry's soliloquy. It's about how he loves his

young wife and thinks she's going to leave him, about wanting the war to come and take the competition away, or take himself away. I did it pretty well. Sophie nodded and smiled a lot.

'Thank you so much for that, Ham. A real privilege. I'll be in touch.'

The inflated being who'd entered that space was no more. I knew for certain there wouldn't be a part for me. Sophie had taken a huge pin and stabbed the balloon I'd floated about in so happily for the last two weeks. My shrivelled little self would have found it difficult to get out of that room if it hadn't been for one thing, one hope, left. I looked Sophie in the eye. 'You're seeing Jane – next? Brilliant actor, she is.'

'So I understand. Lovely to have met you. Susie will show you out.'

IV. 6

When I first started acting, politics came into things much more. A lot of directors had causes, left-wing causes, not quite so extreme as the Scally Roos – who were much too radical to believe in directors – but going that way. The few women running companies I met, unsurprisingly, were strong feminists. They didn't look anything like Sophie and terrified in a completely different way.

I've often asked myself what makes people want to direct and I reckon sex is a big driver. Many directors, male and female, are what you'd call predators. The job allows you to box well above your weight in terms of who's willing to strip off and get into the ring with you, and good-looking actors will go a bout or two with downright bus-ugly directors in the cause of a decent part.

Spiders, some of these directors are. Dressed in black, with long legs and arms, lurking silently at the back of the stalls before pouncing, tying the inexperienced into knots and unwinding them slowly only when they tearfully acknowledge they know *nothing at all* and open themselves to be totally *re-made* by the director. Re-made in all ways, that is, including in bed.

Other directors wouldn't dream of screwing actors. 'Did it once, Ham,' Greg had confided. 'Completely fucked up the play.' By which I think he meant having an awkwardly intimate relationship with one of the actors got in the way of communicating his vision of things to the audience, which, however small, however regional and however working class, to him represented the world. His productions were fragile things with very short lives, but, like butterflies, beat glorious wings. I think up to *The Blaydon Races* that was all Greg needed; not success on the big stage, but that tremulous flutter of beauty, a tiny piece of perfection.

In Britain, there's a short cut to success in theatre via the posh universities. People get to direct at the national companies never having humped scenery or played to a non-middle-class audience. You get some funny situations when very serious young directors, fresh out of Oxford or Cambridge, come up against hardened troupers. I did a play at the Royal Court once with a very well known old *actress* – which was what she'd insist on being called – who was famous for playing loveable old dears. The young director went to great lengths to explain to her what her character's *objective* should be in the scene and what particular *actions* in that scene combined to achieve her character's *superobjective* in the play. 'Remember,' he said, 'one sentence, one breath, one action…' After a while she leaned forward and patted him on the shoulder, 'Scuse me dear, but I think you've mistaken me for one of those actresses who gives a fuck.'

I don't know where Sophie fits in to my index of directors. A new category, I thought, as I walked slowly back through the theatre.

A middle-aged woman sat in the foyer, talking to the box office girl, cupping her chin in her hand in that particular, unforgettable way I found I'd forgotten. She turned her face slowly towards me and our eyes met. Jane. Everything went slow motion for a moment. The girl swivelled her head from Jane, to me, to Jane. Then normal speed resumed. We kissed cheeks.

'You haven't changed a bit,' Jane said, as we both clocked the changes in each other. No sour lines, but wrinkles, quite a lot of wrinkles – the sort you get that emphasise a basically good nature; not fat, but heavier; hair still unruly, streaked with grey. Susie called her in. 'I'll wait for you here,' I said. Forgetful, still, because she had to come back for the script and handbag she'd left on a chair.

'Silly of me…' Bending to pick it up, she blushed, and for a moment she *did* look the same.

Amazing, I thought after she'd gone, how the moment of seeing Jane again, imagined so many times in my head, had passed off so quietly. But now, she was actually here. So bloody what about the part, I thought, I'd got Jane for a whole evening, and like a child knowing there's a treat coming his way, I started chatting happily to the girl on the desk. Ticket sales for the cabaret were a bit slow, she told me. 'Get's tedious sitting here all day.' I tried to tell her how cold it had been in the seventies, when this was not much more than a draughty warehouse with no heating at all, whereas now… She looked really bored.

The sound of a door swinging open, a shout of greeting and a small wiry man, wearing a tweed cap, drainpipe jeans and Doc Martens arrived. Stafford. We hugged, slapping each other on the back, laughing.

'Jane's here too.'

'She never is! What the fuck's going on?'

'Search me.' I told him. 'All I know is Sam's doing it.'

'Is he?'

I left it to Stafford to work out what that bit of news meant in terms of casting to us hopeful fifty-somethings. He rolled a cigarette before noticing the signs and putting it back in his tobacco tin.

'You've had that tin a while.'

'Good tin. Changed a bit down here, eh?' He leaned forward and murmured, 'Full of young lasses running around with bottles of water.' He grinned, showing stained teeth, perfect for the kind of parts Stafford usually gets. I asked him about work.

'Doing all right. Film coming up in March or April. You?'

'Nothing much. Writing a bit these days.'

'Might be something in this film, like. Mining story. I'll put your name forward.'

'Great. How's the family?' Stafford had married in his forties and there were now three kids; two sons, Lester and Frankie, and then a girl to spoil the racing theme, Juliet instead of Jonjo. Stafford chatted on about their various doings until Jane returned, followed by Susie, now carrying a small blue plastic bottle. Stafford winked and I burst out laughing.

'What's the joke?' Jane asked, looking from one to the other. We were all quite pink with the delight of being together.

'Tell you later,' Stafford called, following Susie into the theatre. 'Mine's a pint of Stella.'

'We may as well wait for him,' Jane said, and I wondered if she felt reluctant to be alone with me. As it happened, the girl in the box office only kept us company for a few minutes more before she pulled down the shutters and left, explaining she had to get ready as the staff were having a bit of a party in the bar after the auditions, sort of their Christmas 'do', like. There was a silence.

'Sophie seemed nice.' Jane said.

'Did she ask you about the play?'

'Asked me who was in love! Bit of a funny question.'

'What did you say?'

Jane picked up a publicity leaflet. Studied it. 'I said I didn't know.'

'How did the audition go?'

'Okay, I think. She looked up. 'I'd love to do it. What about yours?'

'There won't be anything. Sam's got the only part I could play.'

'Sam?'

'I think that's who this is all about.' I explained.

'Couldn't you do…' Jane faltered. I remembered how she hated anyone to feel rejected; '…the army man, remember, when they go down to join the Durham Light Infantry.'

'He's all there is and *I* wouldn't cast me. It's not big enough to justify another actor.'

'Maybe they're rolling in money.'

'Maybe. Rolling in money for foreign trips, new writing *teams*, administration *teams,* fucking script vets, marketing *teams*, posh carpets, bottles of water. Look around you at the posters. All those plays *we* did, the few they've done since. Makes me—'

'I know. I know… It's kind of lost its purpose, hasn't it? I always liked its noble purpose. Makes me feel really old and sad.'

'Makes *me* feel angry! Who'd come here to see plays? Who'd feel comfortable here? Just the middle classes! And it'll be even worse when they do the redevelopment. They don't even want to *tour* any more. Did you read that? I tell you all that's left of our ideals is a pile of clippie mats the actors use in their fucking warm-ups! Did you see that girl? No shoes! Since when have theatres been the sort of *sterilised* places you can walk around in barefoot? Theatres should be dirty, a bit dangerous and come to that they should put on a few plays! All that crap and no product, no fucking *plays*. They don't even do their own Christmas show!'

Just then Stafford arrived back, face dark. 'I need a drink. Come on.'

Leaving, we passed a young TV soap actor on his way in. He nodded at us. 'All right?' he said. He definitely had a bit of a spring in his step. As soon as I saw him I knew he'd been lined up for Morris.

Stafford breathed in a blast of icy air and spat out, 'I tell you what, fucking Wankin Theater Kunts is the right name for that lot. Halfway through, it clicks. So I says, "Hang about then, Sophie Pet, if Sam's playing Harry, what the fuck am I doing here? What have you got me down here wasting me time for? Learning fucking lines for nowt? I passed up a nice afternoon's badger-digging to come here." Her mouth drops open, like. I don't think many people talk back to her. Came as a bit of a shock.'

Jane said, 'You don't really dig up badgers, do you?'

'Course not. What do you take me for? But theatre, fuck me, I'm sticking to films from now on. The cheek of it!' He fixed me with a look 'You knew the score before I went in, didn't you?'

'I realised when I was in there. Wish I'd said what you did.'

'Thing still puzzles me is why did she ask us to come. What's going on?'

Jane said, 'Maybe Sam asked her to see us.'

'What? Just so's we could be rejected? He's not *that* much of a bastard.'

I said, 'Maybe she doesn't understand the play. She can't ask Sam without looking an idiot, can she? Cuff's not here to answer her questions.'

Jane said, 'Nor Greg, come to that.'

Stafford thrust his hands deeper in his pockets. 'That young lad. *Coronation Street* isn't it?'

'That's him,' I said. He'll get that part, *my* old part, even though he's not much good.'

'Not much good? Thirty-two carat shite, I'd say.'

'Doesn't need to be good though, does he? They just cast people to play themselves, these days. Got rid of us proper actors years ago.'

'Look – will you two stop whingeing, *please*.' Jane's voice rose to a squeak. 'The good thing is that we're together after all these years and I want to enjoy it. Don't you?'

We'd arrived at what used to be our pub, a place where, over many years, Stafford, Jane and I had laughed, gossiped, argued and got extremely drunk. It had gone through several incarnations over the years and its exterior could barely be recognised as the rough sawdust-on-the-floor boozer we'd known back then. *Advocates Wine Bar & Brasserie*. 'Shit,' Stafford said, 'Shall we go somewhere else?'

Jane shivered. 'Make up your mind. I'm freezing.'

I didn't like the look of the place, but something other than the cold was bothering me, or rather some*one*, and I wanted to get inside. The river running just a few yards away, the weather, and the time of year, all made me think of Matt. 'Let's give it a try.'

'It'll be crap. Nothing like the old days.'

But I reckon there's something in buildings that survives change, as though the old bricks under the new décor, or perhaps even the rocks and soil beneath the floor, bear the impress of all those who, at one time or another, have rested and taken refreshment. One day, they'll probably download the images and unscramble the million murmured conversations etched into the stones. We'll see jolly girls with holes in their stockings and sideburned, stovepipe-hatted shipowners. There'll be hungry-looking clerks, sailors bound for the Bosphorus, and, far, far back, colours fading, outlines blurring, perhaps we'll catch a glimpse of a battle-scarred Viking, or even a lonesome Roman…

LIGHTS UP ON *ADVOCATES WINE BAR AND BRASSERIE*. POLISHED WOODEN BOARDS, GLEAMING BRASS FITTINGS AND CHAPS IN LONG WHITE APRONS, FRENCH STYLE. AROUND A TABLE ON A RAISED AREA TO THE RIGHT SIT A GROUP OF SMART YOUNG MEN APPARENTLY ENJOYING A CHRISTMAS PARTY. THE DOOR OPENS. ENTER THREE POOR PLAYERS, *HAM* FIRST, FOLLOWED BY *STAFFORD* AND *JANE*. THEY LOOK AROUND WITH INTEREST.

WALL   *(stage whisper)* Welcome home.

Act V: Deus ex Machina

V. 1

VOICE OF CHORUS   Become a god. Part the heavy curtain
of grey sky and peer down on
Newcastle, early in the afternoon of
this dull December day in the year two
thousand and six. Observe, as you
descend, lightly treading air, the
curious way the town tumbles down
the bank to the river. See the streets
crowded with shoppers, humming
with traffic and musical trash, bright
with Christmas lights. There. You've
landed.

GROAN OF TRAFFIC, HUM OF VOICES. WHAM SING 'LAST
CHRISTMAS I GAVE YOU MY HEART'... A QUEUE OF WOMEN AT A
BUS STOP SHUFFLE FORWARD, CARRYING BAGS OF CHRISTMAS
SHOPPING.

DIONYSUS   I'd forgotten the cold. *(he looks around
him)* It's wall-to-wall women down
here! Wonderful! *(the queue moves
forward)* Hello, beautiful one. *(the
woman does not respond. He waves a*

hand in front of her face) She's in some kind of trance! *(Dionysus goes down the queue to other women, sliding his hands over their bodies. None responds)* They all are! *(the women, clutching their bags of shopping, faces set, turn to front, each raising one hand they clasp an imaginary strap and sway to left and then to the right. Dionysus moves among them whispering)* They're ripe for me, I can tell. They'll sense me in a minute...

CHORUS   The great Dionysus, on a bus! It has its funny side.

EXHAUSTED HISS OF BUS STOPPING. THE WOMEN EXIT HURRIEDLY, LEAVING DIONYSUS ALONE ON STAGE FOR A MOMENT.

DIONYSUS   Some great lust consumes them. *(he takes out a gold-edged white handkerchief and dabs at his eyes)* Rather unsettling. Gods are not immune you know. We experience feelings of rejection too... *(sniffs)* But I smell beer... wine... What? Later, you say? The bridge? Oh very well. EXIT. *(in cloud of dry ice)*

CHORUS   And he takes to the air again, flying over the city towards the Tyne Bridge. It is the last working day before

290

Christmas. Beneath him as he flies some of the god's worshippers are already drinking at his fountain in the Bigg Market and barmen are busy restocking their shelves, polishing glasses and phoning security in expectation of a Big Night.

VOICE OF DIONYSUS
FROM ABOVE This sense of savagery to come – it's so enticing!

CHORUS Watch him! Wheee! There he goes, skimming the roofs of Grey Street's elegant restaurants, where waiters slide tables together, fold napkins into fantastic shapes, lay up bright silver for banquets. Now picture the god on the arch of the Tyne Bridge, beneath him the great empty river, once carrier of the trade of nations. Beside its banks, high buildings turn glassy eyes towards the Tyne, blind to its beauty, its power to lure and destroy.

VOICE OF DIONYSUS Brings it all back. A lovely view, I always thought. But I can't see a single crane! How is this all going to work, if I may ask?

CHORUS He's right, of course. There are no more ships – and no more *building* of ships in the Tyne. These days, the business of the quayside is *law*. And

                          law, today, is also the business of the
                          god.
VOICE OF DIONYSUS Look, now where? Hurry up. I'm not
                          dressed for this.

DEAN WHITAKER, ALONE IN THE LARGE OFFICE, SQUINTING
INTO HIS COMPUTER SCREEN. HE PRESSES *PRINT* AND THE
PRINTER IN THE CORNER OF THE ROOM COMES TO LIFE AND
STARTS TO SPIT PAPER. DIONYSUS ENTERS THROUGH THE
WINDOW, HUGGING HIMSELF, BLOWING ON FROZEN FINGERS.
HE GOES OVER TO THE PRINTER AND PICKS UP A SHEET.

DIONYSUS   Ah! The device!

HE WATCHES AS DEAN STAPLES THREE SETS OF PAPERS AND
TRANSFERS THEM TO HIS BRIEFCASE. YAWNING, DEAN SHUTS
DOWN THE COMPUTER AND SHRUGS ON A CRUMPLED COAT.

CHORUS   Now follow, as into dwindling daylight
                          our Dean plods. He steps off the
                          pavement, and, narrowly avoiding
                          being run down by a judge heading
                          home in a silver Mercedes, crosses to
                          the bright corner of the quayside
                          presently occupied by *Advocates Wine
                          Bar and Brasserie*. Before the door
                          Dean hesitates.

LIGHTS UP ON THE INTERIOR OF *ADVOCATES* WHERE, AROUND A
LARGE TABLE, LOPSIDED PAPER HATS ON THEIR HEADS, DEAN'S

                              292

COLLEAGUES SIT, IN VARIOUS STATES OF ANIMATED OR SOMNOLENT
DRUNKENNESS, NOW NEARING THE END OF A LONG CHRISTMAS
LUNCH. DEAN PUSHES THE DOOR OPEN AND ENTERS, FOLLOWED
BY DIONYSUS. THE MANAGER HURRIES TOWARDS THE DOOR.

MANAGER	Can't you see the sign? Private function till six this evening.
DEAN	Oh I'm sorry but actually er…I'm with them. The party I mean.
DIONYSUS	*(glaring at the manager – to whom he is invisible)* Officious slave!
CHORUS	They're finishing their feast, the fifteen or so young lawyers seated at a huge round table, with liqueurs and arguments. In their bellies bob pink slices of filet de boeuf; figgy pudding slowly sinks.
DIONYSUS	*(following Dean to the raucous table)* But this is delightful! I could be in Rome! The end of a feast!

DEAN LOITERS FOR A MOMENT IN SHADOW, UNSEEN BY THE
REST, THEN HE STEPS FORWARD.

DEAN	Hi everyone.
ALASTAIR	Witterer! At last! You're bloody late, you poor bastard. That Sophie's had you by the short and curlies hasn't she? Sit down here. Got rid of the females an hour ago. And the old man's gone,

293

	too, thank fuck. Have a mint. Can't
	stand the things myself. *(Dean sits,*
	unwraps a mint. Dionysus, in shadow,
	stands behind his chair)
DIONYSUS	*(whispers)* Come on! Come on!

THE DOOR OPENS AGAIN. HAM'S FACE PEERS IN. THE MANAGER
BUSTLES OVER.

MANAGER	Can't you read?
DIONYSUS	*In* we go!

DEAN'S CURLY HEAD SNAPS BACK. HE INHALES A HUGE BREATH
AND HIS EYES FLY OPEN, LIPS STRETCH INTO A WICKED GRIN.
STANDING UP, HE BRINGS THE PALM OF HIS RIGHT HAND SO
HARD DOWN ON THE TABLE EVERYONE STOPS TALKING AND
STARES.

DEAN / DIONYSUS	My friends! Come on! You, Slave! Yes,
	I'm talking to *you*, permit my guests to
	enter and get us some more of this! *(he*
	waves a bottle of champagne) Now! Quick
	sharp! *(Ham, Jane and Stafford advance*
	uncertainly) Welcome! Welcome!
ALASTAIR	I say, Witterer, what's got into... *(he*
	looks at Dean for a moment) Good idea.
	Liven up the party.
DEAN	*(swooping to take Jane's hand and kiss it)*
	Let me guess. You are a daughter of
	Thespis?

JANE	*(charmed)* Well, yes. How did you know?
DEAN	I read it in your beautiful eyes.
HAM	Look. It's very kind of you and all that but this isn't the sort of evening we had in mind.
STAFFORD	Just what I was thinking. Come on Jane.
DEAN	*(resting his arms about Ham and Stafford's shoulders)* Oh no. Please stay! You must! We have so much in common – lawyers and actors. Deliverers of lines, persuaders, performers, stirrers of emotions… Am I not right, fellow justicers? And yes! Now I have it! A competition! A battle of rhetoric! Barristers against thespians. Some Euripides – or better still, some Sophocles! *(Dean claps his hands)* Chairs for our guests please! BLACKOUT.

I'll blame the champagne for getting sucked in to the game; Dean's, the mad lawyer's competition, that is. Perhaps I also needed to assert myself – as an actor, like – in the face of my most recent rejection, and Jane's little squeeze of my hand as she volunteered me, 'Ham's very good at Shakespeare', must have had something to do with it, too.

The other big-mouth barrister there, name of Alastair, offered to do *Hamlet*. 'I was bloody good at school, you know. Did a bit at Oxford, too.'

So he stands on the table and gives it the old 'To be or not to be'. Crucified it. Not that it stopped all his mates cheering and banging their cutlery on the table.

'Crap,' I said, when the noise died down. Stafford gave me a look. Enjoying the champagne, I suppose. 'Complete and utter shite.'

'Wonderful!' says the mad one. 'Discord!'

'Who the bloody hell are you calling crap?' Alastair thrusts his big red face at me.

'That's not Hamlet. Doesn't show you his state of mind at all. Just *words* in a posh accent. Like you were in court.'

'I suppose you want to mangle the verse with your appalling Geordie?'

'Think I'll deliver the lines as they were spoken in Shakespeare's time. That be all right for yous? Give us that carving knife would you?' And up on the table I go, to do my second *Harry* soliloquy in one day. Harry V, this time. I made a few thrusts and parries in the air. I love stage fighting. 'How about some Henry V.'

'What, *you?*' sneers Alastair. The other lawyers shout derision; cheers and whistles from Stafford and Jane. Stafford always had one hell of a whistle.

I kick myself a space out of the ruins of the feast. 'I am *the king*. And I address *you*, my soldiers, in the midst of battle, surrounded by the bodies of our comrades, our boots slipping in their blood, the great walls of Harfleur in front of us, walls in which hours of fighting have succeeded in making only one small opening. Once more I urge you forward.'

'Get on with it, then, you big girl's blouse.'

'Silence!' shouts mad Dean.

I remember to get the *mores* out from the back of my throat, make war into *wahrr!* tiger into *tigger*... 'Once more unto the breach, dear friends, once more...'

Alastair booms, 'Ooh arr moi luvver, if I don't be Jethro—' but I touch his throat with my sword and he sits back in his chair sharpish:

'But when the blast of wahrr! blows in our ears,

'Then imitate the action of the tigger;

'Stiffen the sinews, summon up the blood...'

It's nearly a full rhyme at the end, *charge* and *George,* and you only get it if you stay west of Weymouth. I raise my sword over my head and leap forward among the crockery.

'The game's afoot;

'Follow your spirit; and upon this charge,

'Cry – God for Harry! England and St Jarge!'

A burst of clapping. 'St Jarge!' they shout. I sit down. Jane pats me on the back. 'That showed them.'

'Grrrrr! I love it,' shouts mad Dean. 'I declare the thespians to be the winners! All rise please.' He filled his glass and sent another bottle round, 'To actors!'

This started a round of toasts, 'The bard!'

'Sophocles!' A clash of glasses. 'Euripides!'

'Look, Witterer,' Alastair says, 'you're boxing above your weight, old boy. Don't tell me you studied Greek at the Comp?'

I don't hear Dean say a thing in reply. He just puts his hand on Alastair's shoulder and I swear you can hear the hiss of escaping air as Alastair deflates, withers, fat jowls quivering, then slumps in his chair, silenced. As, for a moment, are the rest of us. 'No stamina, Alastair. That's his trouble,' says Dean, holding out his glass for more champagne.

Dean and Stafford seem to be getting on like a house on fire, Stafford confiding, 'All that health and safety bollocks, couldn't get away with it now, you know. Every blade has to be blunt as fuck…'

Jane breathes into my ear, 'I came to see you play Rosencrantz.'

'Did you? Why didn't you come backstage?'

'And you can't even light a candle without getting the fire brigade in to approve it first.'

'I don't know. Didn't like to, I suppose. But I felt so proud of you.'

'And as for heights, you have to use all sorts of straps and stuff…'

'Ah! It's height I need. To stage an event tonight. I need to descend from a great height…'

Stafford laughs. 'Well, as far as jumping goes, your best bet's the Tyne Bridge.' Then he stops, looks at us, realising what he's said.

'You want to keep away from Tyne Bridge after a few drinks,' I say.

'Actually what I'm after would be more of a crane.'

'You'll be lucky,' Stafford snorts. 'They all went years ago.'

'Or a machine of some kind—'

Stafford laughs again. 'You're fucking cracked you are.'

The danger seems over. There's no more talk of the Tyne Bridge, anyway. The flow of champagne slows to a trickle and the question 'What now?' becomes uppermost in people's minds. Dean says he has something to deliver to Sophie at Kicking Theatre – and Stafford remembers the 'Parteeee!' going on there right then.

And we stampede.

298

V. 2

Kicking's Christmas do turned out to involve Sophie and her team partaking of wine and canapés in the company of favoured Young Soap and a few other people I didn't know. All eyes turned to us as we came to a skidding halt just inside the bar and for a moment stood in a bunch, rolling our eyes and snorting, like a herd of bullocks confronted by an electric fence.

Sophie advanced a little uncertainly. 'Dean,' she said holding out a hand, 'You've brought my report?'

Dean held the briefcase aloft and drummed on its leather with his fingers. 'Your report. Yes. It's in here. But first a little wine, perhaps? For my colleagues…and my friends… I believe you are already acquainted.'

Sophie glanced at Stafford, Jane and me and managed a bewildered smile. Her eyes returned to Dean. 'Yes. Of course. Help yourselves, all of you.'

I was more than happy to have a drink on Kicking while taking Jane for a nostalgic tour of the old posters lining the corridor to the gents, and didn't notice Stafford and Dean disappearing upstairs. First I knew of anything was hearing Stafford's yell of 'Everybody outside!'

We joined the crowd following Stafford out of the door. 'Look. What on earth…' But Sophie was swept along with the rest and a few moments later we were all in the street, hugging ourselves against the cold and staring up at a square of light on the top floor, into which stepped the slight figure of Dean Whitaker.

My heart flipped.

'Mad fucker,' breathed Stafford admiringly. 'I told him that rope might not hold, but he's determined.'

'Ooh! I can't look!' squealed a nymph. 'He's so brave!'

Dean waved a sheaf of papers and then thrust them down the front of his trousers.

'Don't!' I screamed. Dean leapt, his legs bicycling in the air… I shut my eyes and prayed.

The rope held. Dean abseiled expertly down the brick walls in gigantic hops. He landed, whisked two documents from his trousers and bowing, presented one to Sophie. Then he turned to Stafford. 'This is for you. Now, girls,' he said, 'time for some fun!' He offered one arm to a bewildered Sophie and the other to a gushing water nymph, and they set off up the hill towards the town centre.

Very soon, it seemed, only the silent three of us remained in the street. After a bit Jane said, 'Did that really happen?'

Stafford nodded slowly. 'Takes me back… Fancy the hoist still being there after all these years…'

'Original feature, so they had to keep it,' I said. 'Shame it doesn't apply to us.'

Young Soap moved out of the shadow of the building. 'Raving nutcases round here.' He handed me a glass. 'Take that back inside for me would you?' He set off at a run.

'Very good looking, wasn't he?' Jane breathed.

'Who, him?'

'No! *Dean*, I mean.'

'Definitely gay,' I said. A huge sense of relief and wellbeing washed over me. Danger had been averted. No one had died and the night was yet young. 'You hungry, Stafford?' I said.

Why don't you come back with me and Jane for some steak and kidney pud?'

'All right then, I will.'

'What were those papers he gave you?' Jane asked as we started walking.

Stafford held the document up under a streetlight. *The Way Forward: A Report on the Assets of Kicking Theatre Company.*

'Riveting reading,' Stafford said.

The steak and kidney was a great success, and while we ate I rooted in my trunk for old programmes and photos. One I'd taken at Cuff's place. Him, Greg and Jenny. Stafford laughed. 'I was thinking about that when I was learning the lines. Jenny certainly had the hots for Greg. Remember the night of the Feast?'

Jane started looking in her handbag for something. She probably didn't remember it like I did. Out loud I said, 'Anybody hear anything of Greg?'

'Saw him about five years ago,' Stafford said, 'In an airport. Said he wasn't doing theatre any more. Wouldn't tell me what he *was* into, like.'

'Maybe back to his old ways?'

'That's what I thought.'

There was a photo of Stafford and Nic sitting on the terrace at no. 12, Nic in shorts, her lovely long brown legs stretched out, one hand shading her eyes. Jane said, 'Oh I'd *love* to see Nic. Do you know where she is?'

'Still snake dancin' for all I know.' He paused and then went on, his voice a touch unsteady, 'That fucking snake. Preferred him to me.'

'What?'

'Did I never tell you? When she finally left, like, or rather just before. We were staying the night at me father's. Ate Nipper.'

'Nipper?'

'Me dad's Jack Russell. Poor thing was dead old, slept all day in his basket. Nic's snake ate him. I told her it was him or me after that. She chose him.'

Jane and I looked at Stafford, who was staring down at his empty plate, blinking. Jane patted him on the shoulder. 'Tell you what you need.'

'What?'

'Bit more of Ham's snake and pigmy pudding.'

Soon after that, Stafford got a call on his mobile from his wife, wondering where he'd got to, and he went, promising to be in touch about the film and saying we must meet up again soon. That left me and Jane sitting on the saggy sofa. I looked at her. She laughed and rolled her eyes, but there was no stopping me. 'I've dreamed about this.'

'Ha-am.'

'Never loved anyone as much I as loved you.'

She squeezed my hand. 'Sweet. Long time since anyone said something like that to me.'

'But what did *you* feel?'

'I don't know. I sort of loved you, but I was so screwed up. Took me years to stop being a doormat. You started that process, you know, so I finally had the courage to leave Gerry. I've always been really grateful to you for that—'

'Glad I had some uses.'

She laughed. 'I didn't mean it like that.'

'So who *was* in love then, during the play?'

'All right. *We* were. And then – you know what happened.'

'Matt died.'

'Yes.' She got up and started collecting the dirty plates. 'Let's get this cleared up. I must get the nine-thirty train.'

I walked her through the streets to the station, the town no longer a beautiful blur but headachingly bright and filled with litter and drunken kids. I hadn't got the part and Jane was about to slip away again, but I felt strangely peaceful, holding her hand. Maybe it was because she'd admitted she'd loved me once, so it was a sad kind of happiness, but happiness all the same. Waiting on the platform, our hands still joined, I said, 'Tell me when you felt you really loved me.'

For a moment I thought she wouldn't answer me, or she'd say 'Ha-am!' again, but she took a breath. 'When I saw you on stage doing Rosencrantz I ached with love for you. You were so brilliant, all those little bits of business so right—'

'But you never came to find me.'

'It was all over. It didn't feel right. We weren't…equal…any more. My best time had come and gone, with Kicking.'

'I see that as my best time, too.'

She looked at me. 'Do you?'

We walked on down the platform. 'What do you remember most, about us I mean?'

She took a breath. 'I remember being on stage together, near the end of *The Blaydon Races* and the spot on you, talking about joining up, leaving me and going to war and then the lights widen and the audience can see I'm sitting there on the bed, listening.' Jane had tears in her eyes. She squeezed my

303

hand. 'We were so bloody *good* together.' I knew at once she was right. We had our closest, most intense moments on stage. She looked at me, her head on one side, 'This sounds stupid, but I think I'm better at being other people than I am at being myself. I've always thought we were the same species that way.'

It came as a bit of a jolt, but I knew she was right about that, too. Like in the old days, being with Jane made everything clearer, as though in her company I breathed different stuff, a pocket of pure mountain air.

The train appeared in the distance. 'I miss what we had so much,' she said.

Of course she meant acting with me, being in theatre with me, not loving me. I understood. Completely. The train came in and I gave her a hug, breathed her apple smell, her hair crisp on my cheek. 'Maybe you'll get lucky. There is still a part for *you*, after all.'

She got into a carriage and pulled down the window.

'It was lovely, Ham.'

I blew her a kiss. 'I'll see you *soon*.'

What a day, I thought, walking home. Felt more like a week had passed. And at the end of it, nothing was like I'd hoped, but oddly, I felt great. I even decided to look down on the Tyne from the bridge for the first time in a quarter of a century.

I gazed down at the water. At least I'd *had* a career, unlike poor Matt. I wanted to talk to someone, to tell someone about my day, talk about Jane, about Matt, and it came to me with a sort of shock that the person whose voice I most wanted to hear was Najib. Strangely, Najib and I had become friends.

Getting pissed off with him for knowing more than me was completely missing the point. I'd learned a huge amount. He'd opened my mind to all sorts of things. I started walking, speeding up as I realised I would probably still catch him at the shop, and could give him the good news that I'd be working for him for the foreseeable future, maybe suggest he crack open a bottle of cooking brandy to celebrate.

When the wailing engine passed me I didn't give it a thought, not until I turned into the street and saw it. The shop. On fire.

V. 3

As Christmases go, it's been one of the worst. Worse even, perhaps, than the one after Matt died. Pity me in Pity Me, no, hang on, they'd moved by then – in Hetton-le-Hole, Christmas 1978, partaking of the joys of the season with my brother Joe, his kids and Frances. There I am, see? Helpfully getting stuck into the annual Lego impossibility with my two young nephews, thinking dark, regretful, miserable thoughts about Jane and Matt, and listening to Frances going on:

'I was saying to Joe, wasn't I Joe? Wasn't I saying? He doesn't look much like an actor, your Ham…'

Over the many years I've spent Christmas with Joe, Frances has enjoyed my failure marginally more than my success. 'I said to him, your Joe, "He'll be thinking himself too posh for the likes of us, you mark my words…"'

When night finally fell on Christmas Day, 1978, I remember lying on the put-you-up in their front room, the lights on the tree blinking on and off because 'it looks so cheerful from the outside so Ham'll not mind leaving them on', thinking about Jane and what she and Gerry were doing at his parents' house in Alderley Edge.

I phoned Stafford the next morning. 'I was just going to call you,' he said, 'Cuff's in hospital. Thought he had 'flu, but it turned out to be his heart.'

'What? Is he okay?'

'Not too good, apparently.'

He drove over to pick me up. When we arrived at no. 12

306

Hardley was settling down to *The Great Escape* with a huge tray of food on his lap. He offered us a couple of his turkey and sausage sandwiches and munched away gloomily as Steve McQueen rode his Norton up and down the wire. The phone rang. Greg thundered down the stairs to take the call. 'Lower the fucking volume!'

Steve silently revved his bike for the leap as Greg murmured for a few moments into the receiver and then slowly set it back with a little clunk.

'Cuff's dead,' he said. Everything stilled. Hardley turned off the television. Greg pressed the heels of his hands to his temples, his face contorted. 'I'm going out.' The back door slammed.

History repeating itself, you could say. Twenty-five-plus years on I'm at my brother Joe's on Boxing Day.

'I was saying to Joe, that Sam, he's done well, hasn't he, out of acting? It's been a while for you, like. Do you still call yourself an actor? I mean, after so long?' I look at Joe, who never defends me, just waits for the chance for us to escape on some errand and grab an hour or so's drinking. Joe's Christmas treat.

I say, 'Why do you keep going on about acting, Frances? I'm not an actor any more, am I? I work in a shop.'

'I didn't think there was anything left of that shop.'

She never fights fair. Joe gets to his feet. 'I'll just gan down the Spar, shall I? I think we need some milk. Come on, Ham, you keep me company.'

Your fucking wife. What a fucking bitch. Ask me why I've never got married Joe, go on, ask me! That's what I want to say, but

307

stumping down the road, our hands deep in our pockets, collars up against the north wind, he says, 'Take no notice of Frances,' and looks at me with his sad eyes, watery not from the wind, but from all the blows she's rained down on him over the years. So I say nothing. 'Tell me what happened,' he says.

Egg and Chips filled a bottle with petrol, jammed a pair of Fat Sue's tights in its neck, applied a match and threw. It was just on ten; the grilles were down, the shop secured at the back; only the front door remained open. The Christmas tree I'd just decorated was the first thing to go up in flames.

By the time it arrived on the front page of the *Evening Chronicle*, the bottle had turned into 'a fire bomb'. Egg and Chips also got transformed into Richard Carter (34), unemployed, who was heard to shout, 'This is for you, Billy!' as with one strong flick of his wrist he turned the premises into an 'inferno'.

As far as the paper went, it made a nice, neat story. Egg and Chips had a half-brother called William Denton.

Denton (22) died from his wounds in Helmand Province on Tuesday last. Carter apparently held Mr Najib Khan, the Afghan proprietor of the business, responsible for his half-brother's death.

Newspapers don't go in for the complexities of subplot; if they did, my name should have been mentioned, too, as the unwitting agent of it all, the source who supplied Carter with the information, and thus the motivation, to commit the dreadful act. Come to think of it, the *Chronicle* wouldn't have put it in quite those words. More 'Ham to blame.' 'Ham's Shame.'

When I saw the fire, I hoped for a minute Najib had shut the shop early and gone home, but still I bellowed his name into the flames shooting out where the door used to be. A fireman yelled in my ear, 'Do you think there's someone in there?' and I thought please God, please Allah, don't let him be in there. Then this kid yells, 'There's someone at the back,' and I ran round and in the upstairs room overlooking the backyard you could see through the smoke belching something banging on the glass, then falling away.

They were fast, the firemen, fast as they could be getting a ladder swung across the wall and up to the back room, smashing their way through the glass. They laid Najib on the ground like a great smouldering log while a paramedic gave him mouth-to-mouth. All I could do was stand there staring at his hands. Black and shredded looking, the lower arms raised where the muscles had contracted as they burned.

I'd promised Joe I'd stay until New Year, but on the 28th I told him, 'I've got to go home.'

He nodded. 'I understand. I'll run you back. Maybe we could have another pint on the way?'

The one thing about going to Joe's is that it makes my flat feel almost homely, if only because it's empty of Frances. I even found a bit of mail on the mat to welcome me, but just put it on the table, hardly looking at it, and sat staring into light-polluted city dark. What made it worse was that there was no one to phone to talk about Najib. At least with Matt, with Cuff, there'd been people to share things with.

I got up to look in the fridge and found his last free gift. A

Cornish pasty, 'Still in date, you see!' I left it there and went to bed.

The following morning, I opened my mail. One was franked *Northern Arts*. Long time since they'd been in touch. Perhaps I'd been awarded a bursary after all? I unfolded the slim sheet of paper.

> *Dear Mr Nicolson,*
>
> *As someone who has contributed so much to the development of Kicking Theatre, you will no doubt be delighted to hear the Company's Expansion and Redevelopment Proposal has received Provisional Approval from the Lottery Fund. In preparing the paperwork for the next stage in the process, however, we have discovered a slight legal anomaly that you can help us resolve and thus expedite the company's moving forward at this most exciting time in its development. I would be grateful if you would sign the attached document and return it to me in the pre-paid envelope as soon as possible.*
>
> *Yours sincerely,*
> *James Allen*
> *Projects Officer (Theatre)*
> *Northern Arts*

The other letter, handwritten on very posh Kicking Theatre stationery, came from Sophie.

> *Dear Ham,*
>
> *Just to reiterate what an enormous pleasure and privilege it was to meet you and see your work. I am only sorry that in this particular instance there was nothing I could offer you.*

310

We at Kicking want very much to keep in active touch with our past, and I will have you at the forefront of my mind when casting in future. In the meantime, how is your Afghanistan play going? I greatly look forward to reading it.

Best,

Sophie

Well! As good as a commission, surely? Now I didn't have a job any more it seemed like a miracle. I switched on the computer to see if any more consoling news had arrived by email. During its long and noisy start-up process I looked again at the first letter. Of course I wanted the company to go ahead with its expansion... As far as I could make out, the attached very boring–looking document set out changing a partnership into a charity or something. I nearly got that over with there and then, making use of the helpful crosses that had been inserted, indicating where I needed to sign. Thought I could stick it in the postbox on the way up to Ameena's.

I looked back at the computer. Yes! One from Jane, *three* from Stafford, and three others from addresses I didn't recognise. Jane first.

J.davidson@btinternet.com

Ham,

Have you had a funny letter from Northern Arts? What do you make of it? By the way, I didn't get the part. Took their time in telling me. Had to phone.

Jane x

Arkleneverbettered@tesco.net

*DON'T SIGN A FUCKING THING! HAVE YOU GOT
HARDLEY'S ADDRESS?*
Stafford
WHY'S YOUR MOBILE NEVER ON?

Arkleneverbettered@tesco.net

I've found Hardley. Where's Lynette at these days?
S

Arkleneverbettered@tesco.net

*I've got a lawyer – that one we met in the Wine Bar the
night of those auditions. Name's Dean Whitaker. Meeting
Weds 6pm at my place. YOU'VE ALL GOT TO COME.*
S

V. 4

Six of us made it to the meeting. 'Still can't find Greg or Rod,' Stafford said, ushering Jane and me into his kitchen. 'But I'll track them down, don't you worry.'

Lynette was already there. 'Eeeh Ham! Jane! I don't believe it!' she shrieked, jumping up and giving us both a hug. 'Nice fur coat,' I said.

She twirled around for me. Still childishly slim. 'Do ye think so? Got it off Ebay. Fifteen pound.' A decade in London hadn't done much to change how she sounded, either. The doorbell went again.

Soon, six middle-aged-to-old people sat around Stafford's big pine table, waiting for Dean Whitaker to arrive. It felt a bit like a séance, and Dean did look a bit satanic, striding in, grinning at us all, before settling himself in the big carver chair and beginning. 'This is a bit of fun, isn't it? I *adore* subterfuge.'

'I've got a question, first,' Stafford said. 'Aren't you supposed to be working for Kicking?'

'Well ye-es. On their redevelopment. But in the course of my investigations I found out something I thought would be of great interest to you. That's why we're all here, isn't it?'

'None of us have any money to pay you,' I said.

'Oh I'm aware of that. Think of this by way of payment for your performance in the bistro that night. And don't breathe a word of my involvement. I come with a little advice, that's all.'

Alice fixed him with one of her stares. 'I don't know what this is all about, but some of us have got things to do. Spit it out.'

'I thought you actors enjoyed secrets.' He looked around, hopefully. 'Oh well. Here it is then. The fact that you have been partners in Kicking Theatre Company for almost thirty years, though everyone had forgotten about it, means that you have, at times, been in very vulnerable positions. Had the company run into debts, you would have had to pay them, possibly selling your houses in order to do this. However, that was true only when the assets of the company were worth very little – as in the 1970s, when all you had was a derelict warehouse. They increased in value when the present theatre was built twenty years ago—'

Hardley butted in, 'I raised the funds for that.'

'But during recent years, when the quayside area has taken off as a whole,' Dean paused, leaned forward, and lowered his voice, 'you have become partners in a very valuable piece of real estate.'

We all leaned in, breaths suspended, fingers on an imaginary Ouija board. 'How much?' squeaked Lynette.

'Maybe three million pounds. Redeveloped as planned, four or five.' Dean leaned back, fingers interlocked against his chest, grinning.

Stafford looked around the table. 'But they cannet redevelop it unless we sign over the assets.'

Alice burst out, 'Let's shut down the company and sell it.'

Dean twiddled his pencil. 'You could do that. Though that would be very bloody – and the wrangles and legal battles might take years. No. I want to suggest you refuse to sign over the assets unless you're compensated for the risks that for many years you undertook on behalf of the company.' He got up. 'Must go. Do that, all of you, and see what happens.'

We argued it out after he'd left. Hardley wanted to follow Alice's suggestion – he was very bitter and understandably so. He'd worked for the company for quite a few years longer than the rest of us, carrying on with the thankless task of balancing the books until it was decided his face no longer fitted the new company image. Being older, he'd not been able to find another job and had hardly worked since.

Eventually, though, we decided to follow Dean Whitaker's advice.

The first reaction from Northern Arts was an outraged letter reminding of us of our duties to the company and to arts in the region. We stood our ground. Then an emissary arrived. Sam. Another meeting at Stafford's. A more uneasy gathering round the pine table, the spirit of envy whispering in the ether.

'All right, Ham?'

He looked older. Tired.

'I'm all right, yes.'

He got to the point fast. 'Look. We all owe a lot to Kicking. We'd be nothing without it.'

'Some of us are nothing,' Hardley interrupted.

Sam looked awkward. 'All they want is for you to sign the papers and then they'll be loads of work for everyone with the redevelopment. They've promised that.'

'Crap.' Stafford told him about the 'auditions'. 'There's been no work there for any of us for fucking years.'

Lynette came in, 'And what do you know about it, anyway, Sam? You're always doing telly.'

'Yes!' Alice came in. 'Just because there's nothing in it for *you* – you want to spoil it for the rest of us.'

Sam spread out his hands. 'Look. In memory of the past. You don't want the company to fold, do you?'

That's when I made my little speech. 'It's my memory of the past that makes me want to say fuck 'em,' I told him. 'All that good work we did, all that great writing. Now look what they do! Hold workshops and visit wankers in Germany.'

'Bloody *cabaret*,' Stafford added. 'All those *teams* doing nowt.'

Sam sank lower and lower in his chair. 'No other theatre companies are partnerships.'

I stood up and knocked over the jug of coffee. 'Shakespeare's was,' I shouted. 'There were eight sharers, just like us. Funny that, isn't it? Shared the risks and the profits. Worked for them. Used to work for us.'

Somebody knocked loudly. Stafford went to the door and came back to say Sam's driver had arrived to take him to the airport. Sam went out, then came back in. 'I've told him to wait,' he said. He looked at me. 'I never knew that. About Shakespeare.'

'Well it's true. Looked after people in their old age, that company did. Rather than dump the old actors, like. Leaving them to struggle on. Only the *fortunate* doing all right.'

Sam shouted. 'It's not so fucking fantastic being fortunate, you know!' Then he held up his hand to ward off the tongue-lashing about to come his way from Alice and Lynette. 'Look. I'm *trying* to understand.' A car horn tooted. 'Hang on a minute.' He went outside again.

'Fucker's gone and left!' Alice exploded, looking, with the stained dishcloth in her hand, like some dangerous bloody female from Greek tragedy.

'No he hasn't,' I said from the window. 'He's told his driver to go. He's coming back.'

Stafford made some more coffee while Sam talked and the tension slowly drained. 'I think about those plays a lot. Especially Cuff's. The shite I have to learn these days, you wouldn't believe it. That's why I wanted to do *The Blaydon Races...*'

We all went out drinking. Amazing amount of free booze you get when you're with someone famous. I don't remember much about it except going down the Bigg Market, reprising our tech roles of Romeo and Benvolio with Lynette standing in for Cindy Edwards. I do remember waking up in a posh hotel and having a very good breakfast with Sam. And I remember him making clear he remembered a lot more than it said in his autobiography. And some other clarifications.

'You never did meet Ava Gardner, did you?'

'Saw her.' He burst out laughing. 'Like two hundred yards away. She waved. Pretty sure she waved at me.'

The emissary having failed in his mission – instead having indulged in a drunken roustabout with his fellow rogues and vagabonds – and the region's premier new writing company and all its shiny, lottery-funded redevelopment plans about to go down the swannee, Northern Arts made us an offer.

'Getting there,' whispered Dean Whitaker, in a dark corner of Advocates. 'But not enough. Not nearly enough. Stand firm for Harry, England and St Jarge!'

Finally, we accepted one hundred thousand pounds each. I'll say that again. One hundred thousand pounds. Each. On the proviso we kept it quiet, enabling the august organ of

317

government funding to bury this handout somewhere in the bottom of its accounts.

Stafford's going to buy a steeplechaser. Rod (located at last in Marbella) seems keen on running a bar. I don't know about Greg. In a scribbled airmail letter to Stafford, he asked that it be transferred into an account in Larnaca, Cyprus, giving the number. We couldn't make out the postmark. The others paid off mortgages or just looked forward, like Hardley, to a comfier life. I think Lynette's investing a lot in shoes.

Sam's taken to phoning me every couple of weeks. 'What are you going to do with it?' I knew what I *wanted* to do, but he had plenty of suggestions. 'Get a house, man.' Or 'How about a BMW series 5. Lovely car. Just got one meself.' Or 'enough money there to pay for quality sex the rest of your life.'

Finally, I told him. 'Me and Jane want to set up something in memory of Matt. Theatre group for kids, you know, *lost* kids. Not just acting, but writing, design, lights, computer stuff, the whole lot. There's a problem, though.'

'What?'

'Well, like Jane said, "The funders will hate us for ever now. They'll never help us and what will happen when our money runs out?"'

'Hmm. See her point,' Sam said. 'Good idea, though.'

He sorted it. Set up a charity, the Matthew James Young People's Performance Project, put in a hundred thousand of his own money and guaranteed fifty thousand a year for five years, so long as Northern Arts came up with at least the same in matched funding. And because it's Celebrity Sam, the project's had loads of publicity. Jane and I keep getting sent huge forms to fill in so as we can apply for other funds from all over the shop. Youth and Community, the Gulbenkian Foundation. It's a pretty well full-time job applying for money, never mind using it.

Sam suggested we buy a base but I'm determined not to. The last thing we want is to own a building.

Forget all that stuff about September; I reckon it's time to celebrate renewal where it belongs: in spring. Maybe it was Ameena Khan's swathes of many-coloured tulips that convinced me. She was very busy in her kitchen when I went round last week, cooking to celebrate the Afghan New Year.

'Your garden's a picture,' I said.

She smiled. 'Thank you, Ham.' Ameena's a tall, handsome woman of sixty odd with wonderfully arched black eyebrows. She'd had her hair done for the party and sparkly tights and high-heeled shoes showed underneath her apron. Two of the largest cooking pots I'd ever seen rested on top of the gas cooker.

'How many you feeding?'

'Forty-five I think will be coming. Some from far.'

I hadn't realised that an Afghan community even existed in Newcastle, but after the fire a lot of people appeared to help Ameena.

'It's kind of you to invite me,' I said. 'Can I do anything?'

She folded her arms and looked at me, head on one side, the attitude clearly questioning my ability as a man to be useful in any way whatever, but said finally 'I need many tulips in the room for the party. Could you pick, please?'

A watery April sun felt warm on my back as I bent among the clumps. It made me think about spring and hope and change; how life can be renewed, however old you get. You could say it's a feature of our time, along with climate change and DNA, us fifty-pluses moving on, having adventures. I keep hearing of people retiring and going off to Africa to build schools, or white-water rafting down the Amazon, never mind some women having babies in old age.

Jane says she's had enough of the country, wants to try life in the fast lane of Jesmond or Heaton, and she's suggested I come in with her on a place, 'to get a toehold in the housing market'. So we might live together, after all, just as friends and colleagues, like. I haven't quite made up my mind. On the Project Matt front, we've found a good space to rent dirt cheap – St Cuthbert's Church Hall, the place where we rehearsed *The Blaydon Races* – and we're already operational three nights a week, plus all day Saturday.

The urn's still there. Still works. Even if it didn't, we'd keep it. We're using Sam's money to buy a van, some instruments, rostra and lights. Lights are very important. The grand opening's at the end of this month so I guess that still qualifies as spring. Sam's bringing along some of his telly star mates and I've invited all the old Kicking bunch, including Cuff's widow, Jenny. I ran into her the other day and asked her back for a drink. She looked great; the same round childish face only a little worn, though she must be nearly as old as me and she told me she's got a granddaughter in university. Little Sally's daughter. I couldn't believe it.

Jenny told me it took her ages to get over Cuff dying. 'I felt so guilty, Ham. And it made it worse because Cuff carried on supporting us after he died. I still do all right in royalties. Never had to go out to work.'

320

I told her Cuff would be so happy to know that, which of course he would. Jenny's on her own now, after a couple of relationships, and says she feels really happy. I believe her. Funny thing was, it turned out *The Blaydon Races* would never have gone on, because Sophie had neglected to get Jenny's permission. 'She phoned me, that woman, once they'd cast it. I said "No Way!" I bloody hate that play!' She poured herself another glass of Merlot and refilled mine. 'Makes me into a complete monster!'

We even talked about the Bhagwan Shree Rajneesh's weekend. The Bhagwhan – there was a Dionysus figure for the twentieth century – *Go ye forth, girls, and shag!* 'Make a good radio play,' I told Jenny. She had a laugh at that.

As a matter of fact I've been out with Jenny a couple of times since then. I think she actually *likes* me, you know, in that way. It's very tempting, but the idea of Cuff still gets in the way somehow, even after so long.

There were hundreds of tulips in Ameena's garden. I took a great armful back to the house.

Najib met me in the hallway. 'Ah! My talented assistant!' He looked at the tulips. 'Thank-you, Ham,' he said. 'My bally fingers still do not yet permit such delicate doings. Come and sit down.'

One of Najib's arms had to be amputated just below the elbow. The other is shiny and tight with burn scars, but with tremendous effort, he's managed to get some mobility back into his hand and fingers.

I didn't think Najib would ever get over what happened, but his resilience has amazed me. When I first visited him in

321

intensive care, I cried. He'd reminded me of that later, sitting up in bed looking very much the old self I never thought I'd see again.

'Poo! You looked so down-in-the-mouth,' he'd wheezed. 'The problem with you British is weakness. You have become weak because you have not suffered. What has happened to me now is nothing compared to the torments my family suffered in Herat.'

Now, in the sitting room of their comfortable bungalow, I sat down as ordered. 'Hadn't I better give Ameena the tulips?'

'Wait,' he said, clamping on his spanking new artificial forearm and hand. 'I will perform a magic feat for you.' With little whirrs and clicks, the hand reached out towards my bunch of tulips. It slowly rotated. Najib's face was a study of intense concentration, tongue slightly protruding between his teeth. 'Do not move!'

The hand's index finger and thumb parted, then closed about the stem of a deep purple tulip, slowly lifting it from the bunch. 'My favourite colour,' he said. I gave him a clap.

Then I asked, 'Why do you grow so many tulips?'

'To remind us of home, of course.'

'I thought tulips came from Holland.'

Najib shook his head. 'Ham, you are very ignorant in certain matters. The tulip is the national flower of Afghanistan.'

'Oh.'

'Ignorance is a terrible thing,' he went on, looking at the hand holding the tulip. 'That foolish person threw the bottle because his brother had been killed fighting the people I hate.'

We thought about that for a bit. Ameena came in with a

cup of tea for me. She looked at the tulip and smiled at her husband. 'Isn't he coming on, Ham?' she said, bending to relieve me of the bunch of flowers and momentarily bathing me in her lemony perfume. 'Thank you for the picking.'

After she'd gone, Najib turned his burned wrist slowly to look at his watch. 'Tell me of this theatre project of yours,' he said. 'We have still time for a bit of a chin wag.'

CURTAIN

MORE FROM HONNO

Short stories; Classics; Autobiography; Fiction

Founded in 1986 to publish the best of women's writing, Honno publishes a wide range of titles from Welsh women.

A Diamond in the Sky

Margaret Pelling

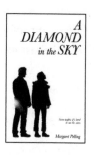

Some nights it's hard to see the stars… A touching and compelling story of love and loss from a new Honno voice, set among the dreaming spires of Oxford, rural West Wales and urban North London.

"A rich and imaginative work with a powerful story… A beautifully written book, with touches of Welsh magic and Oxford Gothic."
Jane Jakeman.

"Pelling has an enviable knack for catching the cadences and inconsequentiality of everyday speech."
Chris Sladen, *Oxford* Magazine

ISBN: 9781906784287
£8.99

All Shall be Well

eds. *Penny Thomas and Stephanie Tillotson*
25 at 25: A quarter of a century's great
writing from the women of Wales

Honno's 25th anniversary anthology
brings together a wonderful and
absorbing collection of writing by Welsh
women taken from the fiction and non-
fiction anthologies published by the press
over the last quarter of a century.

"Hooray for Honno!"
Sarah Waters

"Honno so magnificently lives up to the headline – 'great books,
great writing, great women!'"
Glenys Kinnock

"A wonderful and incredible achievement…"
Niall Griffiths

ISBN: 9781906784331
£9.99

Winter Sonata

Dorothy Edwards, ed. *Claire Flay*

Young clerk Arnold Nettle arrives in a
small village as summer fades. Repulsed
by his crude working-class landlady he
becomes enamoured of the respectable
Neran family, who have their own
difficulties…

First published in 1928 and well received by author David
Garnett and his circle, this novel sees Dorothy Edwards
delineate class and gender boundaries with a deft hand,
using the unique device of structuring the work by imitating
a musical form.

ISBN: 9781906784294
£8.99

Sweets
Jo Verity

Gordon has to go… Tessa and Lewis
decide that something must be done
when the arrival of baby Gordon
threatens their, so far, perfect childhood.
A bittersweet story of sibling love and
rivalry. The third novel from award-
winning Jo Verity.

*"A ripping yarn…pitch perfect evocation of childhood and
sibling relationships"*
Marcel Theroux, *Daily Telegraph*

"A richly detailed and absorbing narrative journey in the
company of two completely believable – and believably
complicated – characters."
Andrew Cowan

"Intelligent, well-observed, and immensely readable."
Catherine Merriman

ISBN: 9781906784003
£7.99

The Great Lie: A Nicholas Talbot Adventure
M. Stanford-Smith

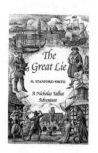

Nick runs away from the clutches of a
tyrannical guardian with a troupe of
travelling players. They bring him to
London – a hotbed of political and sexual
intrigue, where he must find a way to
survive… The first in the *Great Lie
Trilogy.*

*"A tremendous ride through the swirl and bustle of
Elizabethan life."*
Emma Rea, *New Welsh Review*

ISBN: 9781906784164
£8.99

Short stories; Classics; Autobiography; Fiction

Founded in 1986 to publish the best of women's writing,
Honno publishes a wide range of titles from Welsh women.

All Honno titles can be ordered online at
www.honno.co.uk
twitter.com/honno
facebook.com/honnopress

ABOUT HONNO

Honno Welsh Women's Press was set up in 1986 by a group of women who felt strongly that women in Wales needed wider opportunities to see their writing in print and to become involved in the publishing process. Our aim is to develop the writing talents of women in Wales, give them new and exciting opportunities to see their work published and often to give them their first 'break' as a writer.

Honno is registered as a community co-operative. Any profit that Honno makes is invested in the publishing programme. Women from Wales and around the world have expressed their support for Honno. Each supporter has a vote at the Annual General Meeting.

For more information and to buy our publications, please write to Honno at the address below, or visit our website:

www.honno.co.uk

Honno
Unit 14, Creative Units
Aberystwyth Arts Centre
Aberystwyth
Ceredigion
SY23 3GL

Honno Friends
We are very grateful for the support of the Honno Friends:
Gwyneth Tyson Roberts, Jenny Sabine, Beryl Thomas.

For more information on how you can become a Honno
Friend, see: http://www.honno.co.uk/friends.php